A WRINKLE IN THE MIND

The Mind Sleuth Series Book 5

Bruce M. Perrin

TITLES BY BRUCE M. PERRIN

THE MIND SLEUTH SERIES

Of Half a Mind

Mind in the Clouds

Mind in Chains

From the Mind of a Witch

A Wrinkle in the Mind

STANDALONE NOVELS

In the Space of an Atom

Killer in the Retroscape: A Near Future Mystery

For all the latest on new releases, promotions, and book reviews, please subscribe to my blog: brucemperrin.com

*For my family and
their boundless love and support*

Contents

*There are some people who live in a dream world, and
there are some who face reality;
and then there are those who turn one into the other.*
DESIDERIUS ERASMUS
DUTCH PHILOSOPHER

WEDNESDAY, APRIL 6

Morning, The National Mall, Washington, DC

"At least you didn't have to take a bullet for the guy."

Renee Portnell heard the words but made no attempt to find their meaning in the fog of pain that filled her mind. Rather, she watched in numbed disbelief as a trickle of blood inched closer to a Washington Senators baseball cap that sat on the sidewalk. She had to be ten yards away sitting on a park bench and the sun was just beginning to crest the buildings ringing the National Mall, but with a half-dozen Washington DC Metropolitan Police Department cars now parked on the grass, all with their headlights blazing, she could move another ten and the horror of the scene wouldn't fade.

"Government, right?"

Portnell slowly turned toward the sound of the voice beside her, an MPD officer, his name already forgotten. "What?"

"The guy? I heard he was a senator or something. Figured you'd have to take a bullet for him if it came to that."

"U.S. Representative Alan Barclay," said Portnell, every word drawn out like she was from the deep south rather than

Connecticut. "Although, that's Secret Service, not private protection services."

Portnell shook her head to clear it, each of her senses slowly returning to the here and now, each becoming preternaturally acute for an instant before succumbing to the next. She heard the murmur of voices filled with urgency and authority all around. She registered the acrid smell of car exhaust mixing with the sickly-sweet of cherry blossoms that had reached their peak the week before. She tasted gunpowder on her tongue, her saliva no match for its bitterness. But when her gaze fell on the woman lying on the sidewalk, the round-robin of sensations ended. She couldn't pull her eyes away. And all the while she wondered, how could Barclay's ball cap have landed so close to the woman and so far from him?

The police and paramedics had already moved away from the female. Portnell wasn't surprised. She'd always been an excellent shot, and any of the four rounds she'd squeezed off could have been fatal. The only difference between them and the thousand she'd fired before today was that the previous ones had only penetrated paper. These last four had found flesh and bone, blood and muscle. As she watched, the woman's blood inched ever closer to the cap.

It wasn't supposed to be like this, Portnell knew. In her eight years with the military police, she had never fired her sidearm in the line of duty. And when she had retired, her recruitment into the private sector had emphasized the fact that female bodyguards were often instrumental in de-escalating violence. But when the threat is shooting at your client, gender is not going to stop the onslaught. Only a bullet could.

"Renee, look at me." The drop in his volume pulled Portnell's eyes to the officer's face. "From what I hear, you got nothing to worry about. The shooting was righteous. She shot first, and you have the right to protect yourself and others from deadly force. Only question seems to be, she get off two shots or three?"

Portnell thought it could have been more. Hadn't she stared in disbelief for seconds? Hadn't she fumbled with her firearm when drawing it from her shoulder holster? The only thing that had gone smoothly was the Weaver stance-aim-fire sequence, a routine that was burned into her muscle memory from those thousand practice shots at targets that she couldn't harm.

"Not that you need insurance, but she was obviously a wacko," said the officer. "I mean, what the hell was it she said?"

Portnell stared at the man's face, wondering how many times she was going to have to repeat those words? Of course, it wasn't like she'd ever forget them. "When she first approached, she said, 'You must find it hard to represent the folks back home.'"

There was nothing particularly memorable in that part of her statement, but her voice was so melodic, almost childlike. Perhaps that was why, when Portnell started forward to ask the woman to move on, Barclay had given her "the signal"—a hand held low at his side, palm facing backward. Of course, the woman's physical appearance may have played a part in his decision as well. Although Barclay had a reputation as a family man, even he could dream and the woman was the stuff of men's dreams—a dark, exotic beauty in a pure white dress.

"Then, she said, 'I mean, it's gotta be tough for the spawn of a Martian whore like you.'"

"Spawn of a Martian whore," said the MPD officer, chuckling and shaking his head. "Where the heck do these kooks get this crap? I mean, you knew the guy better than me. There's no truth to her words, right?" The officer laughed again like it was the funniest thing he'd ever heard. Portnell just stared at him.

She suspected that it was the incongruity of the hate in the woman's words and the lilting tone that had carried them to her ears that had caused her hesitation. She remembered thinking, could this be real? She knew, of course, that this might happen one day. But in her mind's eye, it was always the silhouette of a crazed man. It was the practice target of the firing range given life.

But while her response had been hesitant, the woman hadn't vacillated. A gun materialized in her hand where moments before there had been none. The crack of her first shot brought Portnell out of her trance. She reached for her handgun, but it caught for an instant on her jacket. The woman fired again. Portnell saw Barclay spin to the ground out of the corner of her eye, perhaps as a defensive reaction, but probably from the impact of the round. His cap flew from his head, which now explained where it had landed on the sidewalk.

Her handgun came free, and from that instant on, she no longer needed to think. Each of her four shots produced a new bloom of red on the woman's simple white dress. But unlike Barclay, she stayed upright, as if she was one of the paper targets hung from the carrier at the firing range. Finally, the woman crumpled to the ground.

"Two," said Portnell, the words indistinct in her ears.

"What?"

"She fired twice."

The officer didn't say anything, but Portnell could hear him moving. After a moment, the man crouched down in her line of sight. Her vision dimmed and she collapsed to her back on the bench. The officer yelled, "Get a paramedic over here. She's going into shock." It sounded like he was twenty yards away, not standing over her.

Lying down helped, and Portnell's vision and hearing cleared a bit. She rolled to her side, watching as the trickle of crimson reached the bill of the baseball cap. Now, the darkening fabric marked the slow march of the woman's blood. She stared at the woman's face. Once, it had reflected an energy to match her voice, but now, it looked more like frozen stone, her naturally dark complexion faded from the loss of blood. Only her eyes seemed to show signs of the person she had been; they twinkled with an inner light, although Portnell knew that was impossible.

Another man appeared in her line of sight. "Stay with me, ma'am." He turned away. "Get that stretcher over here. Now!"

It was help, and Portnell thought she should feel relieved. She didn't. She knew no one could help her with what she needed most—getting the image of the beautiful woman in white with the melodic voice out of her mind forever.

Evening, Samantha Rowles's Apartment, St. Louis, MO

"You're sure this stuff is safe?" asked Samantha Rowles, holding the glass up to the light as if there was something to see in the clear liquid. Despite her thirst for thrills, tonight's events would be pushing her limits, so once again, she was glad she had made Scott Anders come to her place in the Central West End area of St. Louis, Missouri.

"No one's died yet, Sam," replied Anders, raising his eyebrows.

It was a flippant response and it irritated Rowles, but she knew she wanted to try the drink. She wouldn't have come this far if she hadn't.

"It's Samantha," Rowles said.

Although she used the nickname, she reserved it for friends, and Anders hadn't quite achieved that status. As to exactly why he hadn't, she wasn't certain. He was a hunk with those rippling muscles under the knit shirts he favored outside of work. She even found his shaved head sensual. She'd never had anything like a five-date rule. Not even a five-minute rule, if the guy was right. But in Anders's case, she wanted to see how tonight went before she let things go further.

"So, let me get this straight," Rowles said. "This drink is not illegal?"

"Correct."

"And it produces hallucinations, but you can't tell me if I'll enjoy them?"

"Which is not really any different from alcohol or any other drug. Negative thoughts can pop up, but you can't focus long enough to get stressed anyway. Right?"

"I guess," she replied slowly, thinking his response sounded too well-practiced. But then, in his line of work, he'd be answering the naïve questions of anxious people every day.

"Well, this stuff is a little different when it comes to focus. You get started down a path and it may meander and morph, but the basic theme can go on for what seems a long time. You could start out nude bodysurfing on a Hawaiian beach and end up relaxing in a bathtub ringed by scented candles. And like I said, sometimes these hallucinations seem to last for hours, even days. But in fact, it's all out of your system in less than ninety minutes."

"And just why do all these illusions involve me being nude?"

Anders only shrugged in reply to that question, then added, "I'm just here to make sure you don't continue down a negative path. If you start, I'll turn your thoughts toward something more positive. And with clothes on, if that's what you want."

"Yeah, I'm sure you'll have me in something modest but elegant." The undertone of cynicism was clear even to her ears. "And you're not just going to wait until I'm under and then take advantage of me?"

"We can take sex off the table if you want, but I think you're doing yourself a disservice. You may end up begging for it before the ride is over."

"I'll take that chance," replied Rowles somewhat sharply. "And remember, I need to text someone tomorrow to say I'm OK or the police will be knocking on your door."

"Yes, yes. I know."

Anders was beginning to sound exasperated, not that Rowles cared. He wouldn't let her invite any of her friends to the evening's festivities—her trip had to be kept completely secret— but she had told someone he was coming over. And while most people would fear for her safety after she said, call the police if I don't text you tomorrow, this person just said, "I think you're nuts, but I will."

Rowles wondered if Anders would be surprised to learn that her ace in the hole was his office assistant, Susie Wu. The woman rarely missed an opportunity to deride Anders, to which Rowles had always responded with cautious assurances about her own skills to control the opposite sex. But in secret, she also found the OA's warnings exciting.

For a moment, Rowles wondered why she was being so cautious. She'd been with men she knew no better than Anders. She'd tried drugs that had made her paranoid, afraid of every sound, jumping at every shadow. She remembered nights where her only thought was to cling desperately to the floor so she wouldn't be flung into a wall by the spinning world. But even after those nights when she swore it was the last time, she always came back for the thrill.

But in the same moment that the question came into her thoughts, so did the answer. She was being more wary than usual because, unlike everything else she had tried, she knew nothing about this drink. And unfortunately, there was no chance of filling that void. There were no tales from users. No warnings from the medical community. There were only assurances from a man she hardly knew. Would he enjoy suggesting that she carve his initials into her flesh while the drug made her believe she wanted the same? Would he put her behind the wheel of her car just to see how long she would survive? Could the drug make her believe she was being buried alive? That had been the subject of too many nightmares for her to want to repeat it again this evening.

There was, however, another possibility—that the man and his potion would make her night something special, something that she'd want to repeat again and again. And if that was the case, she'd let Anders do a lot more than call her Sam. Perhaps they'd even exchange roles. She was certain she could plant a thought that would bring him tantalizingly close to the point of ecstasy for hours before she let him cross over.

That sounded too good for her to resist. "What the hell," she said, picking up the drink and swallowing it in one long gulp.

THURSDAY, APRIL 7

Morning, Samantha Rowles's Apartment

Rowles rolled over, her eyes opening to find Anders sitting in a chair beside her bed. She blinked. The sunlight streaming in through the bedroom window hurt her eyes. Sunlight?

"What the hell time is it?" she demanded loudly as she sat up and threw the sheet off. Then, realizing that she wasn't wearing anything, she grabbed it and pulled it back up around her neck. "And where are my clothes?" She waved a hand. "Never mind. I'll find them as soon as you get the hell out of my apartment."

Scott Anders made no move to leave, but rather, just sat there with a Cheshire-cat grin on his face. "Easy there, Sammy. It's only a little past 7:30. And as for your clothes, I think ...." He looked around, his brow wrinkling as if he was trying to unravel a mystery. "Oh, yes, your bra is right there, hanging from the lampshade." He pointed. "And the rest are somewhere between here and your living room."

"You're an ass," said Rowles. "And it's not Sammy. It's not Sam. And from now on, it's not even Samantha. To you, it's Ms. Rowles and that's only if we ever end up at the same function, which I don't intend to let happen. I thought you'd behave yourself, here in my home. But you have no shred of decency. I remember everything from last night."

"You remember what you imagined, which obviously doesn't include the strip you did. Otherwise, you would have known where your bra was." Anders chuckled. "And I admit, I've never seen a woman who saves her bra for the finale ... though in your case, it was worth the wait."

Rowles shook her head in disgust. "The peep show's over, you perv. Now, get the hell out of here."

Anders stood slowly, walked to the lamp, and removed her bra. But when he bent down to give it to her, Rowles lashed out with a hand, slapping Anders hard on the cheek. He stumbled backward.

"Jeez, what was that for?" Anders asked. "I stuck to my word. I didn't lay a hand on you when you were under."

"Maybe not a hand, but you laid a lot of vulgar thoughts on me. You were quick with those, weren't you? Just give me my bra and get out of here."

Anders started forward, then stopped, perhaps concerned about the reach of her right hand. He tossed the bra toward her, but it fluttered to the floor about halfway there.

"You can't do anything right, can you?"

Anders released a long sigh. "I was hoping that last night would lead to a lot more nights because, I'll admit, you're one fantastic brown-eyed black-haired beauty and I'm betting the sex would have been amazing. But you obviously have a screw loose. All I did last night was steer you away from the downers. You get started on one of those and you end up slitting a wrist, not tossing your bra over a lampshade."

She laughed, her tone matching the scorn she felt. "And underaged sex with your father isn't a downer? If that's the case,

I gotta meet your family." In her head, her diatribe continued with questions about what he'd done with his mother, his sisters if he had any, but she wasn't going to stoop to his level.

"Look, I don't put thoughts into your head," Anders said. "You were definitely turned on, with one hand rubbing your chest and the other down ...."

"Enough," Rowles shouted. "I don't need the image." But she couldn't help wondering what he was going to say before he'd started fantasizing. "If you're saying I had ideas about having sex with my father before last night, you're full of it."

Anders raised both hands. "I don't know where the thought came from, but you were ... you know, and then, you said something about your dad. I couldn't see that coming; no one could. But when it did, I said I was with you. Yeah, you can blame me for the picture of us together, if you want, but nothing else. And certainly, nothing that involved your dad. In fact, I didn't even know if you knew him."

Rowles flopped back onto her pillow, Anders's words bringing more of the hallucination from last night back into her thoughts. The incident that she'd relived was based in real life, at least in its beginnings. She had been fourteen, and she and her older boyfriend had been in her parents' basement doing what kids did. She was worried that they would walk in, and then, in her reimagination of the evening, her dad had appeared. But rather than yell or grab the boy and throw him out, somehow he ended up on top of her. He said, "I'm here," and it was his voice. Then, it was Anders on top of her.

Rowles covered her eyes with a hand for a moment as if the darkness could erase the vision. "It was so real," she whispered to herself.

"I'm sorry, Samantha," said Anders almost as softly. "I don't want to tarnish your memories of family or anything, but maybe you should see a counselor ... or a hypnotist, or something. I mean, could there be something there? Something you tried to forget and this just brought it back to the surface?"

Rowles wanted to scream. She wanted to slap him again, only this time, she wouldn't open her hand. But in the end, she couldn't. In the few minutes since waking up to find Anders sitting beside her bed, a seed of doubt had taken root in her thoughts. She had been devoted to her father when she was a child. She still remembered following him on weekends as he puttered around the house.

But about the time of this incident in the basement, it all changed. She discovered there were other males in the world, ones only a few years her senior, not more than twenty. Her father became ... well, almost the enemy. She remembered hiding things from him and lying about the things she couldn't hide. And her mother? She was irrelevant for all practical purposes, never supporting her, but never taking his side either.

The questions flooded her thoughts. Was the timing of her disenchantment with her dad a coincidence? Or had he done something to repulse her, something that she had repressed until last night? Did the graphic detail of the image of him straddling her mean it was a recovered memory, not just some creation of a drugged mind? Rowles had long wondered how her mother could maintain her neutrality; perhaps now, she understood. Maybe her mother had withdrawn because she was powerless to stop her father? If he had forced himself on her, a lot of things that hadn't made sense did now.

Unfortunately, no one could answer her questions. Her parents had died in a car crash the next year. Her aunt and two uncles, both on her father's side, had never been involved in her life. They hadn't even been willing—or able if you believed them—to take her in when her parents died. Instead, she had been left in foster care until she was of age.

Out of the corner of her eye, she saw Anders starting to move forward, perhaps to comfort her, but the thought of even a touch from him made her feel ill. Her hand shot up. "I need some time to think. But," she said slowly and deliberately, "one thing I don't have to think about is the fact that these drug parties are over. And so are we. I don't know what's in that crap you served me, but it's scary as hell, and I'm finished with it and you."

"We could cut out the refreshments, just enjoy each other, if you know what I mean."

Was that supposed to be subtle? She shook her head at the man's crassness. "Sorry," however, was all she said. Better to move on, since if they went out again, she'd be wondering if he'd spiked her drink. And with enough of that stuff, she'd probably spend her days drooling into her pillow in a padded cell. She watched him walk out of the bedroom. She stood, wrapped the sheet around her, crept to the hall, and watched as the door closed behind him.

"Last time I'll see that loser," she muttered to herself as she locked the front door and went to get ready for work.

FOUR MONTHS LATER, WEDNESDAY, AUGUST 3

Morning, The Ruger-Phillips Complex

Dr. Sam Price—or "Doc" to virtually everyone who knew him—entered his office in Ruger-Phillips Building number 2 in St. Louis, Missouri. He dropped into the chair behind his desk and held his head in his hands, elbows propped on the desktop. Sleep had been elusive last night, as it had been for weeks. So, when he woke up at 5:00 AM and knew slumber wouldn't return, he came into work to get a start on his assignments ... or equally important, a start on his distractions.

When Nicole Veles, his fiancée, had been kidnapped nearly a year ago, Doc had set out on a quest to find her. Ultimately, he hadn't, and it was law enforcement that had happened upon the bloody scene. The void left after she was ripped from his life was vast, but eventually, he felt the pain would fade. That much of his fate he'd accepted. But what Doc couldn't accept was how he had missed the warning signs leading up to her abduction. He had a mind that was constantly collecting information, sifting and re-ordering the individual pieces to find the hidden figures lost in the noise. And since no crime was perfect—an assumption he knew, but a highly defensible one—how had he completely missed the clues to her peril? He had to know why he'd been so blind.

So, at first, he had replayed those weeks before Nicole's disappearance, again and again, retreading the same mental ground in hopes of finding something new. He hadn't. He did, however, recognize that his recollections had become less detailed and more the gist of the situation. Basically, he was recalling the story that had formed in his mind rather than the events themselves. Given his background in psychology, he wasn't surprised. The transition from low-level detail to high-level generalizations over time was well documented in psychological research and theory.

He needed something to stimulate his recollection, but therein lay another peril. If he tried to jog his memory with new information, say typical methods used by kidnappers, he ran the risk of creating false memories. Any time both original observations and new information were brought into awareness at the same time, they might become inextricably intertwined in later versions of events. Of that scientific finding he, too, was well aware.

To avoid that problem, Doc decided to prime his recall with data that was true of the actual kidnappers. False memories might not be prevented, but hopefully, any errors would still point in the right direction. And during his search for Nicole, he had amassed a wealth of information on them, as well as all the police reports leading up to and after her abduction. The documents and news clippings he had accumulated during those months filled the trunk of his car and almost half of the backseat when he was searching. Now, they took up an equal amount of space in his closets and filing cabinets.

Last night had been a marathon session with this information, as he poured over it until almost 1:00 AM. From previous evenings when he'd done the same, he expected little sleep, as his unconscious would continue to massage the data until he awoke. That, too, was part of his plan. Insights that had come to him in the morning had served him well over the years, although none had involved anything this painful. And perhaps that was why, in this case, nothing had come to him yet. But it would. It had to because he wasn't sure he could live without knowing how he'd failed the woman he loved and who had once loved him.

With these efforts being fruitless, he had sought other ways to shut the pain out. Working with his friend, Private Investigator Rebecca Marte, had been one of them. Perhaps her cases would give his unconscious something besides his failures to ponder. And besides, after her last investigation had upended a nearly open-and-shut case—a self-proclaimed witch caught red-handed in a ritualistic murder—there should be no lack of work.

So, Doc had screwed up his courage to make a rather unorthodox offer of his help. She had feigned pleasure but had accepted out of pity, for what else could it be? He had no skills; he hardly even had a life. He didn't deserve the gesture, but he readily accepted with the hope it was the distraction he needed. Because if he could relax, perhaps the missing key in the mountain of data would come to him.

Unfortunately, working with Rebecca hadn't been the boon he hoped. In fact, their continuing association was having the opposite effect. Based on the publicity from the witch case, Marte Investigative Services was busy, but there were no cases relevant to his background in cognitive psychology. So, rather than becoming involved in solving someone else's problems, seeing Rebecca only served to bring his own failures to the center of his thoughts. And invariably, after he left her office with nothing new to ponder and restless sleep came, so did the voice, more strident than ever, that he had failed his love.

So, he was going to have to end the unofficial collaboration he had with Rebecca. He just needed a little more time to decide how to do it because someone as supportive as she deserved more than an easy lie.

Doc's second ploy to bury his pain was more traditional; he had tried to lose himself in work. Soon, he found himself at the head of the line, volunteering for more and more responsibilities. And when he could pry nothing more from his management, he found make-work assignments and turned them into long-term crusades. Nothing was too small for his full attention if it meant he could forget for a few hours.

"Doc?"

He jumped at the sound of the voice in his office doorway, his head snapping around to find the visitor. "Dani. My favorite buyer. Come in. Have a seat. And thanks for coming in so early. I didn't think anyone's calendar was as full as mine, but I think you have me beat."

Dani Gustafsson's official job title was Procurement Specialist, but everyone at Ruger-Phillips called the individuals in her department "buyers." The shorthand reflected the close relationship of designing a technical solution, Doc's job, and procurement, hers. Doc provided the theoretical and research knowledge of training and learning; Dani had the expertise to translate his requirements into hardware and software specifications for the purchase. And since her background in the theory-to-physical translation was extensive, Doc's statement that Dani was his favorite buyer was, in his mind, fact not flattery.

"Yeah, busy times," she said somewhat noncommittally.

"I just wanted to go over this web server you spec'd out for Newbuilt Products."

"Yeah, you mentioned that in the email, though I'm a bit surprised. I mean, it's not government. We were able to go with best commercial practices, and I think you pushed the requirements pretty well to the top of the range, so the specs followed. You have concerns about them?"

"No. It's not that. I just thought we could go over the requirement on computer memory. Make sure we've allowed enough room for growth. You know, software just keeps getting bigger since memory has gotten so cheap."

"Right," Gustafsson said as she slowly entered Doc's office, her head turning from side to side as if inspecting the corners for lurking threats. She took a seat. "I brought all the paperwork. Let's go over the sizing stuff, make sure I didn't miss anything."

For the next 20 minutes, they did, easing Doc's mind. In fact, her analysis was so straightforward that Doc wondered if the concern had been real or if he had only invented it so he could fix it? Were his unconscious motives really becoming that twisted? The thought was troubling, and unfortunately, it wasn't the first time he had had it.

"You don't seem convinced," said Gustafsson, breaking into his reverie.

Doc shook his head, realizing his feelings must have shown on his face. "No, sorry, Dani. Everything looks fine. No, better than fine. You nailed it, and I should have known you would."

The woman's expression transitioned from a shy smile at the compliment to a slight frown, and she started fidgeting in the chair. Doc was puzzled by her unease until she spoke.

"I'm glad you're happy with the paperwork because frankly ... well I was a bit distracted when I worked up this buy. I usually don't let outside worries into the building, but .... Well, everything seems to have turned out OK." She shook her head slowly.

"What were you going to say?" asked Doc. The frown on the woman's face deepened causing him to backtrack, "I'm sorry. That's personal. I didn't mean to pry."

"Personal? Yeah, if a lie shared on the front page of every paper in the country could be considered personal." Gustafsson stopped, her face turning red in embarrassment. "I'm sorry, Doc. I shouldn't be troubling you what with ... well, you know."

"You mean because of my own problems?"

Gustafsson answered him with a guilty nod. Nicole Veles's kidnapping had been in the news, of course, but unlike the short attention span of the public, the story hadn't yet faded from the Ruger-Phillips consciousness.

"It's OK," said Doc. "Misery loves company, don't they say? That is, if you want to tell me."

Gustafsson released a long sigh, drew her lips into a tight line, and gave a single nod of determination. "It's my cousin, Violet Cruz. Maybe you've heard the name?"

"Not sure," Doc said with a slight shake of his head, although it sounded familiar.

"How about Alan Barclay?"

"The U.S. Representative who was shot? In broad daylight? On the National Mall in DC?" Gustafsson gave a slight nod to each of his questions.

That context was more than enough for Doc to place the name, Violet Cruz. Her attempt on Barclay's life had been in the national news for several days and the St. Louis news even longer, as she was from one of the small towns west of the city. But her act had only been an attempt and a somewhat amateurish one at that. Although she had been fairly close—about three yards—even a well-practiced marksman would have had trouble placing the small caliber rounds she was using so precisely that they would have been fatal. And according to the press, Cruz had no training at all. And while chance could have intervened to defy the odds, it hadn't, and she had barely clipped Barclay on the right buttocks as he dodged reflexively and spun to the ground. Of course, the location of his injury had been repeated incessantly by the press. Cruz's wounds, on the other hand, were more numerous and any one of them would have been fatal. She was pronounced dead at the scene.

"I think the press would leave her in peace if not for the whole spawn of a Martian whore thing," said Gustafsson. "They seem to think there's something in her past that could explain that statement and there isn't. At least as far as I know." Gustafsson paused as if checking her memory again, although Doc doubted it. He'd bet she'd been over what she knew of her cousin hundreds of times since the shooting.

"But the lack of anything doesn't keep the media from digging," Gustafsson said with a single, disdainful laugh. "You know, they even went to my daughter's school, hoping to find a picture of the solar system she made for the third-grade science fair. They probably think Mars will be twice as big as it should be. And my son made a tinfoil hat for some pirate game he was playing with the neighbor kids. That got crumpled up and buried at the bottom of a trash sack. They won't find evidence for any sick conspiracy theories around my house."

"It's DC," said Doc. "The place is crawling with off-the-wall claims ... like the long bursts of gamma radiation from deep space that the Russian mafia is focusing on the U.S. Capitol building."

It was an attempt to lighten the mood a bit, though Doc recognized it was somewhat pathetic. Gustafsson's brow wrinkled, making him wonder if she might even think he was serious. But then the buyer rolled her eyes dramatically and smiled. "Well, I guess that explains why my representative forgets to vote so often."

"Just stay the course," continued Doc more seriously. "Don't give the reporters anything they can turn into a story and eventually they'll look elsewhere."

"Yeah. Unfortunately, elsewhere may be Violet's ex, Roy. Roy Freemont. He'd been staying out of the spotlight, somehow, but his name popped up a few days ago. That's why I thought I might have messed up your buy. They'll have a field day with his beliefs ... and drag my cousin through the mud once again."

Freemont's beliefs? Doc was picturing a balding, overweight man in white robes, sandals, and a "welcome to earth" sign. But if he came from some of the more rural areas of the state, a man in overalls, baseball cap, and a "go home ET" sign was probably more likely.

"Roy is harmless," said Gustafsson as if reading the uncertainty in Doc's thoughts. "He'll be railing against public education one week—turning us all into robots, you know—and the next he's worried about water rights in the southwest United States. It's just that .... Never mind."

"There are some topics where perhaps he isn't so harmless?"

"No, it's not that," replied Gustafsson quickly. "If it was just him, I'd say there is no chance my cousin was influenced by one of his crackpot ideas. His causes don't last beyond the next news cycle. But for the last few years, he's been hanging out with a group whose ... well, for want of a better word, their bigotry is a lot more firmly entrenched. He even got Violet to go to one of their meetings, maybe more. And when I think of weirdos she's been exposed to, the Council for the Right is about the only group that comes close."

Doc leaned back in his office chair, crossed one arm over his chest as he massaged his forehead with the other hand.

"You know them?" asked Gustafsson.

"Not really, but I've heard of them. You remember that shooting when a medical professor and several of his graduate students got killed a little over a year ago?"

"Oh, my God. I never heard they were involved in that."

Doc's head was shaking, and a hand was waving off her statement even before Gustafsson finished it.

"They probably weren't," he replied, hoping to end his statement there. But the quizzical look on Gustafsson's face told him that wasn't going to be possible. "I only know that the FBI suspected the Council early on—I saw that in an online news story. But after they identified the killers, I never heard their name. Maybe the Council had nothing to do with it. Or maybe the

FBI had an informant in the group and wanted to keep that name out of the papers."

Doc was in his element when citing all the data he had on a question and all the inferences he had drawn from them. He wasn't particularly good at holding back, especially from a friend, as evidenced by his last statement. True, he suspected the FBI had someone on the inside, but why had he brought it up? And not only did he think they had someone watching the Council, he thought it might have been Rebecca Marte before she left the Bureau. It was nothing she had ever said; it was just small things in her reaction when their name came up. And if that was true, only she and the FBI would know if the Council had been involved in the massacre.

The buyer, however, merely shrugged, then said, "I'm hiring someone to look into the Council for the Right. Who knows what they might have done to my cousin? And if it's not them, we'll go from there because someone really messed up her head."

Though a simple statement, it produced a rush of questions in Doc's mind. What could the Council have done to produce Violet Cruz's bizarre idea about Barclay's parentage? When he'd first heard the story, he thought her statement might be some sort of odd taunt, an insult that hadn't quite gained widespread usage. But her social media posts made it clear that wasn't the case. If she wrote them, she truly believed his mother was a space alien.

Besides the question of what the Council could have done to implant this delusion, there was also the issue of when? Surely, nothing like this happened at a meeting with her husband watching … unless he was part of the scheme. And why would the Council do something like that? Was there something specific about Barclay or did they just want to topple all of government? If it was something specific about the representative, how had they linked an obviously delusional thought with a very real person? He looked no more like a little green man than anyone else in Congress.

But the question that Doc asked Gustafsson was none of these. "Are you really going to hire someone to investigate what happened to your cousin?"

Gustafsson nodded. "We are, but this talk is not the reason if that's what you're wondering. My husband and I decided a few days ago that we were going to get an investigator. There's something that stinks in this whole situation, and we want to get to the bottom of it. I just need to figure out how to get started."

Doc nodded slowly. If his feeling about Rebecca having a history with the Council was right, she would either be perfect for the case or perfectly wrong. She'd be perfect if she could use her familiarity with the group and completely hamstrung if she couldn't. There was only one way to find out.

"I may know someone who can help."

Morning, The Basement of Kluge's Home

The man who called himself Kluge stopped at the basement door of his small bungalow-style home in south St. Louis. His gaze moved left and right as if surveying his domain. The morning sun had just appeared at a small window set high in the wall to his left and a pale shaft of light, weakened by both the hour and the security frosting on the pane, fell on the bare concrete floor. The warmth it produced, though little, was comforting; nonetheless, Kluge walked to the window and closed the shades. He moved past several sets of floor-to-ceiling cabinets, a sink, and a bed, its frame marred by years of use, before reaching a plain wooden desk that sat in one corner.

Kluge fished a set of keys from a pocket, took the chair behind the desk, and flipped on a small desk lamp. Then, he unlocked the bottom desk drawer and removed a laptop. Once booted, he opened the computer's settings and increased the brightness of his screen to its maximum. For his current efforts, he would want every bit of brightness, every lumen that his laptop was capable of delivering. After all, it was exacting work, searching among the hundreds of images to find just the right woman to be his next conquest.

The link to his special database beckoned. And yet, he faltered, his hand trembling on the mouse, his breathing uselessly accelerated. He pushed back from the desk, preparing his mind for the same mental ritual, the same balancing act that he had performed dozens of times before. On one hand, his fear of detection and, ultimately, death by legal injection was debilitating. He held no misconceptions about this fact; he would receive the death penalty if all he had done came to light. But on the other hand, his aching need to master another woman and use her for his ends only continued to grow. His state was the proverbial irresistible force meeting the immoveable object ... except that his fear could be nudged. It could be manipulated if he learned from his mistakes. And he had. He just needed to remind himself once again.

The first woman he had killed had given him considerable grist for his self-education mill because it had been a near disaster. He and the woman had a relationship if a month together could be considered one. But they had been brought together by a common vision of an impending apocalypse when even the sanctity of one's inner being wasn't safe from the prying eyes of the rich and powerful. But regarding the means to avoid that catastrophe? On that front, Kluge and the woman could hardly have been more different. Her method was to claim the limelight, to shout to whoever would listen that the end was near. And if imprisonment or even martyrdom followed, so be it.

But while the woman's path lay in the spotlight, Kluge had always traveled in the shadows. His feet were guided in the dimness of his world by misinformation and deceit; his sight in the feeble rays was aided by cunning and guile. This had always been his way. Even from an early age, his mother had known. She'd often called him "a sneaky little bastard"—among other things. So, as if to prove her right, he'd stolen from the local liquor stores to add to her "secret" stash of alcohol—anything to hurry her inevitable demise from drink and so, stop her abuse. And when she died, he feigned his grief at the gravesite, while inwardly, he reveled in his part in her passing.

But perhaps his new partner in life was right. Perhaps progress could be made in public confrontation. So, for her, Kluge hid his true nature behind barriers he built in his mind.

At first, all was good. The woman seemed to know that this was uncharted territory for him, and she accepted his hesitancy, his fitful starts and stops. But soon, her patience vanished. She began deriding him mercilessly for his half measures. She begrudged him his job, taunting him when he failed to spend every waking hour striving toward their goal as if the work that kept them fed, clothed, and sheltered was irrelevant. Without pause or pity, she picked at every crack in the barriers he'd erected in his mind. She had become the same as the woman who had bought him screaming into the world, and this was more than Kluge could stand.

So, one evening, just when she had started to list his many failings, he grabbed her by the hair, dragged her to the basement, raped and beat her. Never before had he felt the crack of bones and the crunch of cartilage under his fists. Never before had he heard the retort of his hand striking bare skin and it was ... satisfying. And afterward, as he watched her naked body shivering on the cold concrete, he knew he had awakened a beast within himself. No longer were empty promises and insincere flattery his only tools. Violence had been added to his kit. He would finagle what he needed, but if that failed, he'd take it by force.

This awakening would be short-lived, however, unless he dealt with one remaining problem—the woman. The evidence of his rebirth had to disappear. So, he wrapped an electric cord around her neck and pulled. At first, her struggles were feeble, but soon she began kicking at him fiercely as some of her strength returned.

There were no exposed rafters, so he tossed one end of the cord over a door and pulled it taut from the other side. The wood around the top hinge split, allowing the bottom outside corner of the door to drop to the basement floor. The other two hinges, however, held, leaving one side of the door sitting on the floor, the other wedged against the frame. He pulled on the cord again, the dark strand biting into the skin of his hands while the sounds of her feet striking the wood intensified. But even as he listened, her struggles lessened.

He glanced around the edge of the door, finding that she'd managed to slip her hands under the noose. Or perhaps she had clawed away enough skin to create the gap because blood now ran from her neck to the white T-shirt she wore. Her eyes blazed with a mixture of fear and loathing, but that light was fading from the lack of oxygen. She would never summon the strength necessary to swing her body away from the wood, hoping the backswing might bring the makeshift gallows to the ground. So, he left her, returning after a few hours to wrap the body in plastic and bury it in a wildlife area forty miles from his home.

Kluge had no more than washed the dirt from his hands, however, when he knew that disposing of her in this crude manner had been a mistake. It was the work of his new ally, violence, and violence is never patient. Violence is never clever. As his eyes traveled over his subterranean world, the evidence of his murderous rage was everywhere. Even the abrasions on the broken door from the electric cord might be enough to convict him if law enforcement ever found the body. And sooner or later, they would. He'd read too many stories of hunters or hikers stumbling across corpses left in shallow graves to believe otherwise.

So, he drove back to the wildlife area and retrieved the body. Then, over several days, he dismembered it, pulverized the bones with a sledgehammer, and ground up the flesh. He flushed the entire bloody soup down the public sewer. He burned the broken door and replaced it with a new one. He thought one of the cabinets might have gotten some blood on it and though he could see nothing, he destroyed and replaced it, too. He dumped the electric cord in a dumpster behind a convenience store several miles from his home. Then, he cleaned and bleached every surface.

But still, he wasn't satisfied because all this cleaning said one thing to him—no one goes to these lengths unless they have something to hide. It was time to call on misdirection to see what help it might provide. And when he considered the situation dispassionately, he knew the floor and walls were his nemeses. There were simply too many cracks and crevasses to believe there was no DNA hiding in them.

To cover his crime, he rented a commercial grinder intending to remove a thin layer from the floor and walls, which he would replace with new concrete. The plan, however, had problems. This much work would take him weeks, if not months, and create enough dust that it might catch someone's attention. And in the end, this solution was hardly any different than bleaching everything. So, if they were going to think he was hiding something, why not give them what they expected?

Carefully, he taped around each imperfection in the floor and walls. He made sure each area was at least eighteen by eighteen inches—big enough to slide a body into what would appear to be a hole cut through the concrete. He marked other areas with a length of sixty-two inches, which not coincidentally had been the woman's height. Then, he picked another dozen random locations, marking each with squares and rectangles of varying sizes, lengths, and widths. After these mock grave sites were marked, he ground out about a half-inch of the concrete and replaced it with new. Finally, he got some soil from outside and ground it into the fresh patches.

Not that Kluge ever expected the police to find this room, but if they did, opening more than two dozen of these apparent grave sites to find nothing would discourage even the most experienced detective.

Once he felt safe again, Kluge returned to his troubled vision of the future. Surprisingly, he found it intensified by the passing of the woman who had shared his fears. Now, he alone bore the mantle of responsibility for saving humanity from itself. And since he was free of her demands for a public assault on the approaching Armageddon, he pulled back from the limelight and returned to the shadows where he felt at home.

It didn't take him long to come up with a plan because the core of it was based on an idea he'd long-held but hadn't implemented. He hadn't tried it because, while it featured his old friends, guile and misdirection, it would leave a trail of his subjugations behind—women who would have to die in service of his vision. That had been outside his nature before. But now, with the beast within him awakened, the need to call on it from time to time was an acceptable cost because eventually, he would be vindicated in the pages of history.

Whatever lingering doubts Kluge had about his method were answered by his second and third killings. Both women were gone and buried, each allowed to serve a purpose greater than herself before her death, and no one was the wiser. No one suspected him.

With his fear now nudged to the background, Kluge turned back to his computer and opened the database. He moved quickly and smoothly among the images and the pages of information because there was much to be done and little time. In only a few hours, he had to be back at the job that was merely a stepping-stone to his place in a world where he was the savior.

Noon, Marte Investigative Services

"Dani, this is Private Investigator Rebecca Marte," said Doc, nodding his head toward Rebecca. "Ms. Marte, Dani Gustafsson, a coworker at Ruger-Phillips." He turned back to Gustafsson. "And just so we don't start repeating ourselves, I've told Ms. Marte about your connection to Violet Cruz and your interest in looking into the Council for the Right."

"Thanks for meeting with us over lunch," said Gustafsson. "I would have put it off until later in the week, but lunches are about all I have open for a while. And Doc thought it was important that we get started."

"Good advice," replied Rebecca, nodding toward Doc. "Like you, I'll just get a bite later." And a bite was all it was likely to be, since her schedule was full, too.

Rebecca glanced at Doc. She'd nearly fallen out of her chair when he called to set up the meeting and mentioned the Council for the Right. How had he known she had been involved in their surveillance? But in retrospect, perhaps he hadn't known. The Council was "of interest" to the FBI, along with several other groups; that much had been leaked to the press. And at the time, she was FBI. Ergo, she would at least be familiar with them. Maybe that was all it was.

But as soon as she convinced herself it was nothing, she decided that was just a blatant attempt at self-deception. When Doc became interested in a topic—and the Council would have tugged at him like metal to a magnet—his mind would ponder the facts continuously, looking for a pattern. Or he'd find some piece of data that just couldn't be made to fit, meaning the theory or the information wasn't quite right. In this case, perhaps she had used the Council as an example too often when they talked? Or maybe she had hesitated when naming the other groups of interest but not them? Whatever it was, Doc had picked up on some subtlety in her behavior and had followed it to its logical conclusion—she wasn't giving him the whole story.

As Rebecca saw it, Doc's ever-assessing, ever-questioning mind was his gift. Although scientific research wasn't her background, she was certain it was why he was so good at what he did at Ruger-Phillips. It even explained why he enjoyed the statistical hunt through a complex set of data when most others wanted nothing to do with it.

But Doc's restless mind was also his curse and Rebecca had seen that side of this trait, too. When Nicole Veles had been abducted, locating the kidnappers had dominated his every thought, waking and sleeping, to the point where he had turned his back on the rest of his life. That case was over. But in Doc's head, she wondered if it was still going on? There were definitely things in his actions that suggested that was true.

After her initial surprise about the Council possibly coming back into her life, Rebecca had decided there was no reason to claim ignorance to her potential client. The fact that she knew something about them wouldn't reveal anything about the FBI's methods or their interests. So, because Rebecca didn't want to make any promises to her potential client that she couldn't keep, she had contacted the owner of the catering company that had been her cover when she worked for the Bureau, asking if she could reprise her role as a member of the team. The owner had accepted immediately, saying she could schedule Rebecca for a Council meeting the next evening. She went on to mention how hardly a week went by without someone asking when she'd be back. Rebecca, however, interpreted those comments to mean they missed ogling her and swatting her butt, rather than anything about how she served beer and wings.

"I've also asked Dani to make some notes about anyone else suspicious in her cousin's recent history," continued Doc. "And with that …." Doc extended a hand to turn the floor over to Gustafsson when she spoke.

"If it's OK with you, Ms. Marte, I'd like Doc to stay?"

"That's up to you, Ms. Gustafsson. If you want him here, that's fine."

Fine, however, was an exaggeration. Rebecca was finding Doc's casual closeness to his coworker annoying. He'd patted her on the back when he introduced her. He'd called her Dani, while she was "Ms. Marte." She'd told herself that his silence the past few weeks was because this was time that he needed to close the last chapter of his life, but here he was, being chummy with a coworker. Perhaps she'd misread his remoteness.

And though she hoped it was just coincidence, Gustafsson was gorgeous. True, she was married, but Rebecca wasn't sure that made much difference. If the buyer wanted to test the infidelity waters—or if she was a frequent swimmer—she would be hard to resist. About the only flaw on the surface was a mismatch between her name and her looks. Truth be told, Gustafsson's last name should be hers. With Rebecca's light blond hair and blue eyes, she could be Scandinavian; Gustafsson, on the other hand, was dark and exotic, though Rebecca had no guess as to her nationality.

There were, of course, rationalizations for all Rebecca had inferred from Doc's behavior. His pat on the back could be a gesture of support for a victim and addressing her as Ms. Marte was consistent with the roles they were playing—professional PI and concerned friend. And although she had long wondered if the connection she felt to Doc could be more, Rebecca had no claim on him, no reason to be bothered by his and Gustafsson's closeness except for one. If he was involved with her, he might lose objectivity and be of no use on the case. He might even become a detriment if he let things become too personal.

Rebecca pushed those thoughts aside to be dealt with later. She extended a hand toward two chairs, and they sat, Doc and Gustafsson on one side of her desk and she on the other.

"So, I had the impression from Doc that you might know something about the Council for the Right?" said Gustafsson. "I'm uncomfortable with them, although that's based more on what I don't know than what I do."

"Yes, I'm familiar with them. And if you decide you want me to pursue the case, I can attend an upcoming meeting—tomorrow night actually—and ask around about your cousin."

"That would be great."

"Good," said Rebecca. "So, let's take a look at the list Doc asked you to put together, see what other directions things might go."

Gustafsson handed Rebecca a piece of paper, then grimaced. "I'm afraid it's not much of a list."

A glance told Rebecca that the disclaimer wasn't an exaggeration. She counted six entries.

"It's short because Violet was always pretty quiet," said Gustafsson. "Even in high school, when all her friends wanted her to try out for cheerleader or run for some student government position, she'd pass. It was the same in college. She didn't date a lot either. Mostly stuck with one guy through college. And then, after graduation, along came Roy. Roy Freemont. He didn't fit the pattern, so no one thought it would last. I still remember being shocked when they got engaged. But after a time, their differences caught up with them and they divorced."

"So, Cruz is your family name?"

"Correct. I took my husband's last name, which, I suppose, is obvious," she said with a soft laugh. "I don't really look like a Gustafsson. Anyway, maybe Violet foresaw problems with Roy, but whatever the reason, she never changed her name."

"And I see Mr. Freemont made the list," said Rebecca.

"Mostly for completeness," replied Gustafsson. "He introduced her to the Council. But as for creating bizarre conspiracy theories? Well, I can't imagine him talking about bursts of gamma radiation from deep space used by the Russian mafia for mind control."

Doc stifled a chuckle. Rebecca, however, just stared at them in confusion.

"Sorry, that's just a weird example Doc used when he was trying to cheer me up," said Gustafsson. "Violet's delusion was about Martians procreating with humans. But you probably already knew that."

"It was pretty widely covered," replied Rebecca. "Other than perhaps where Barclay took the bullet, nothing has gotten more press than your cousin's delusion."

Her elaboration, however, was mostly to cover some internal accounting. Apparently, Gustafsson and Doc had inside jokes, making the score for keeping him on the case zero, while the tally for being blinded by personal feelings was two. Again, she pushed the question aside to be considered later.

"Do you know who asked for the divorce?"

"Violet did." Gustafsson paused, releasing a long sigh. "Violet and I were about the same age. Growing up, I thought she was boring, much too straightlaced. It wasn't until about junior year in college that I started to appreciate her approach to life. She really had her act together and we became close. And at first, Roy seemed similar, just more passionate about"—Gustafsson held a hand up—"well, about whatever caught his attention. And when something became his cause, he was all-in, sometimes leaving for days to join a march or attend a protest. Then, in a month or two, it was something new.

"She never told me this exactly, but I think Violet got tired of his chiding her for lack of commitment, even though it was never about the same thing. And I think she got tired of being alone while he tilted at his windmills. She finally had enough and asked for a divorce."

"Do you know how Mr. Freemont reacted to the request?"

"No, but I'd guess he wasn't that surprised. I know he went to Kansas City right before the final hearing. He was even a little late getting to the courthouse. So, I don't think he was serious about making things work—at least, at that time."

"Any of the causes he adopted seem odd or bizarre to you?" asked Rebecca.

"Doesn't one side always think the ideas of the other are bizarre?"

"Probably."

"But if you're asking, were any of Roy's beliefs delusional, no, not that I remember."

"So, let me see if I have this right," replied Rebecca rubbing a hand over her chin. "Your cousin was quiet and generally focused her life on a limited number of things she found important. Mr. Freemont, on the other hand, was more mercurial, more or less going with the latest social cause. Is that about right?"

"Close, but it didn't have to be a popular social issue for Roy to jump on the bandwagon. I think I mentioned to Doc that he once campaigned against public education, suggesting that it was turning us into robots. Basically, he thought mass education killed individuality. That issue comes up from time to time, of course, but Roy was promoting it during the COVID pandemic. At that time, a lot of people just wanted their kids back in school, whatever the curriculum."

Freemont's willingness to go against public trends didn't necessarily sound that innocent to Rebecca. How big of a step was it from mass education kills individuality to alien infiltration leads to world domination? But then again, when it was space aliens who were invading, rather than some foreign country, perhaps that was a major leap.

"Any idea where he got his causes? Any favorite news channels or TV personalities? Or perhaps, someone in government?"

"No, and I doubt there was any one person who influenced him. I'm not sure anyone but Roy could be as hot and cold on an issue as he was."

With Freemont's beliefs seeming about as stable as the weather, Rebecca still wondered if some strong wind hadn't blown him to the delusional side? But if that had happened, Gustafsson apparently hadn't witnessed it, so it was time to move on. "You've got two other names on here. William Abbett, who goes by Billy, and Scott Anders?"

"She dated Billy, off and on, for the last three years ... after her divorce from Roy. Billy seems nice, but he certainly spent enough time with her to affect her thinking." Gustafsson paused, slowly shaking her head. "Affect her thinking about how often the lawn needs to be watered or whether the speed limit in Missouri should be

75, but this space alien stuff? That can't be just normal peer pressure, can it?"

Rebecca noticed Doc shifting in his seat out of the corner of her eye. Gustafsson's question bordered on social psychology, and he probably had something he wanted to say. But when she glanced in his direction, he just settled back in his chair. Had he decided his thoughts were too technical for this setting? Or perhaps, it was some type of reassurance he wanted to give Gustafsson when they were alone?

"I only have limited knowledge about things like this," said Rebecca, "but peer pressure over a long enough time can have profound effects on a person. And if physical or emotional abuse is added to the equation, you can get radical shifts in beliefs, even delusions. So, if the investigation moves in that direction, I know a few people who can help. And Doc might have some ideas, too."

Rebecca didn't really believe that Doc would have much to add because he'd often mentioned that his background in cognitive psychology focused on how individuals generally think, learn, and remember. Disruptions in those capabilities were the subject matter of other areas within psychology. So, if he suddenly claimed to be an expert on brainwashing, he'd probably put his impartiality in the rearview mirror.

"You're better off going with the experts you know," said Doc.

Well, at least he hadn't totally abandoned objectivity. "OK," said Rebecca. "I can check on both Mr. Abbett and Mr. Anders, see what I can pass on to the experts if it comes to that. Now, back to Mr. Abbett."

"Just a second," said Gustafsson, her brow wrinkling. "I don't want to sound inconsistent, since I'm the one that used the phrase, peer pressure, but .... Well, I can't imagine that Billy Abbett believes in Martians. You can check if you want, but I'd be amazed if he held those kinds of beliefs and tried to pressure Violet into thinking the same."

"And I doubt that, too," said Rebecca. "If he did, that would make my job awfully easy. Instead, I'd be looking for problems in their relationship, something that was significant enough for him to want her out of the way. Then, Mr. Abbett doesn't need to believe in Martians. He only needs to believe he can make Ms. Cruz accept the idea through emotional and psychological pressure. And when she acts on her new belief, not having any skill with firearms, things go very badly for her, very quickly."

Gustafsson sighed. "Yeah, I guess that's what we're looking for, although it sounds so cold and calculating when you say it. That's really hard for me to believe about Billy."

"Of course, I'd be looking for the same thing with Mr. Anders. But back to Mr. Abbett. How did he meet your cousin?"

"At my wedding. He was a friend of the best man. I asked him at the wedding, kiddingly of course, if he had come for the free food. He turned to Violet and said he came to meet her." Gustafsson's eyes went to the ceiling before returning to Rebecca's face. "He could be a little corny like that, but Violet liked it."

"So, do I have the timeframe right? You got married recently, after your cousin's divorce?"

"I made it sound that way, didn't I?" Gustafsson wrinkled her nose in a way that said she'd made a mistake, although Rebecca also recognized it as a cute *mea culpa* that would draw a lot of attention from the opposite sex. "No, I got married a little less than a year before Violet. As far as I know, she and Billy never ran into each other during the time she and Roy were married. Then, Billy reappeared after the divorce, probably to give Violet some emotional support."

"Did Ms. Cruz tell you that?" asked Rebecca.

Gustafsson paused, her lips drawn in a tight line. "No, I suppose not. I just have trouble believing Billy could do anything like what we're suggesting."

"Which is normal. But don't worry. We'll need a lot more evidence before we accuse him of anything other than being a friend."

It wasn't ground-breaking detective work to move an ex-husband to the top of a list of suspects when a woman was murdered. Nor was it unusual to put the male friend who had materialized after a divorce right alongside. The ex-spouse had become infuriated by being displaced by the friend. Or the long-standing friend had become enraged when his patience wasn't rewarded after the divorce.

Rebecca, however, wasn't sure these possibilities had ever been laid out more neatly. She'd even think that it was an attempt to frame one of the men for Cruz's actions, except the perpetrator would have wanted Abbett or Freemont to have a much clearer motivation to want Cruz out of the way. Then, this mysterious third person could hide behind that desire, ridding himself or herself of Abbett or Freemont by making it look like one of them had been behind Cruz's half-baked attempt to kill the representative. Right now, however, she didn't know if either the ex-husband or the current boyfriend had voiced any interest in getting away from Cruz, making a frame unlikely.

Of course, all these possibilities were based on the assumption that there was a perpetrator other than Cruz's own mind. The idea that she'd somehow lost touch with reality and believed her delusion still seem the most likely.

"OK. So, what's the story with Scott Anders?"

"You know about Violet's problem with migraines, right?"

"I saw something about it in the papers, but not much. Is he a doctor, treating her for that?"

"Not exactly," said Gustafsson slowly as she rubbed a hand over the back of her neck. "Like I said before, I have trouble believing Violet's radical change came from a normal relationship. I can't see any guy pressuring her enough to make her act the way she did. So, drugs seem like a possibility, but so does medical technology. And he works for a company that makes a biofeedback device they were going to try on her migraines."

"What's the name of the company?" asked Doc, apparently no longer constrained by whatever had silenced him before.

Rebecca didn't try to re-establish control of the interview because, frankly, she was interested in where this might go. At some point in the past, Doc had mentioned using physiological feedback to make sure trainees were alert and reacting to the instruction. Biofeedback was sort of the opposite. Measures like heart rate were taken so people could learn to control them and so, relax. In effect, it was training to not pay attention, meaning that Doc's background could be a boon to the investigation. He'd speak Anders's language. He'd know the questions to ask. And he'd sift through the answers and the way they were delivered until a picture emerged.

There was another possible benefit to his involvement—working the case might give him a chance to forget about his problems for a time. When he'd made his suggestion that he work with her in an informal consulting role, he hadn't mentioned distraction as a reason, but it was apparent enough to Rebecca. Unfortunately, there hadn't been any cases where his expertise fit, so instead of helping him move on, which she would like to do, he'd been left to ....

Well, hell, she didn't know what he'd done since that offer, except perhaps playing house with her potential client. That situation needed to be resolved soon, preferably today.

"He works for Healthtech," said Gustafsson. "You know them?"

"A little," Doc replied. "And they were using some of their equipment to treat your cousin's migraines?"

"It never got that far," said Gustafsson. "Her doctor ran tons of tests, and they were getting ready to try some of Healthtech's equipment."

She paused, turning toward Rebecca.

"You should know, her doctor's name is on the list, too, but only because of the possibility that drugs are involved. In fact, his reputation is spotless."

Rebecca nodded and Gustafsson turned back to Doc.

"After one or two initial interviews at Healthtech, where she met Anders, her doctor found out that her migraines had worsened because of a change to her birth control prescription. He changed it again and the problem disappeared. So, she never had the chance to try Healthtech's equipment."

"And that was the only contact with Mr. Anders?" asked Rebecca.

Gustafsson slowly shook her head. "I'm not sure. Anders did something to make an impression on her because Violet mentioned him a few times. They may have even gone out, but that's a complete guess."

"OK. And then you have two organizations on your list—a food pantry and a museum?"

"She volunteered at the first and worked at the second. Those two, plus home, Billy, and her ex just about defined her life. I've racked my brain trying to come up with others, but there just aren't any that I can think of."

"Your list is actually a pretty good starting point," replied Rebecca. "Your cousin's social and work life are both represented, as well as her medical history. And, yes, I agree that anything involving drugs, medical technology, and her health are important parts of her recent history to consider. If I work this case, I'd take the names you provided and follow the leads from there. Take her doctor, for example. Even if he's clean as a whistle, like you said, maybe someone at his office isn't? Of course, if you come up with other people, let me know, but I think I have a decent shot at finding some leads with what you've given me so far."

"I hope you're right," replied Gustafsson. "I hope you can find who or what did this to her because the Violet I knew couldn't have shot anyone."

Rebecca paused, mentally reviewing what she had heard. A straitlaced do-gooder had gone off the deep end by accusing a United States representative of betraying humanity. He was the first of a wave of interspecies beings that would pave the aliens' way to world domination. She had, however, put a positive spin on what

Gustafsson had given her to work with because there were major voids in this picture that would be very hard to fill.

What was the motive and was it a motive to get rid of Cruz or Barclay? A U.S. representative seemed the more likely target than the quiet, beautiful Cruz, but maybe the woman had a seamier side she'd kept hidden? Or maybe her quiet, reserved approach to life had driven one of the men in her life to murder? And what was the means to induce Cruz's break from reality? The list contained names of people who had an opportunity to plant a delusion, but none seemed to have the means except perhaps Anders. And he was weak on opportunity unless they had dated almost from the instant she appeared at Healthtech. If she took the case, she'd earn her fee.

"If you want me to investigate, I'll start by checking out the Council. I have to say, though, they're a really long shot. Unless Ms. Cruz was still going to their meetings after her divorce, she wouldn't have been around them for three years. After checking them out, I'd work through your list, starting with Mr. Freemont, Mr. Abbett, and Mr. Anders. Then, I'd check out their associates and the organizations on the list because, as the scope of the hunt broadens, the case will become more time-consuming. And, of course, I'll keep you updated on progress and next directions. Do you have any questions or anything more you'd like to add?"

"No, not really," said Gustafsson with a half-shrug.

"OK. Here are my standard fees. You can study them and get back to me."

Rebecca slid the pages across the desktop, thinking she'd either get a call back in a few days or not. Gustafsson, however, had a different schedule in mind. She took them and quickly leafed through. "These appear to be the same as the copy Doc showed me," she said when she reached the last page. "The terms are fine. I'd like to hire you."

When the paperwork was signed, everyone stood, and the women shook hands. "OK, I'll be in contact," said Rebecca, then turned to Doc. "Would you mind staying for a minute? I have something we need to discuss."

He paused. "Um ... we drove together, but I can call you later."

During his moment of hesitation, Rebecca thought Doc looked like the kid who got caught with his hand in the cookie jar, making her wonder, once again, just where his hands had been. A cookie jar, however, was not at the top of her list. Unfortunately, this picture was popping into her thoughts much more frequently than she'd like. Though she wanted Doc involved both for her benefit and hopefully, his, she didn't want him around if it came at the expense of the case. Of course, she couldn't stop him if he went on alone, but she could keep herself out of his and Gustafsson's drama. And maybe she'd find another way to help Doc, although she was starting to wonder if getting him out of her life permanently wasn't better for both of them in the long run.

"I have a full day finishing up some background checks that are due tomorrow," replied Rebecca. "Can you call me tonight?"

"I have a better idea," Doc replied. "How about I get something from that Thai restaurant down the street from me? I'll get the food and we can eat at my place—say 6:00? That'll give us a chance to talk through ... well, a lot of things without any interruptions."

Although his words sounded a bit like a proposition—come to my place where we can be alone to "talk"—Rebecca was under no delusions. In fact, when she added the slight uptick in his tone and the set of his jaw, she was pretty sure that talking without interruption was code for pouring over case data on suspects and evidence until the wee hours of the morning. He might even have it all in a spreadsheet by then.

Internally, she smiled at the image that, for some reason, she found amusing and attractive at the same time. "Sure."

Evening, Doc's Apartment

How do I play this? How?

The question kept running through Doc's mind as he paced the twenty-one feet from his front window in the north of his apartment to his back wall in the south. Yes, he'd measured, wondering if it could really be that little. It was. And while his place stretched—if he dared use that term—thirty-six feet east to west, that distance was broken by a bathroom wall, the stove in his kitchenette, and a bed. In his 756-square-foot apartment, those twenty-one feet were his only pacing territory and he needed every last inch of it if he was going to come to any conclusions.

He hated to play on Rebecca's sympathies. He hated to ask her to make a role for him on Gustafsson's case when, in fact, she'd undoubtedly be better off going it alone. After all, look at his track record. It was littered with people who had been vivacious and brilliant, but who were now empty, broken, or dead. Why would she jeopardize her livelihood just because he needed to forget about his failings for a time?

And yet, didn't this case have the potential to be more than a diversion? Couldn't it at least partially remove the stench of his failure if he and Rebecca broke it? That, of course, assumed there was something to break because the prevailing view was that the case was exactly what it seemed—a woman had suddenly and unexpectedly developed a mental illness and had tried to act on her delusional beliefs. Some of the media had even gone so far as to ask, who could blame her? With all the infighting and backstabbing that had characterized Congress for some time, why wouldn't she see violence as a reasonable response? That, however, felt like a bit of a stretch to Doc.

The theory he held as the most likely alternative was that the incident was an attempted murder and successful suicide. That Cruz had basically committed suicide wasn't a new conjecture; several reporters had raised the same possibility and Rebecca had alluded to it during the "peer pressure" discussion. But the similarity between what the reporters believed and what he and—he assumed—Rebecca hoped to prove ended there. The two of them were investigating the remote possibility that someone had manipulated Cruz into her self-sacrifice. If that was the case, Barclay had been the target of some mysterious mastermind who had pulled Cruz's strings like a puppet master to achieve his or her political objectives. Basically, her death was the way to further this mission without risking detection.

Why did Doc think a third person held this objective rather than Cruz herself? Because she had no apparent political motive, not counting the delusional one. There was no public program that Cruz had lost or was about to lose because Barclay opposed it. And if Cruz was going to give her life to stop Barclay's political actions, then her cause wouldn't be a secret. She would want the world to know.

This mastermind theory, however, was going to be the devil to prove. Other than a traumatic brain injury or a remarkably rapid onset of some neurological disease, murderous delusions didn't appear overnight. And if it was injury or disease that the perp behind the scenes had used, he or she would have had no control over the focus of her delusion. How could this individual direct Cruz's misguided beliefs toward Barclay, a man she had never even met?

Brainwashing was another possibility, and it would give Cruz a villain to loath, but it took time for mental and physical abuse to work. And from what Gustafsson had told them, few people had long-term access to Cruz in a setting where this could have occurred. That, of course, would need to be verified. And finally, why would anyone brilliant enough to orchestrate a delusion-driven assassination leave the outcome in such ill-prepared hands as Cruz's? If she had been selected for this mission, her shooting expertise was obviously not the criterion that had been used.

Then, why had she been chosen?

The knock at Doc's apartment door broke into his thoughts, leaving only an instant for him to realize that he had to throw himself on Rebecca's mercy. There was no other option. He just had to make it sound like she was getting something out of the arrangement besides a liability.

"Evening, Rebecca," he said, opening the door.

"Hi, Doc. Can we talk over dinner? I'm starving thanks to a meeting over my lunch break today."

On a good day, Doc probably would have come back with something of the ilk, what, you only want cases from retirees because they eat lunch at ten? This, however, wasn't a good day, and Doc slapped his forehead with an open palm.

"I totally forgot the food." He paused. "I mean, I thought the ambience at the restaurant would stimulate the discussion. How about we eat there?"

"That recovery would have been lame even if you hadn't said you forgot. Let's ...." But before she could finish, she glanced down at his feet. "Were you planning on playing footsy with me during dinner? Go put your shoes on."

"Socks are better for thinking," he replied as he went to his bed and pulled a pair of tennis shoes from underneath. "Well, they're better for the pacing part of thinking anyway. And I've been thinking."

Rebecca scowled, making him realize he was talking, not putting on his shoes. He slipped on a shoe and started tying the laces.

"Scott Anders and Healthtech are right in my wheelhouse. Not that you won't want to verify whatever I discover. Or even run your own separate investigation."

This was his sales pitch? You can do it yourself because you're not going to be able to trust what I give you? Why didn't he just say, I'm dead weight, but please, let me tag along? All he'd done right so far was to finish putting on the first shoe. "Of course, I'll try to verify everything I give you."

"Let's talk on the way."

"OK, sure." Doc started on the second shoe when a thought came to mind. "Different topic. The patrolman who was the first on the scene at the shooting at Nicole's apartment? I can't find his incident report. Do you still have a copy?"

"Your shoe?"

Doc looked down, realizing his hands had stopped. Of course, he could tie a shoe without thinking about it, but there was just too much circulating in his head to even let him go on automatic pilot.

"I don't think I have a copy of the report, but why do you need it?"

"I just want to make sure my files are complete," Doc lied. He wanted to tell Rebecca what he was doing, but he worried that it might lead to a get-on-with-your-life chat. And although she had probably suggested moving on less than just about anyone else, he could tell that "You're living in the past" was on the tip of her tongue. She just didn't understand why his search was important.

Rebecca shrugged, seeming to sense the half-truth, but apparently, she decided to let it go. As he finished tying his last shoe, Rebecca reached down, grabbed him by his collar, and pulled him up off the bed.

"Easy there," Doc said, only needing to partially feign discomfort.

"You want me to guide you around with my hand placed gently on the small of your back?"

"What?"

Rebecca was obviously angry about something—angry enough that she didn't bother explaining herself. Had she decided to make the missing report an issue? If so, hustling him out of his apartment was for the best. He could change the subject and get back to promoting the skills he didn't have.

Rebecca released his collar at the door so he could lock it. When he turned back to her, he had to jog a few steps down the hallway to catch up. "You've probably thought of this already, but finding out how someone planted that space alien delusion in Violet Cruz's head is key to cracking this case. And Healthtech might well have the technology to do it. You know what biofeedback is, right?"

"I do."

Did she really? Clearly, she wasn't going to elaborate, and he needed to avoid misunderstandings ... or another one, anyway. "With biofeedback, you use sensors to pick up how your body is reacting, like measuring brain waves," he said as they stepped out the front door of his building and onto the darkened sidewalk. "Then, with practice, you learn to control those reactions and so, relax."

"And I said I already knew that," replied Rebecca.

"Yeah, I just wanted to make sure we were talking about the same thing. Anyway, I don't know how, but Healthtech may have found a way to use a derivative of that technology to influence thought. I mean, there's been a lot of work on creating depictions of what someone is thinking by using their brain waves. If they flip their technology around—push the waves into the brain rather than pull them out—maybe they can create an illusion that seems real. Like a memory of Barclay's mother in the throes of passion with a Martian."

Rebecca partially stifled a choke, then turned sideways to stare at him as they continued down the sidewalk. "Seriously? Cruz comes in for migraine headaches and they say, let's put some images of little green men in your head. That should take care of the problem."

Doc started to reply, but Rebecca waved him off with a hand. "Sorry, I know you're just thinking out loud and you'll need to do a lot more digging before you have anything reasonable. But remember, you're not ...."

"I'm not a PI," Doc said, finishing the first and most important of her oft-quoted guidelines for his involvement with Marte Investigative Services.

"Right. If you talk to anyone at Healthtech—and I do mean *if*, not when—then you're only interested in how their technology might be used for training. That's part of your job and sticking with that story keeps you out of trouble. Now later, if their methods look like they could be twisted in a way to create delusions, fine. That fact could break the case, but don't force-fit anything."

Good advice, he knew, and normally, something he lived by. But wild speculation about what Healthtech might be doing was more likely to get him a spot in the investigation than a dispassionate look at the data. So, he simply replied, "Yes, ma'am."

"Good. You could be a help with this part of the investigation, but I have one other question first. And I'll ask straight out because beating around the bush will get us nowhere."

"OK," Doc replied, trying to keep the unease he felt out of his voice. At last, she was going to address the elephant in the room—that she was allowing him to play PI out of pity. It took him a moment to realize that she had stopped walking. He turned back to face her.

"Are you having an affair with my client?"

Doc stood there a moment, dumbfounded. "What? Dani?"

Rebecca just stared in reply.

"No, I'm not having an affair with Dani Gustafsson. I'm still .... She's married."

"You're still what?" Rebecca asked slowly, her eyes narrowing.

Doc couldn't look her in the face and found his gaze sweeping the darkness around them as if looking for an answer. The void, however, had nothing for him, and finishing the sentence the way he'd intended—I'm still investigating the kidnapping—would only lead to a talk he didn't want to have. Finally, into the night he said, "I'm still a little off-balance with all that's happened."

"A little off balance?" Her tone dripped incredulity.

He looked up at her. Even in the dim streetlight, Doc could see her run a hand through her hair, then turn to walk a couple of paces away, only to turn and come back. She slowly shook her head.

"The guy who stumbles on the edge of the sidewalk is a little off balance. You? Your sense of balance disappeared with Nicole, but unlike her, it never came back. And now, you're lying to everyone, me included. You just want the police incident report so your files are complete? That's bull. But the biggest lie is the one you're telling yourself—that there's something in the past that will magically change history."

"You don't know what you're talking about," Doc shot back, a bit too loud for the distance between them. He could see the people on the sidewalk drop their gaze and shuffle by as if trying to be invisible. He didn't care.

"Oh, don't I?" she replied, her voice now rising, too. "Why else do you keep going over those days when you lost Nicole? You're not going to learn anything new from them. And even if you did, so what? You can't change a damn thing. You told me once that you have trouble leaving problems before they are solved. Well, this one is solved, over and done. I'm sorry you hate the answer—we all do— but it's still history."

Doc could feel his blood starting to boil. "That's easy for you to say, isn't it? I doubt you've ever loved anything enough to mourn its loss." The second the words left his mouth, he knew he'd stepped over the line, but something kept him from taking it back. Rather, he just stared, chin jutted, waiting for her anger to boil over.

Curiously, however, it didn't. Rather, Rebecca just stood there, hands on her hips as she looked down the street for a moment. When she turned back to look at him, she said, "I think it's better that I go it alone on this case. I can't be worrying about you pulling out on me in the middle of it to chase your ghosts."

Though the taunt he'd directed at Rebecca a moment earlier had given him pause, banning him from the case redoubled his anger. "Fine," he shouted. "I don't need your permission to look into it anyway. And besides, I'm sick of playing on your pity."

"Pity? What the ...." Rebecca paused, taking a breath. "Accepting help from you on this case or any other has never been out of pity," she said somewhat more quietly. "I wanted you involved for two reasons. First and foremost, you're good at digging out the facts. For someone without training, my old partner thought you were one of the best he'd ever seen. He just worried that despite doing everything humanly possible to save Nicole, you'd blame yourself and crawl into a bottle. But no, you had to crawl inside your head and beat yourself senseless from in there. So now, you're a liability, not a help. I'm out of here. I'm going home for cold leftovers and better company on the television."

She turned and started stomping down the street.

"Aren't you forgetting something?" asked Doc, calling from behind. "You said there were two reasons you wanted me on the case, and I'm just dying to hear the second."

Rebecca stopped but didn't turn. But even from the back, Doc could see she was looking at the ground and slowly shaking her head. "You said that I'd never loved anything enough to mourn its loss, and maybe that's true. I didn't have brothers or sisters. I didn't know my grandparents well, and my parents are still alive and healthy. But I'd like to think that even if I'd lost them, I wouldn't give up. And I'm certain they wouldn't want me to."

"What the hell is that supposed to mean?" Doc shouted to Rebecca's back as she continued down the street. "Because that's exactly what you're telling me to do. Give up. And I won't ... ever!"

Doc heard footsteps behind him. He spun around, ready to ask, "What the hell are you looking at?" but it was unnecessary. The couple who was approaching had their heads down, staring at their feet. So, he turned toward his apartment, adopted a similar posture, and started the short walk home.

THURSDAY, AUGUST 4

Morning, Doc's Apartment

"What the hell does Marte know?" Doc muttered to the walls of his empty apartment, spinning for the return trek across the tiny space. He'd called in sick for work, allowing himself some time for his anger with the woman to subside. So far, it hadn't. If anything, it had grown.

Before two years ago, he never would have used the I'm-under-the-weather line to get out of work. But during his search for Nicole, falsehoods had become his best friend. The true story, of course, opened a lot of doors—what could be more pathetic than a man searching for his kidnapped fiancée? But when he needed to locate someone other than Nicole, that person was an old college friend. Or when he needed food, someone had mugged him and stolen his wallet. Or when he needed access to an official document? "Just a quick look and maybe I can swing by later and take you to lunch?" It had worked more often than he'd ever expected, and he didn't feel the slightest bit of remorse for any of the falsehoods.

Had his ease with fabrications followed him back to St. Louis? Perhaps, but the line to his OA wasn't that far from the truth. He was sick. He was sick and tired of people like Marte judging him. And it wasn't just the sanctimonious PI. His own family—mom, dad, and both brothers—had told him it was time to move on. But family had to say that, right? And friends? Ditto. He'd been thrown for a while when Nicole's parents took up the same chorus, but that, too, could be explained. If he closed that chapter of his old life, then he wasn't trying to reinsert himself into their daughter's world. Only Jen, Nicole's sister, shared his belief that in the long run, he was part of the solution rather than all of the problem.

Doc paused mid-stride, the pieces of a puzzle that refused to fit together drifting in his thoughts. If he'd become such an accomplished liar, how had Marte seen through every little fib he'd told her? Of course, he'd been uncomfortable when he brought her Dani's case and then tried to insert himself into it for his personal reasons. Who wouldn't be when one's concern for a friend was being overwhelmed by a need to forget for a while? In the past, he'd met issues head-on. That trait, however, now felt like a myth.

As for asking for the patrolman's incident report, that had to be the biggest rookie mistake he'd ever made. Of course, Rebecca would see through the request. And she'd interpret it as proof that he just wanted to beat himself up. Like he'd said before, what the hell does she know?

Doc restarted the 21-foot circuit of his apartment, thinking that tomorrow, he needed to start jogging again. His runs had been an opportunity to clear his head and organize his priorities for the day. That habit, however, had died when Nicole went missing. At that point, he didn't need to organize his day because his priorities had become totally static—find Nicole, eat, and sleep, in that order. There was no time for luxuries like a run to clear his mind.

For a fleeting moment, a surprising thought entered Doc's head. What if Rebecca was right? What if all the data he had collected on the kidnappers didn't hide an insight? If so, then all the information was good for was torturing himself. But when he tried to consider that question dispassionately, he couldn't. He was still too angry with her to admit anything beyond her stubborn, backward attitudes.

But while the PI's rant about his self-destruction left him at a dead-end, at least it had some meaning that he could ponder. Her second reason for wanting him involved in the case, on the other hand, was meaningless. Or contradictory. Or something. What did it mean that she didn't believe she would give up if she had loved and lost? He'd loved and lost, and yet, she wanted him to give up. Why couldn't she just say what she meant ... assuming she knew.

Whatever she had been thinking, he couldn't waste any more time trying to discover it. He pulled his cell phone out of a pocket and hit a number in his contacts. "Ruger-Phillips Training Technology. Linda Oats. How may I help you?"

"Hi, Linda, Sam Price. I'm feeling a lot better. I'm heading into work."

"Sure, Doc. I'll let Ken know."

"And tell him it'll be an hour or two. I thought I'd take care of some things around here while the local businesses are open. I'm going to run by and talk to some people at Healthtech."

Afternoon, Treadwell's Tire Barn

Play the odds.

How many times had Rebecca heard her old mentor at the FBI repeat that dictum? And in this case, the numbers could hardly be clearer. Nearly half of all women who were murdered were killed by romantic partners, putting the spotlight of suspicion directly on Roy Freemont and William "Billy" Abbett. And since they were solid suspects that she could check out before she made the trek down south for another evening with the Council for the Right, she did, starting with Abbett.

Until she met him, Rebecca had considered Abbett the slightly more likely perp. He had waited through a marriage only to start, if Gustafsson was correct, a lukewarm relationship with Cruz. "Off and on" had been her description of their dating history. Depending on his personality, Abbett could see Cruz as a tease and he, the man to teach her better ... until the lesson went too far.

When she called Abbett to set an appointment, she had learned that he, like Cruz, had majored in art. But where she had gone to work for a museum, he taught in a local high school. And when she told him the reason for the meeting, he had suggested his home during a block of time when he had no classes. That made sense, but it was also risky if he was a killer. Rebecca wished she could tell someone where she'd be, but there wasn't anyone. She had even delayed hiring an answering service until her finances were more settled. So, in the end, she left an entry in her online planner. Bread crumbs were better than nothing.

Within the first two minutes after arriving at Abbett's home, however, Rebecca felt it was unlikely that he had orchestrated Cruz's death. He had the quiet manner of an introverted artist intertwined with the patience of a high school teacher. The precipitous drop in her concerns about the man, however, wasn't based on his manners. After all, Ted Bundy, confessed killer of thirty women, was supposedly extremely charming. Rather, it was everything else that painted a consistent picture of Abbett and Cruz as kindred spirits and good friends ... and nothing more. And every time she had tried to find a slight imperfection in that image to expose a lie, the evidence repainted it as clear and consistent as ever. Photographs were signed "To my best friend". Gifts were hand-woven scarves—a bit amateurish but cherished by Abbett nonetheless—rather than negligees or sex toys. And even leading questions were gently corrected by the man.

"And where did you go on this date?" Rebecca had asked at one point.

Abbett had rubbed his chin in thought for a moment, then said, "We met at a coffee shop near the museum, Best Dregs or something equally cute but meaningless. If you don't see it on the map, I'll get you the exact name. But as for this being a date? Not really. She was working late on an exhibit at the museum on her own time. They had a tendency to pull that on her. I'd just finished grading some really dreadful mid-semester projects. We each needed someone to commiserate with, and she always understood my frustrations. And I hers. At least, I always thought so."

Later, Rebecca had tried to explore some of the common motivations for murder—sex and jealousy topping the list—but Abbett indicated that intimacy had never been a part of their relationship. Their association had started as a friendship during her marriage, and he'd never given much thought to changing that fact. In his view, good friends were hard to find. But perhaps because he knew how that sounded, he had produced a photograph of his fiancée, a bespectacled woman with a pale complexion and curly brown hair—a near-perfect inverse of Cruz. Even the longshot that it was some sort of love triangle gained no traction in Rebecca's suspicions, as despite efforts for the three of them to get together, the scheduling had never worked.

Rebecca ended the interview knowing that a person is never taken off the suspect list entirely—any evidence can be falsified. But in Abbett's case, she was close to making an exception.

So now, she was down to Roy Freemont on her list of ex-romantic partners, wondering how he might have felt, seeing his ex-wife out on the town after their divorce. If his wounded pride had festered, he might have decided to make Cruz pay with her life. And that scenario, or a similar one, was why she was sitting in the parking lot of Freemont's place of employment—a tire store where he was an assistant manager. She checked her phone, finding she had another ten minutes to wait. She leaned back in the seat, her fingers idly tapping on the steering wheel.

Unfortunately, no story she had been able to concoct for Abbett or for Freemont explained how one of them had produced the delusions in Cruz. The means to do that, as Doc had said, could be a key to solving the case. Or rather, it was "the" key, in his mind. And he had a point. But to her, the domain of means was vast and vague. It would contain everything from old-fashioned social deprivation to physical abuse to futuristic technology for mind control.

Doc, too, knew the space of possibilities was vast, but he figured he'd narrow the search by looking at the intersection of suspects and means. And that, of course, was why he wanted to start with Anders and Healthtech. The approach wasn't bad. In fact, it probably had the potential for a quicker solution than hers. But Rebecca preferred playing the odds, as she had been taught.

"Ah, Doc," she sighed, sinking a bit lower in her seat. She hadn't really told him the second reason she'd wanted him on the case when he'd asked the day before, although if he'd quit thinking the world revolved around his loss, he could figure it out. She hadn't said it because she was angry, and that was no time to say she wanted to give the two of them a chance. And besides, that feeling was fading into history. She'd given him time, options to keep his mind busy, support, advice, and finally, a piece of her mind. Nothing had helped. All she could do now was avoid watching his slow, painful self-destruction, which was exactly what she planned.

Rebecca glanced at her phone again. "Close enough," she muttered. She picked up her notebook from the passenger seat, exited the car, and entered the building.

To her right, tire displays and promotional signs filled the front window. On the wall straight ahead were two doors with signs that read "Private" and "Restroom." There was a long counter on the left with a wall behind it, the latter featuring a list of services and prices, a door to the work area, and a window. Through the window, Rebecca could see several cars on lifts and one worker rolling a tire around on the floor. Spaced along the counter were three cash registers, two of which were manned. As she'd seen pictures of Freemont, she knew he wasn't one of the cashiers.

"I'm looking for Roy Freemont."

A man at the counter pointed a thumb at the door marked private, but the woman next to him said, "He's not in there," then turned to Rebecca. "He's in one of the bays." She opened the door. "Hey, Roy. Someone here to see you." Apparently confident that her summons would work, she went back to her place at the counter.

After a moment, Freemont appeared, looking a little confused. "Mr. Freemont?" He might have nodded, but if so, the blank stare overshadowed the gesture. "I'm Rebecca Marte. We spoke a while ago on the phone."

"Yeah, sure. Let's go to the office."

In person, Freemont looked much the same as the photographs she had found online. He was pale, but not excessively so. His eyes were brown without a hint of green or gray. And his hair was a color that she had achieved in grade school art class by mixing every watercolor she had—sort of a washed-out brownish gray. If it was true that the CIA sought nondescript individuals for field work, she was certain that Freemont would be the perfect candidate.

Freemont closed the door to the office. "Can I see some ID?"

Rebecca pulled the holder from a back pocket and held it out to him. His gaze went back and forth between the laminated card and her face until finally, he said, "Yeah, OK. Have a seat." He started around his desk. "Can't be too careful with these reporters. They've been using all kinds of tricks to get to me."

Rebecca nodded, then carefully laid her notebook on the edge of his desk. With his remote connection to a case that was rapidly fading from everyone's mind, Rebecca wondered if he'd actually seen more than a couple of reporters. "Well, I'm not part of the press."

"I don't have much use for PIs, either," he said matter-of-factly.

Now, her curiosity was piqued more than she could ignore. "Bad experience with one?"

"Too many people telling me what I can and can't do. I like my freedoms and I don't want anyone telling me different." He paused as if waiting for her to ponder his words. "You agree?"

Although familiar with the sentiment—you can't tell me what to do being her motto through much of high school and some of college—Rebecca had a more nuanced view now. The change had something to do with realizing that if she wasn't going to chase criminals, she would probably end up one if she continued to follow that dictum. A degree from the Criminal Justice Program in college followed by a stint at the FBI had completed the alteration in her worldview.

"Absolutely. People should exercise their freedoms up to the point where it starts hurting others."

"Well, I'm not hurting anyone," Freemont replied, his tone adding that he wasn't certain if she had just agreed with him or not.

Rebecca didn't address his unspoken doubt, but instead said, "I understand you were married to Violet Cruz until about three years ago."

"Correct." Freemont's pause made Rebecca wonder if that was all she was going to get when he continued. "And regardless of what you may have heard, we parted friends. Well, not best buds or anything like that, but we spoke ... from time to time. And that's a lot more than you get from most couples who split without kids."

His halting disclaimer addressed a question about motive that Rebecca hadn't asked—were you angry when Cruz asked for a divorce? But when she considered what had loosened his tongue, simple nervousness seemed more likely than guilt. Still, it was best not to jump to that conclusion too quickly.

"When was the last time you spoke with your ex-wife?"

Freemont raised his hands in the air, his head making a couple of quick shakes. "With her gone now a half-year or so, how the hell am I supposed to remember that? Eight months ago? A year?"

"Do you happen to remember what you talked about?"

His eyes narrowed; his forehead wrinkled. Then, after a moment, he smiled.

"Yeah, I do. I called her about seven or eight months ago, before the rally for that kid in St. Charles who needed that surgery." He snapped his fingers. "It was two days before the rally, and you can find that date in the papers or online. I remember because it was short notice, but Violet liked doing stuff for kids. Anyway, she couldn't make it. Not that she missed anything. Hardly anyone showed up, although I heard they got the money online."

"That kid? And that surgery?"

Freemont shrugged. "Yeah, I don't remember the details. Just search on something like head injury and horse-back riding in St. Charles from about eight months ago. You'll find the story and get the exact date. Hey, you should have asked me that first."

The order of the questions, however, was what Rebecca had intended. Recalling too much detail from a casual phone call that long ago would be suspicious, especially without some background for the question. So, after he had failed to produce a date, she'd asked him to supply the context. With that additional information, he'd recalled more—exactly as it should be if he hadn't rehearsed his answer in advance.

"Did you call Ms. Cruz at home or at one of her jobs?"

"I always call her cell, so I couldn't say where she was."

"OK. Were you—" Rebecca started when he interrupted.

"But now that I think about it, she was probably at home. I remember it was quiet and we talked for a while. It was never quiet at that food pantry or soup kitchen or whatever it is. And she was always in a hurry to get off the phone at the museum. Jeez, I remember a lot more about that call than I thought."

Freemont was looking less like a suspect by the minute. He and Cruz had talked well after the divorce, an assertion too easy to check for him to lie about it. That, plus the way he was reconstructing his memory of the call from small details was typical. So now, it was time to see what a sudden shift in the conversation might tell her.

"I understand that the handgun that Ms. Cruz used during the attempted assassination of Representative Barclay was registered to you?"

"Correct. That's apparently how the media vultures got my name."

"How is it that she had your gun?"

"I left it with her when we got divorced. Figured if she ever got hitched again, I might ask for it back. But till then, a single, good-lookin' woman living alone? She needed it more than me."

Now that he was feeling pretty good about himself, Rebecca said, "That's very generous of you, especially considering she didn't want to stay married to you."

Freemont's head jerked back like he'd been slapped, his face turning red to add to the impression.

"I thought we'd been through that. We had our differences, sure. Doesn't every married couple? But we were OK."

"You're talking about how you feel now, several years after the divorce. But what about when she first asked for it?"

"I suppose I felt like everyone else when something like that happens. A bit surprised. A bit disappointed."

Surprised? Disappointed? Rebecca didn't think so.

"You're saying you never had heated arguments over the things that often lead to divorces—things like money, in-laws, religion, or maybe sex?"

Freemont just sat there blinking for a moment. "I don't think I want to answer that."

"I understand," Rebecca replied in the blandest tone she could muster. She carefully picked up her notebook from his desk and began paging through. Would she need to pull out a pen, too? The question was answered almost before it had formed in her mind.

"I suppose it wouldn't hurt to take all those issues off the table," Freemont said slowly. "We discussed money every once in a while, but isn't that part of living together? As for all the rest of that stuff, it was never an issue. Neither of us was that religious. The in-laws didn't butt in. And at least for me, everything in the bedroom was great."

It wasn't the most enlightened view of intimacy, but more importantly, his comment answered one question while raising another. "So, if there were no problems, why'd she ask for a divorce?"

"Now, there you go, twisting my words. And you ask why I don't like PIs?"

I thought it was because PIs stepped on your rights, thought Rebecca, but to ask that would just make him even more defensive. "Sorry. I'm just trying to make sure I'm clear on what happened to you two."

"I suppose it was because she wanted to ignore a lot of the bad that happens in the world and I'm not a head-in-the-sand kind of guy. I suppose I kinda wore her out, and I feel bad about it. But what are you going to do?"

Good so far, she thought. If Gustafsson was correct about her cousin's feelings, then Cruz was tired of being second to his causes and tired of being alone. From his perspective, that same situation became his wife's inability to keep up with his crusading. And if that was true, Rebecca would bet they had argued about it. Freemont probably wouldn't admit to the tenor of those talks. He wouldn't want to say they'd had a shouting match until he walked out the door to right another wrong, but he would remember some of the occasions. And getting those details would help validate her guess.

"So, you were finding these causes that would help others, but she just wanted to stick with the one food pantry?" Freemont nodded. "And that got her unhappy enough with the marriage to ask for a divorce?"

Freemont's eyes narrowed for a moment, then he shrugged. "You gotta understand. I can get really involved if the movement is right. I even drove all the way to Minneapolis after the death of George Floyd. Like I said, I kinda wore her out."

"And you joined the demonstrations in Minneapolis?"

"Almost. I was close, but it got violent. I hung around the town for a while, but my boss wasn't real happy with me taking off, so I headed back."

"And you've done that other times? Going somewhere to protest or join a movement?"

"Not a lot. Maybe a few times a year. But the way I figure it, it don't do much good to demonstrate against dumping trash in the ocean if you're standing in the middle of a desert."

"I suppose not," Rebecca replied, wanting to keep him talking more than agreeing. "Is that why you went to the Council for the Right meetings? They were starting some movement that you wanted to join?"

"How do you know about them?" asked Freemont.

"It just came up when I was looking at her activities back then." She didn't think Freemont would confront her client about the case, but there was no reason to mention Gustafsson and give him an excuse.

He shrugged. "Naw. They aren't too keen on immigration and importing farm products, but those aren't my thing. See, I grew up down there, even know some of those guys from when we were kids. I thought they were poisoning us with all the pesticides they put on the crops, but it turns out, people like them are the reason more folks aren't starving. I'll take a few chemicals in my cereal if that's what it takes to feed America."

"Ms. Cruz went with you to those meetings?"

"Once and only once. And then, only about fifteen minutes. I think it was all in her mind, but she felt like they were looking down their noses at her. Like she should be working in the kitchen, not sitting down with them for dinner. I tried to tell her they were just a bunch of good ol' boys and wouldn't harm a fly, but she wouldn't have it."

In Rebecca's mind, Freemont was making a grave error in judgment. Based on Cruz's physical appearance alone, some in the Council would see her as a second-class citizen. Eventually, someone in that group would want something—a dance, a feel, her body. Those situations wouldn't end well for Cruz.

"So, just the one time for fifteen minutes or so?"

"Yeah, and I don't need any help remembering that night. It was pretty embarrassing. Never asked her to go again."

Assuming she could confirm these assertions, then it was unlikely the Council had anything to do with her delusions. Unless someone at the meeting had taken an unhealthy interest in her almost immediately, had systematically spirited her from her home each evening for the last three years to subject her to brainwashing, and had done so in a way that escaped everyone's notice, it was very unlikely they were involved. And if she was going to entertain theories that unlikely, then no group or person would look innocent.

It was time for her to change the direction of the interview again. "Before the museum took her bio down, I noticed that Ms. Cruz had an advanced Fine Arts degree. Is that where you met her, at school?"

"Naw, she went to some fancy school back east. I just did some community college stuff around here. We met at a Food for Americans rally and hit it off right away."

Rebecca thought about checking her interpretation of the grin that was on Abbett's face. It looked to her like Cruz had gotten caught up in the moment and they'd ended up in bed, but the question had little bearing on the case. So, instead, she asked, "What did you study at the community college? Art classes, like Ms. Cruz?"

"Never saw the point in them. I mean, knowing one painter from another isn't going to put food on the table. I took a little accounting, but that was deadly boring. A few marketing courses. And some landscape architecture, but those, I finished in December. You ever try to get a job in landscaping in the middle of the winter?"

"Take anything in the sciences? Maybe psychology? Or even something related to medicine?"

Was she really hoping Freemont was a closet mad scientist who had developed mind-control technology based on a few community college courses? Apparently so, since she had asked. But then, wasn't this part of being thorough? She hoped so because she didn't care for the alternative—that she was grasping at straws.

"Nope. Never cared for that stuff. Or understood it, for that matter."

That completed her line of questioning, and though she was tempted to end things there, she didn't. She returned to several issues, phrasing the question slightly differently. And when Freemont said, "I thought we covered this?" she said she just wanted to verify the facts as opposed to the real reason—she wanted to find an inconsistency in his story. None surfaced.

After that final round of questions, she thanked Freemont and headed back to her car.

During the walk to the parking lot, Rebecca had to admit she'd rarely seen two romantic partners with less motivation or weaker means to kill their lover than Abbett and Freemont. It wasn't even clear that Abbett and Cruz were romantically involved. Of course, she'd still need to verify parts of their stories, but she held little hope of finding anything like a lover's quarrel someone had witnessed, a secret degree in neuroscience, or a forged prescription for mind-altering drugs. It wasn't impossible, but progress by elimination appeared the better fit because she doubted it was either of them.

Afternoon, The Ruger-Phillips Complex

"Dr. Scott Anders?" Doc said. "I'm Sam Price."

Anders shifted his briefcase to shake the hand Doc extended. "The name's right," Anders said, "but not the title. I believe you are the only Ph.D. in this conversation." For a moment, Doc thought Anders might have been checking up on him, but then the man added, "And one who goes by Doc, as I hear it."

"A nickname, and please feel free to use it or Sam." The additional detail of his sobriquet undoubtedly came from Liz, the building's receptionist, who smiled and nodded when he turned her way. He returned the gesture while thinking it would be better if she wasn't so friendly and forthcoming—well, better for his purposes, if not for Ruger-Phillips's business.

Doc had been hoping to see the Healthtech facility. You never knew what information might be gleaned from cafeteria walls or company bulletin boards. "Come hear about the future of healthcare with wearable technology that may, someday, make routine physicals obsolete. Wednesday at lunch, with Dr. Julius Sun." A lead like that might prove quite useful. But after he'd suggested a time, Anders had been insistent—it made no sense for Doc to drive across town when he'd be only a few minutes away from the Ruger-Phillips complex. If he'd been faster on his feet, Doc would have suddenly remembered another meeting at the suggested time and offered to reschedule. But he hadn't thought of it.

Doc had found some face shots online, but in person, Anders was more imposing than they implied. He wore khaki pants and a navy blazer over a blue oxford shirt. But even under the jacket, the definition of his arm and chest muscles was obvious; he was no stranger to the gym. Steel-gray eyes looked out from under thick brown eyebrows and over a mouth that alternated only between smiling and grinning. He was bald, although it was probably from shaving; Doc was fairly certain he saw a nick on his scalp. All in all, Doc figured he had little trouble getting the attention of the opposite sex.

"I see you have your temp badge, so we can head back to my office." Doc held one of the double doors open as Anders walked into the work area. "You know, I would have been happy to come by your complex. You didn't have to come all the way over here."

Anders chuckled. "Complex might be a bit of an exaggeration since we only have one building. My company is nothing like the size of Ruger-Phillips, but we're very good at what we do. And like I mentioned, I had to be in the area anyway."

"So, what brought you to our neck of the woods?" asked Doc, just to make conversation.

"A meeting," replied Anders. "Just five or ten minutes away, at Biomedical Associates."

Doc nearly stumbled, the result of his head spinning around to look at his visitor. Was this Anders's idea of a joke? Was he about to be played, this bombshell merely the opening gambit? Or could it just be a coincidence? The questions flew through Doc's thoughts as he struggled to regain perspective. "Mr. Anders?" he said.

"Please call me Scott."

"I'm sorry, Scott, but I forgot a call I need to make. It'll just take a second." Doc turned to walk away, then turned back. "Sorry, security and all. Just stand where I can see you. I won't be long."

Anders seemed happy to comply, a grin and a nod his only reply. He stepped to the edge of the hallway and leaned against the wall.

Doc walked a few yards away, pulled his cell phone out of a pocket, and made a production of dialing his voicemail. He knew he talked to himself, but phoning himself? This was definitely a first, but he needed a moment to think before even small talk with Anders would be possible.

Biomedical Associates had been Nicole's company before she was ripped from his life, so it being Anders's excuse to meet him at Ruger-Phillips felt ... what? Surreal? Threatening? Was this Anders's first visit to her old company or was he a regular? And if the latter, what was his business there? After all, if he could create suicidal delusions in a woman, Cruz, who was quite well-grounded, what might he have done to precipitate Nicole's nightmare?

And then, it hit him—that was completely absurd.

Doc closed his eyes a moment, a hand coming to his forehead to massage some of the tension from his brow. "Marte was right," he muttered into the phone, more to chastise himself than to maintain the illusion he was talking to someone. She was right to be concerned about having him involved in the case. He was apparently at a point in his life where every stranger became a shadowy figure in his fiancée's kidnapping. And yet, that was impossible because the case was solved. There was no room for other suspects, different motives, or new means. There were no more boogeymen to find. And though the final disposition tore at his gut and haunted his thoughts day and night, he had to put these flights of fancy behind him.

And if Rebecca was right about that, what else had she said that he'd ignored. He'd have to come back to that question later.

"Sorry, Scott," Doc said as he returned to his waiting visitor. "I meant to make that call before I swung by the lobby, but it slipped my mind." They started down the hall again.

"No worries, Doc. I'll just have to run about 90 seconds beyond the end of our scheduled meeting to make sure I cover everything." His light tone made it clear to Doc he was joking, but Anders chuckled as if to underscore that fact.

Doc unlocked his office and gestured to a chair as they entered. "And here I was worried we'd run out of topics after five minutes," Doc said, matching Anders's tone.

"Not a chance. We may be small, but we're involved in some cutting-edge technology that will elevate your training products to the next level. I took the liberty of printing some materials on our offerings." Anders pulled two sheaves of papers from his case and handed one to Doc. Then, he returned to digging in his briefcase. After a few moments filled with headshaking, Anders looked up at Doc. "I find talking dry work and always bring a bottle of water. Always except today, apparently. Is there a vending machine around here?"

"Not necessary," said Doc. He walked to a lateral bookcase on a sidewall, pulled open the top drawer, and brought out a bottle.

"I hate to impose."

Doc spun the label toward his visitor.

"Ruger-Phillips bottles its own water?"

"Not quite. We had a water main problem near here a few weeks ago, and the company got bottled water for the duration. Trouble is, they apparently thought it was going to last a month because we have a storeroom nearly full of these. Please, help yourself."

"Thanks." Anders opened the bottle, took a sip, and launched into his pitch.

Doc had to admit, he was good—very smooth, very confident. And while everything he described was state-of-the-art, all of it was technology that could be found elsewhere in the industry. But for his purposes, there was an even bigger problem. All of it was passively monitoring the reactions of the person; nothing involved planting information in the heads of these individuals. Of course, Doc hadn't expected him to say, "And here's our latest tech, which is great at creating paranoid fantasies in people's minds." Even getting a hint about anything like that was going to require some digging.

"That was great," Doc said when Anders finished. "Just a couple of questions. Did you know we routinely package systems with eye tracking, so instructors can be assured that the trainees are paying attention? Dozing or staring off into space will just get that person another round with the same material. Or, at a minimum, they'll get more detailed testing on that topic to make sure their indifference was justified."

"Actually, I did know that," replied Anders. "And I even thought about dropping our eye-tracking product from the talk. But I've also seen your bio online and know you conduct comparative assessments of technology. With a nondisclosure agreement in place, we'd be glad to let you test our tech against yours. We've achieved some great results with our equipment."

"Fair enough," replied Doc. "I'll run that up my management chain. Everything else you discussed—measuring cortical activity, heart rate, skin conductance—that's all in our lab now, with only a few, specialized applications in the field. I'm confident we'd be interested in at least studying your specifications, and we'll see where things go from there."

"Excellent. I can't ask for more than that. Should I send the paperwork to you?"

"Initially, sure," said Doc. "Your point of contact may change later, but I can get the process started."

Now, it was time for Doc to do some fishing for information. He took a deep breath, though he didn't need it. Better, he figured, to look unsure about this topic rather than rush into it like he was hoping to trap a killer—which he was. "You, of course, know the biggest obstacle in training?"

"That you can't open the head of a trainee and dump the knowledge in?" Anders's trademark grin returned to his face.

"More or less," replied Doc. "The transition from words on a piece of paper to usable knowledge is a major hurdle. The same holds true of skills. Knowing the steps to tie a shoe may be something that a toddler can recite from memory, but only after practice can he or she do it quickly, smoothly, and almost without thought. Let's face it— every training technology company is looking for breakthroughs that make these transitions faster, easier, and more reliable. Is there anything that you're working on that would be relevant to those goals?"

Doc was confident his question sounded like what any training technology company might ask. And though a positive response to it wouldn't guarantee he found the capability he sought—the ability to take an absurd notion and make it a belief worth killing for—it would merit a closer investigation. Even Marte wouldn't be able to ignore this admission … if he got it.

For the first time during their discussion, Anders didn't have a ready answer, and that was enough to raise Doc's hopes. He waited as Anders's gaze flitted around the room. Was the man trading off the pros and cons of involving Ruger-Phillips in some ground-breaking research? Or was he, like Doc had done earlier, merely playing a part? Had he become aware of the indirect connection between Cruz and himself? If so, this might simply be a ploy to get him to try the tech and end up as delusional as she had been.

Doc had only started to critically question these notions when Anders spoke. "We have a very small piece of something like that. Unfortunately, it's well above my pay grade to say anything more. In fact, no one in my company could bring you onboard because the project involves a conglomerate of some of the biggest companies in the world, companies that could buy your and my companies with their pocket change. I'll ask, but don't expect to hear anything more about this."

That wasn't the response Doc had expected or wanted. But worse, it introduced some implications that didn't fit his theory. Cruz was local and had only traveled to Washington to make the attempt on Barclay's life. For her to be accidentally exposed to this technology, it had to be here, in St. Louis. So, describing their role as a "very small piece" meant Anders's company wasn't doing the final assembly and test. And though St. Louis had some large commercial companies, none had an apparent connection to something like this. Or did they?

"Do any of the major players in this work have offices in St. Louis?"

"Sorry, but I've said too much already."

"But if your company can't read me into this project, I need to know one that could."

"It's not training technology, *per se*," said Anders slowly. "When it's out in the public, you'll find someone to approach."

"But by then, it could be a mad dash to see who gets involved and who's left out in the cold. Maybe you can suggest some organization I could cozy up to? You know, just so I have a friend when the time comes."

Doc knew immediately that his last plea had been one too many. Anders lowered his head as if he wanted to stare at him over the top of his glasses ... except he didn't wear any.

"I think you can understand why any company involved in training would be interested," Doc said, hoping to reduce the suspicion that radiated from the man. Anders smiled, although Doc wasn't sure he'd ever seen one less real. The look made his skin crawl.

"Right," Anders said, the double meaning of "I agree" and "Like hell that's why you asked" hanging in the air between them. Before Doc could end the meeting and cut his losses, Anders continued. "I'll email you our nondisclosure forms for the other technologies we discussed, but as for the project I alluded to, I won't be forwarding your inquiry up my management chain. Frankly, your curiosity isn't welcome and could be dangerous."

"Is that a threat?"

"Take it as advice," said Anders. "Now, I have another engagement and must be going." He stood and turned to the door without waiting for Doc to respond.

Neither man spoke on the way to the lobby save some small talk about the weather. Once there, Doc said, "I'll be watching for the nondisclosure forms."

Anders nodded. "Good day, Dr. Price." He turned and left the building.

Doc stood there and watched him go. What had he stumbled into this time? If Anders didn't have the final technology, it was unlikely he had polluted Cruz's mind. Or was it possible that his very small piece of the puzzle was enough? And why hadn't he heard anything about this capability? Anything that could make words on a page feel like a real-life experience would be a major breakthrough. And one that, unfortunately, had obvious malevolent uses as well as earth-shattering benefits.

"Well, that's a first," came a voice from behind that he recognized as Liz's. He turned to the building's receptionist. "They are usually slapping you on the back by the time they leave."

"Yeah, this talk didn't go well. Not well at all."

Evening, The Basement of Kluge's Home

Kluge slowly stood up from his desk, walked to a wall, and placed both hands on it. Then, he let his head hang down between his shoulder blades while slowly shaking it side-to-side. "What the hell am I going to do?" he muttered to himself.

Over an hour ago, he'd decided that he must intensify his search. His interest in finding another woman that he could bend to his will had grown to a burning need that he could no longer hold at bay. He could hardly function in his daily life, seeing his next conquest in every set of legs crossed under a table and every derriere that swayed down the sidewalk in front of him.

So, he had gone through his ritual, nudging his anxiety to the background, bringing his omnipotence to the fore. And, as usual, his review of the near-disaster followed by his unqualified successes had calmed him, had given him focus. He then removed the laptop from the locked desk drawer and started it. Although unnecessary because he never changed these settings, he verified that there were no external connections to the computer—no Wi-Fi, no Bluetooth, no ethernet, nothing. This machine was never connected to the outside world where some hacker might accidentally stumble upon it. Rather, when he had new records to add, he loaded them from external drives, which he then destroyed. No one was going to find his digital trail because he had left none.

He opened the database. The images within it were high resolution, and so, initially, the computer renderings were fuzzy and indistinct. Then, over about five seconds, every detail came into focus, every line clear, every blemish apparent. When the contours of the first woman started to materialize, it had produced a slight ripple in his chest. And when the machine finished its task, Kluge could see promise in her smooth, soft lines. If no better candidate emerged, she would do.

He, too, remembered shuddering in revulsion when the next image came into focus. To his trained eye, the woman was hideous, a wrinkled and withered being not worth the electricity it took the computer to complete the rendering. That, however, was the limitation of his method—he received his updates to the database in bulk with no preselection of prospects. And so, the one or two true goddesses in the records were hidden among megabytes of wasted computer storage. He hit delete and moved on. Most of the first hour had gone the same way—he found a couple of possibilities, none as fitting as his last two women, along with hundreds of rejections. But as the hour drew to an end, he found "the one."

Even before the details had sharpened, his breath caught in his throat. He sat mesmerized, his eyes never leaving the screen as if looking away might force the computer to add a flaw where not so much as a slight shadow had existed before. But when the machine was done, there was nothing to spoil the vision of perfection. He reached forward with a trembling hand and lovingly caressed the glass. Never before had he looked upon such beauty.

For every image in his database, there was a corresponding page with personal information, and though he hated to remove the contents of the screen, afraid it might somehow disappear into a vast electronic wasteland, he had to know the name of this magnificent creature. But when it appeared, he cursed the cruel hand of fate. He knew the woman.

It was at that moment that he had stood from his desk and hung his head in consternation. It was a pose he still held. But after a moment more, he pushed away from the wall and turned back to his desk. He needed a reasoned solution, a balance between risk and reward. He sat back down.

The first rule he'd made after awakening the beast inside himself was never to prey upon anyone too close. He'd lost dozens of nights of sleep and spent countless hours in dread after his first kill because she had been an acquaintance. True, only one or two people knew they were even friends. And true, there were few, if any, public records to connect them. For the short time they'd been together, she had kept her apartment, so there were no changes of address filed with the post office. Her name wasn't on any utility bills. He'd even neglected to mention to his landlord that she was living with him, an oversight that had its roots in his finances more than in subterfuge.

His connection to the woman in the database was even more limited and vague. She was a friend of a friend, in a manner of speaking. But then, why should he risk going after her? If he ever came under suspicion for the disappearance of his first, however tenuous and speculative that connection might be, it would be strengthened tenfold if a second set of weak linkages was added to the mix. And besides, his database held hundreds more images. He returned to his task.

The second hour went much like the first, except that he found no more women who were even marginally acceptable. He wondered if finding "the one" had clouded his judgment. Maybe some of them were passable, but his standards had shifted? He wasn't sure. And then, toward the end of the hour, he found perfection again. His rapture was only starting to build, however, when he realized this rendering wasn't new. It was the same woman he had found the hour before. He wasn't sure how that could have happened, since "next" had always meant go forward rather than returning to an image that already haunted him. But somehow, the software hadn't worked that way.

He continued into the third hour of his hunt. After fifteen minutes or so, the image of the woman who had appeared twice before materialized again. And then again, about ten minutes later. And again.

Kluge pushed back from his desk and stared at his hands. Did they have a mind of their own? Was his left hand sneaking over to select "previous" on the menu when he was distracted by the rendering on the screen? And how was a finger supposed to keep track of the precise number of presses to return to this exact image? It wasn't possible. And yet, it had happened four times.

He stood, walked to a wall, and slammed his left fist into it. Searing pain radiated from his hand up through his arm and into his shoulder. He groaned in agony as he stared through watering eyes at knuckles that now dripped blood onto the concrete floor. "Damn you," he swore at the hand he no longer trusted, no longer controlled.

The pain, however, galvanized his resolve. He reseated himself and returned to one of the first two "acceptable" candidates. He checked her contact information. She lived in a small town north of St. Louis, which would make luring her to her fate that much easier. And the best part? He had absolutely no connection to her.

"Yes, my dear. You will do," he said as he shut down the computer.

Evening, Council for the Right Meeting, 30 Miles South of St. Louis, MO

"Damn, girl, you're as skinny as ever," said Wanda Jennings, wrapping Rebecca in a hug so tight she could hardly breathe. "I never expected to see you again. What's it been? A year?"

"Something like that."

"Missed us, huh?"

"Can I reuse my last answer?"

Jennings chuckled and took Rebecca by the elbow. "Well, let me show you around. We've changed a few things since your day. First, the guys all grab their first plate of wings before they sit. And the first pitcher of beer and the veggies are already on the table. They're a lot easier to handle with something in their bellies."

"I thought you had them pretty well under your thumb," said Rebecca.

"I do," countered Jennings. "I meant it'd be easier for you and the other girl."

Rebecca smiled as if appreciating the adjustment to process, but in fact, if Jennings wasn't going to chain their hands to the table, nothing was going to be that different. She'd still have to grin through the squeezes, slaps, and pinches from hands still greasy from the buffalo wings. There were other changes, Rebecca saw, including the location for the meeting, but mostly, everything was the same. It was the same pitchers of room-temperature beer. The same dingy setting, albeit at a new address. The same trays of veggies that would never be touched.

The FBI had set up her cover as part of the "Just Desserts" catering crew, the company name a complete misnomer unless you considered beer a dessert. And if she was going to step back into her role as the "favorite crew member to slap on the butt," she needed some constancy. And since that's exactly what she saw, her smile became real. This just might work.

"And the best part," Jennings was saying, "is that they can smoke here."

Of course, they could, thought Rebecca. Despite its name—the Taj Mahal Party Room—it was the basement of a bar. With all the smoking upstairs, they could probably get lung cancer just sniffing the tables. "Did I miss the memo on the uniform change? Your skirt has to be three inches longer than mine."

"RHIP," she replied, then clarified when Rebecca frowned. "Rank has its privileges. And, besides, no one wants to look at these old stems." She chuckled. "Yours, on the other hand? And wait till you see Cheryl's get-up. She must have taken another two inches off the hem. She's of age ... or so her ID says. But common sense? Not a lick."

Wanda turned to the door of the party room. "And here they come."

Rebecca didn't recognize the first man through, but the second and third were familiar. She relaxed a bit more. And then came a young woman—no, make that a young girl—who had to be Cheryl. Sitting was not an option with her skirt. And as if to confirm the suggestiveness of the attire, the guy behind her slapped her on the rear. Rebecca was hoping she'd crush his instep with the three-inch heels she was wearing, but she opted to giggle instead.

"Becky Ann," called a man across the room. It took Rebecca a moment, but it was Bobby McClaren. He hadn't grown any hair since she'd seen him last, but maybe he'd lost a few pounds. Or maybe he was just a lot calmer. The last time she had seen him, McClaren was out for one particular doctor's blood. "Hell, girl, you're a sight for sore eyes."

The FBI giving Becky as her first name was understandable. She wouldn't fail to react, but Ann? It wasn't her middle name and the two-name moniker seemed incredibly cliché. But that was the Bureau's call.

"Hey, Bobby. How's the wife and kids?"

It was always good to remind these men that they were family men, not that it slowed McClaren any. He swooped in for a hug, which she sidestepped with a preemptory, and unnecessarily firm, slap on his back.

"So?"

It took McClaren a moment. "Oh, the family. They're fine. Whatcha been up to?"

"Same ol'," Rebecca replied, not wanting to get to her questions too quickly. After all, McClaren would stand there for ten minutes making small talk if he thought he might be able to look down her shirt. But eventually, after the weather, the crops, the baseball team, and more of the weather, she said, "You'll never guess who moved in next door to me. The cousin of that woman, Violet Cruz, who shot Representative Barclay in DC."

"Barclay? Oh, yeah, I remember. But I thought she shot him in the keister?" McClaren laughed like it was the funniest thing he'd ever heard. "We could sure use a lot more like her. They just gotta have better aim. Clear out the deadwood in DC." Then, his face clouded. "Wait, Barclay? He supported farm subsidies, didn't he?"

"I think so," replied Rebecca, completely unsure of her answer though it probably made no difference.

"Well, farmer-friendly, plus one," said McClaren after a moment. "A politician, minus ten. Yeah, she had the right idea."

"But her cousin, the gal that moved in next door? She thought maybe Cruz had been to a few Council meetings."

"Beats the hell out of me," said McClaren with a shrug, "but not likely. Not many women come here, 'cept ol' Dingleman. And she only gets away with it 'cause most of the men are scared of her. Not me, mind you, but most of 'em."

"Hmm, that's strange," said Rebecca. "My neighbor was so sure. Maybe you knew her husband, Roy Freemont?"

"Oh, hell, yes, Becky Ann. Why didn't you say so? Roy's been here a few times. Total loser. Came in ranting 'bout pesticides. We told him he could pay twice as much for half the grain and get the bugs on the side if he wanted. Shut him up pretty damn quick."

"Guess she was just mistaken. Hey, your wings are getting cold, and your buddies are halfway through that pitcher."

McClaren's eyes finally strayed from her chest long enough to check on the alcohol supply.

"Yeah, guess I should get over there," he said and shuffled off. "See you around."

"Not if I see you first," said Rebecca, providing the cliched reply everyone in this group would expect.

The rest of the evening was the same. No one could recall Violet, which made sense if she'd made one brief appearance several years ago. But when Roy's name came up, they all remembered him, though not kindly. "Not a complete waste of air" was the most generous reaction she got. If Cruz had fallen prey to someone in the Council, it hadn't been through dozens of visits and a slow erosion of her reality. And the thought that in her one short visit, someone had undertaken a campaign to systematically destroy her mind through drugs, abuse, or both was pretty farfetched.

So, like the cases of Abbett and Freemont, it was progress by elimination. Rebecca just hoped it wouldn't continue this way because when the suspects were gone, so was her client's last hope.

FRIDAY, AUGUST 5

Morning, The Ruger–Phillips Complex

It was going to be a shot in the dark, and there were few things in life that Doc liked less.

He preferred collecting data and, preferably, lots of them. Then, he'd calculate the statistics that separated the pattern from the noise. That part was easy. Every politician and salesman, every advertising executive and stock market analyst, every sophomore in a college math class and sports analyst had statistics. It was understanding them correctly in light of their limitations and interpreting them in light of one's world knowledge that was the hard part. That was the step where, as Mark Twain had said, they became part of the trio of lies, damned lies, and statistics. And it was, easily, the part he liked best. It was the challenge that filled his mind every day and many of his nights.

Did the finding that people who ate caviar have fewer and milder colds mean that fish eggs were medicine? Probably not because, in the context of other facts about these individuals, this statistic most likely meant they could afford better healthcare. And sure enough, if one accounted for socioeconomic status, fish-egg eating and severity of colds were no longer related. Of course, most of the statistics he worked with were considerably more difficult to interpret, but before he could worry about finding their meaning, he needed them. And to get them, he needed data.

The thing about data, Doc knew, is that you have to know where to look, and in the case of Anders, he had no idea. In their meeting, he'd definitely touched a nerve, so asking the man wasn't an option. Neither was getting information from his company; anyone on this mysterious project would be watching for him. Theft from Healthtech? Neither his skills—he wasn't a world-class cat burglar—nor his morals would allow it. All that was left was a shot in the dark. Or rather, a series of them.

So, yesterday, after raising Anders's suspicions, he had fired off his first shot. He waited until after business hours and called Anders's office from a phone at the local public library. Even talking a librarian into letting him make a local call on their phone was a risk, but judging by her reaction—she hardly broke eye contact with the book she was reading—apparently, it wasn't much of one. Then came the second shot in the dark—taking the chance that Anders's recorded message would give the name and phone number of his office assistant as a backup when he couldn't answer. Fortunately, it did.

Today brought volley number three—taking the chance that Anders wouldn't confide all his concerns about Doc with his OA. Her unfamiliarity with his *faux pas* was necessary if he was to use his name and company affiliation to get the first of what he hoped would be a boatload of data on the man. Doc dialed the OA's number.

"Scott Anders's office. How may I direct your call?"

"Susy Wu?"

"Yes," the woman replied somewhat hesitantly. "This is Susy Wu."

"Hi. I'm Dr. Sam Price ...."

"Oh, sure, from Ruger-Phillips. You met with Mr. Anders yesterday. How can I help you?"

Good, it didn't sound like Anders had said anything too negative about him. "Mr. Anders emailed three nondisclosure agreements to me, but somehow, the last one got corrupted. I was wondering if you could send it again?"

"Oh, sure, since I was the person who sent them the first time. But one getting corrupted? That bothers me. Can you call me directly if it happens again? I'd want our IT people on it if we have a problem."

"How about I call you back, success or not, just so you know." Doc wasn't feeling that generous with his time, but the gesture might generate some goodwill.

"That's extremely nice of you." Doc nodded to himself. So far, so good. "Is there anything else I can do for you?"

And now came the long shot. If the previous gambles had been shots in a darkened twelve-by-twelve-foot room where all he had to do was hit the east wall, this one was at a bullseye fifty yards away in the dead of a moonless night at the bottom of a cave. Doc suddenly wondered why he had ever thought this would work, but he saw no other options.

"Actually, there is something. Mr. Anders—Scott—was talking about a woman he had dated six or seven months ago. At the time, the name sounded familiar, like someone I knew in school. But now, I can't recall the name and I wanted to look her up."

There was a pause on the line causing Doc's hope for success to fade appreciably. Finally, Wu said, "Mr. Anders isn't in at the moment, but I can leave him a message with that question."

"Actually, I was hoping to avoid bothering him with such a trivial issue. It even might give him the impression I wasn't paying attention rather than just failing to make a note of her name."

"Well, then, perhaps you should have written it down."

Ouch. The woman's comeback had a bite to it. But she wasn't done yet. "Sorry, but I need to go now."

His long shot now appeared a clean miss. In fact, Doc now wondered if he'd even been facing toward the bullseye at the bottom of his cave. But his dismay made an abrupt turn to confusion when she added, "I'll call you back in a few minutes." She disconnected.

What was going on? Doc was having difficulty making any sense of the last couple of exchanges. Her rebuff was certainly out of character for someone whose job included schmoozing customers. And then, his phone rang. The number was unfamiliar, so he answered with the standard Ruger–Phillips greeting. "Dr. Sam Price, Ruger–Phillips Training Research and Development Division. How may I help you?"

"Hi, Dr. Price. It's Susy Wu."

"But the number ...?"

"I'm on my cell and outside the building. Look, there is no way Mr. Anders discussed his dating history with a potential client. Now, I'll give you one chance to tell me exactly what's going on."

Calling on a personal phone? Outside the building? Seeking a reason to confide in him? Suddenly, the pieces fit together, the key speculation being her relationship with her boss. Ms. Wu wasn't particularly fond of him.

"You looked up the main Ruger-Phillips number online, called them, and asked for me? Just to make sure I'm who I say I am?"

"You have a funny way of using your one chance to be straight with me. Why the heck do you want to talk to a disgruntled old flame?"

"Why do you say disgruntled?"

"Last chance," she said in reply.

"Sorry, my thoughts are racing a bit. I want to check him out, so I'm not interested in a disgruntled former girlfriend as much as one who'll be straight with me." Doc paused but saw no reason not to finish the thought. "And why I want to know is personal, not business, so anything you say won't hurt your company, your boss, or your relationship with him."

"Personal to you or to a woman he dumped on?"

Bingo. She didn't care for Anders. "It's the latter, but look, I'm not a vigilante. I have no thought of taking the law into my own hands, but some information about Anders would go a long way for this woman to close a chapter of her life."

As a summary of why he wanted to help Gustafsson, he thought it was pretty good—all true but not everything. As for the real victim of Anders, if Cruz was, he'd let the law handle that part.

The line went silent. Doc considered making the offer of lunch. Maybe the setting would let her speak more freely? But if he was right about her reasons for letting him get this far, the suggestion might have the opposite effect. There was plenty of research that said rewarding people to do something they intrinsically wanted to do could weaken their motivation. Of course, he did think it a bit strange that he'd recalled that detail at this specific moment, but he had. So, he waited.

"I can't give you a name."

"But ...."

"Just hold on, Dr. Price. I can't give you a name because it feels like I'm betraying my company, regardless of your assurances. But I can say you might find some interesting stories online about a new hospital wing in West County. The opening ceremony was closer to five months ago than six, but Mr. Anders spoke there. And he had a friend along you might want to talk to. Someone he saw until about that time and I'm sure she'll give you the straight scoop."

"Thanks, Susy. And whatever happens, I'll make sure your name never comes up."

"That's because we never talked," Wu said and then disconnected before he could say, "What phone call?"

It only took Doc about three minutes to find the story he wanted online. Anders had been one of the primary speakers at the ceremony, his praise of his own company's products thinly veiled in a speech about the future of medical technology. But Doc had nearly given up on finding the name of his companion until he came to almost the end of the article. Then, there she was, almost stealing the center of a photograph that was supposed to be of Anders.

Fortunately, her name and job title were given as background, the latter a bit of a surprise to Doc. She worked in a law office as Special Liaison to the Missouri State Juvenile Justice system. It seemed an awfully serious title for the girlfriend of a man he now thought might be a player. But the real surprise came when he returned his gaze to the picture. If he hadn't known better, he would have sworn he was looking at a photograph of Violet Cruz—a beauty with black hair, brown eyes, and a dark complexion.

If Anders was a serial killer, Doc figured he now knew his type. But more importantly, he knew the name of the woman who would bring him to justice. He glanced at the picture's caption again to sear that name into his memory. Then, he leaned back in his office chair, stared at the ceiling, and muttered to himself, "Nice to meet you, Samantha Rowles."

Afternoon, The Basement of Kluge's Home

Kluge had left work after lunch, calling to tell his boss he was sick rather than returning. And, in some sense, he was ill. His body was being physically assaulted by his unfulfilled need to enlist another woman in his grand plan.

He'd contacted the woman he'd considered "acceptable." And consistent with the plan's prescripts, he'd described a scenario that should have elicited her cooperation. It hadn't. He'd always known that this could happen, and it had, twice before. In those cases, he'd taken the women's refusals not as a blot on his vision or his methods, but as their unconscious admission that they were unworthy of the honor he was to bestow. Of course, he could have forced them to comply, but violence only played a part in the finale of his plan's script. He needed to keep his new friend, violence, at bay until after the women took the bait.

But he, too, bore responsibility for this latest setback. He had bent his standards to the point of breaking in choosing this woman, and now, his weakness infuriated him. In fact, when she had declined, he'd nearly settled on simple violence for the momentary reprieve it offered. He even knew the perfect object for his wrath—the office assistant of a friend at work. She wasn't acceptable as part of his vision, but her screams of fear and agony as he raped and beat her to death would soothe the beast within him, at least, for a time.

Before he'd left work, he'd even walked to her desk to look down on her, all smug and self-righteous. But as he tried to figure a way to spirit her from his place of business, he knew he'd be trading his life for hers. Even if he got her out of the building unseen, the police would be knocking on his door tomorrow, if not tonight. He and the woman were too close for them to ignore him when she went missing. So, he left for lunch, then called in sick.

Now, desperate for relief from the demons that tormented him, he hurried through his lessons learned to master his unease, then opened the database. He had no delusions about what he would find. And sure enough, the perfect one he'd found before was the first image to come to his screen. It would also be the last during this session because he'd already decided—no more lowering his standards. And with her, that wouldn't be necessary. If anything, her smooth, flawless contours pushed them to new heights.

He paged to her contact information. Although he knew the basics, knew who she was, he wanted to verify the details because he planned to watch her for a time. He normally didn't go to these lengths—he hadn't since number two, his first after awakening the beast. But because this woman was familiar, additional care was necessary. And if he saw anything that suggested that the connection between them was more apparent than he believed, he'd move on. It would be painful to do so but better than death.

With the decision made, the risk seemed to shrink. Surely, no one would discover the connection between them, especially given the way she would die. He shut down his computer and folded his hands in his lap. "Soon," Kluge said to the empty room, "you shall be mine, Samantha Rowles."

Afternoon, The Healthtech Building

If "form follows function" was the principle used in the design of the Healthtech building, then no-frills shelter from the elements was the function. It was a two-story rectangular box of red brick. In the middle of the front façade, a set of metal double doors was flanked on the left by a bank of windows. The monotony of the bricks on the right side, however, was broken only by a slightly too-bright bronze plaque with the company's name. There were no windows on that side, evoking visions in Rebecca's mind of a secret lab isolated from the prying eyes on the street. Given the highly competitive nature of Healthtech's business, that might be the case.

"What a depressing place," Rebecca mumbled to herself as she sat in the parking lot waiting for the appointed hour of her meeting with Anders. After both Roy Freemont and Billy Abbett proved unlikely suspects and the visit to the Council for the Right had produced no leads, she'd been left with the museum where Cruz had worked, a food pantry where she had volunteered, Cruz's doctor, and Scott Anders on the list Gustafsson had provided.

The last entry had moved to first priority for Rebecca primarily because she had a specific person, Anders, to investigate and he had a somewhat shadowy connection to the victim. Had his talk on one of Healthtech's new systems been enough for Cruz to mention him to her cousin? Or had he been something more in Cruz's past? As for the rest of the entries on Gustafsson's list, the family doctor was probably what he appeared, while his office staff and the other two organizations would require some scrutiny into anything that felt out of place. While that kind of broad investigative effort could be pivotal, it was frequently long, boring, and ultimately, unproductive. Nonetheless, she'd set up initial meetings at all three locations for tomorrow.

Moving the investigation forward to look at Anders meant a change in possible motives for the crime. Of the four traditional L's that had been her focus to date—lust, love, loathing, and loot—none seemed that likely because of the limited amount of time Anders and Cruz had known each other. She would check the first three, as strong emotions between them might have developed quickly, but as for the fourth, Anders didn't need the money. He was already quite well-to-do. And even if his greed was insatiable, Rebecca couldn't fathom any way he stood to gain financially from Cruz's death. Apparently, she hadn't even signed a consent form to be in the Healthtech study, much less penned her name to a million-dollar life insurance policy with Anders as the beneficiary.

Rebecca admitted to many other motives for murder besides the four L's, of course, such as killing for thrill or to conceal another crime; they were just not as common. And of the alternatives for this case, politics was the most likely. Barclay was, after all, a politician.

Assuming that Barclay's political leanings had been the source of Cruz's motivation, it wasn't clear when or why she'd developed a grudge that was worth her life. She had never been active politically, save some campaigning for programs to reduce hunger. And Barclay had no record opposing programs of that ilk. She also hadn't prepared herself to kill Barclay, having never fired Freemont's handgun before the day she made the attempt on his life. And finally, after she'd decided to assassinate the representative, she hadn't spent the last 24 hours of her life posting about his political failings. Rather, all of her writing concerned his Martian lineage. Nothing added up.

It was equally unclear what political advantage Anders would gain from Barclay's death. Rebecca's initial search of Barclay's history and voting record had turned up little of interest. Like many in his field, he'd been a lawyer who turned to politics, working his way up to mayor of the state's second-largest city. Perhaps driven by the work-from-home trend in employment—not to mention the natural beauty of his home state—the city had flourished under his administration. That success paved the way for a successful run for the state senate. Four years later, he ran for the U.S. House of Representatives but lost to the incumbent in the party primaries. He returned to his law firm, but when the incumbent retired after four more years, Barclay picked up his endorsement. Even so, the race had been close, but he had won.

Both in the state senate and the U.S. House, Barclay's voting record had been somewhat conservative but not strikingly so. At a very high level, he favored limiting the federal government in favor of state's rights, but there were exceptions. And he supported modernizing the public health system, his position on this issue being moderate to slightly progressive. If anything, Barclay's death would be a blow to Healthtech and Anders rather than a boon. Overall, Rebecca had a difficult time seeing how such a nearly middle-of-the-road stance could lead to murder, but perhaps she hadn't discovered the precipitating issue yet.

But when it came to having the means to weaponize Cruz against Barclay, Anders became a more interesting possibility.

Some of the methods he might have used to turn her took time, and it wasn't clear there had been much. A quick check at the museum indicated that Cruz had been at work regularly until the day before the assassination attempt. The same was true of the food pantry. And Cruz's communications with Gustafsson and other family members had been regular until the end. So, long-term emotional and physical abuse by Anders—or anyone else for that matter—was unlikely. To be even more confident in that conclusion, she planned to verify the timeline of their association when she interviewed Anders.

On the other hand, threats of violence against friends or family required only moments, but there was a problem here as well—the same one that suggested that Cruz hadn't gone after Barclay for political reasons. Her posts on the man were delusional but extensive. Someone, presumably Cruz, had spent hours weaving a convoluted plot of space aliens methodically infiltrating humanity that was truly worthy of the sci-fi masters of literature, television, and the movies. It didn't seem the work of someone worried about kin, although she would need to check that conclusion further as well.

Brain trauma was another possibility—the effect of a head injury could be immediate and the convoluted thoughts it produced totally compelling to the victim. Anders could have delivered the blow accidentally or on purpose, although an accident was more likely. Would anyone club someone over the head in the hopes that he or she would become delusional enough to kill someone and die in the effort? That seemed too farfetched even for a case where farfetched was starting to look normal. And besides, the autopsy on Cruz had found no brain damage due to injury or disease that had existed before the shooting.

None of these natural causes of delusional behavior, however, was what made Anders a more interesting suspect. Rather, it was all the high-tech equipment at his place of work. Considering the capabilities within the four walls of the Healthtech building, it was conceivable that someone had created a reality-warping device. Conceivable, but just barely.

Rebecca's accounting of all the possible sources of Cruz's delusion, however, had always raised a more general concern in her mind—weren't complex yet completely impossible conspiracy theories becoming somewhat common? Rebecca couldn't count the number she'd heard over the last few years. Generally, she'd written them off as attention-getting ploys—or vote-getting ones when promulgated by politicians. But now, she wondered, could they be something else? A sign of the times? The after-effects of modern-day stress? Could Cruz have become a victim to whatever was sweeping through the world from the home's hearth to the halls of Congress? Or maybe it was like Doc said—bursts of gamma radiation from deep space controlled by the Russian mafia had fried her thoughts.

Rebecca rolled her eyes at Doc's off-the-wall example, though she had to admit, it had appeal. It was just bizarre enough to catch on if he ever took it to social media.

Just the passing thought of Doc, however, was enough to make Rebecca shake her head. She could use Doc's expertise on this case, and she liked having him around. And though the anger that had driven her final words to him had receded, the beliefs behind them hadn't changed. He was mistaking self-destruction for self-awareness and closure. She wasn't even certain what he hoped to achieve with his compulsion, but whatever it was, she wished he'd realize his mistake and get on with life. But hoping wasn't going to catch a killer, so she grabbed her notebook from the passenger seat and headed to the Healthtech building.

Inside, the company's security measures were apparent. Doors were equipped with everything from simple keypad locks to thumbprint and retinal scanners. And although visitor badges weren't required, the receptionist—a beefy young man who would intimidate most—never left her side until they reached a door marked only with the number 0623. He knocked and Rebecca heard, "Come" from inside. A man that Rebecca recognized as Anders stood but made no move to come around the desk.

"Ms. Marte. I'm Scott Anders. Or should I address you as Private Investigator Marte?"

Pre-pandemic, his standoffish welcome might have felt rude. Post-pandemic, it might be deemed anything from panicked to pragmatic, although Rebecca's opinion fell somewhere closer to the latter end of that continuum. "Ms. Marte is fine, Mr. Anders."

He nodded, then gestured to a chair across the desk while he sat. "You mentioned Ms. Cruz during our call, so I refreshed my memory of the case. Unfortunately, I'm not going to have much to say. We haven't been released from the HIPPA privacy rule by either 45 CFR 164.508 or 45 CFR 164.512(i)."

It was either an impressive display of memory or Anders was well practiced in using the law to avoid answering questions. Either way, Rebecca was prepared for it. "So, you are in possession of confidential health information on Violet Cruz that warrants HIPPA protection."

Anders drew back, a frown forming on his face. But before he could compose a meaningless disclaimer, the gist of which would probably be that his answer was a standard response whether they had data or not, she continued. "It's not important. I have no questions about Ms. Cruz's health. Only your interactions with her." It was a sequence designed to put him off balance. And since his frown grew fractionally, it seemed to be working.

"My interactions?"

"Yes. How many times did you meet? For how long and where, to start."

Anders paused, drawing his lips in a tight line. After a moment, he shrugged. "One phone call. One meeting here at our building."

"Durations?"

"The call was to schedule the meeting, so maybe five minutes. And the first meeting generally runs from 45 minutes to an hour." His memory for these questions was obviously poorer than his recall of HIPPA regulations.

"And during the meeting, did she try your biofeedback equipment?"

"No," he replied without hesitation.

So, it was going to be the pulling-teeth type of interview—ask a question and get a one-word answer. "And why is that?"

"Use of the equipment would only occur at the second meeting, and she never attended a second meeting."

"You sound pretty certain of that," said Rebecca, watching his face and body more than waiting for a response.

"We don't vary from protocol," he said. "She never gave us her consent, so it was never scheduled."

If there were tells in his tone or posture, Rebecca couldn't spot them. But on the other hand, he was sticking to company policy and doling out information like it was the last rations of a starving man. As to why, that was less clear. He was busy? Impatient? Guilty? Perhaps something more open-ended would provide more insight. "And what is the protocol from initial recruitment to the first use of the equipment?"

Anders released a long sigh. "When doctors in our network believe they have a patient who might benefit from one of our clinical-trial programs, they inform the individual of our work. If the patient is interested, they call to schedule an appointment for an introductory presentation. Ms. Cruz did that. That first meeting is used to describe our technology and answer their questions. I usually handle that part of the process and did so for the group with Ms. Cruz. During the next meeting, the participants would have a supervised session with our equipment, but with her, that meeting never occurred."

"So, you standing at the front of a room of people talking about your biofeedback device was your only interaction with Ms. Cruz?"

"To the best of my knowledge, yes."

Rebecca doubted the veracity of this answer and gave him a moment to consider his words.

"We do these orientation sessions all the time. I don't remember everyone who comes through here."

Rebecca's uncertainty about Anders's truthfulness became less equivocal; there was more to their meeting than Anders was admitting. But what? "So, no chat before or after the meeting with Ms. Cruz? No offer to personally supervise her first session with the equipment?"

With the nearly imperceptible break in his eye contact, Rebecca would have bet a week's worth of her fee that it was one of the two and probably the latter. And that made sense. What better way to make a beautiful woman feel indebted to him and, in turn, establish trust that he could later exploit? And the fact that he was uneasy suggested that he'd done this before. Otherwise, it was just a one-time, magnanimous gesture that Cruz hadn't accepted; there would be no past offers—and presumably some acceptances—to make him edgy.

"Not that I recall," said Anders, now having mastered his urge to glance away.

While Anders using his position and his company's capabilities to make women feel indebted was a serious breach of professional ethics, it wasn't murder. It did, however, suggest a motive to Rebecca. Perhaps his lecherous game had gotten out of hand and he had to dispose of her? However, the journey from being friendly at an orientation meeting to planting a delusion to rid himself of a lover turned bitter was long. Rebecca wasn't certain there had been enough time.

"When was this first meeting with Cruz?"

"I'd have to check the records to be sure?" said Anders.

"Perhaps you remember how long it was before her death? I'd think a research participant dying might make that fact stick in your mind."

"Like I said"—a bit of exasperation creeping into his tone—"Ms. Cruz wasn't a participant. She expressed some interest in our work, attended a meeting, and never came back." He sighed again. "But someone at the office did put two and two together and recognized her name. That did cause enough of a stir that I can tell you that the orientation meeting was a little less than three weeks before the incident in DC. I'm sure you know that date."

The incident in DC? That was a strange way for him to describe a woman's death, but as to why he had or what it meant, she didn't know. That issue aside, if this timing was correct, hard evidence of it might become important. "Where are the formal records that would verify the date of this meeting?"

Anders chuckled. "You're going to need at least a court order to see anything like that."

"And if it comes to that, no problem. So, does that mean you have proof?"

Anders shrugged. "Signed physical consent forms are kept here. They are also scanned and copied, so physical and digital backups can be kept here and off-site. We don't take risks with informed consent forms."

He sounded confident, almost like he was daring her to question the timing of the meeting ... meaning the three-week window was probably accurate. If so, that wasn't much time for Cruz and Anders to become involved, her to become disillusioned with the relationship and threaten him, him to plant the space alien myth in her thoughts, and her to act on it, leading to her death. It wasn't impossible, Rebecca supposed, but it would be the fastest transition from lust to murder she could imagine. But to disprove even this highly improbable scenario, Rebecca made a note to ask her client for Cruz's phone records and her appointment book, assuming the police didn't still have them. Anything as volatile as she was imagining would have resulted in a lot of trysts and dozens of calls between Cruz and Anders.

But even if the two of them had fallen together only to fall out three weeks later, the means to create Cruz's delusion remained the major void in any theory that linked Anders to her death. That void needed to be filled. Unfortunately, Rebecca's research indicated that the design of their biofeedback equipment would have to be substantially different from anything else on the market for it to be the cause of any bizarre change in thought.

"Do you have FDA approval for the device Cruz was to use?"

Rebecca almost didn't need to hear his response, as Anders's confused, quizzical expression already spoke volumes. He hadn't expected the question and didn't see the relevance.

"Well, technically," he said slowly as he rubbed a hand over his chin, "we don't need approval from the FDA. These devices are Class II equipment, and the FDA has exempted battery-operated biofeedback equipment as a group from the Class's approval process. The FDA still recommends the Premarket Notification process and we've completed that."

"So, there's no independent test by the FDA or its representatives of your device's safety or effectiveness. Or for that matter, testing by anyone else other than your company."

"Correct," Anders replied with another shrug.

If he felt any vulnerability making this admission, it didn't show to Rebecca. "Is that because your equipment is substantially equivalent to other products being used?"

Anders's expression changed from one of confusion to a grin, and he chuckled softly. "Substantially equivalent, you say? Interesting choice of words since it's exactly the same phrase the FDA would use if that was their finding. Something tells me you did a bit of homework on the FDA and biofeedback technology, which begs the question, why are you asking me for all this information?"

It was a careless slipup. It was a gaff that her old FBI mentor would have caught in an instant, reminding Rebecca that she wasn't long out of the Academy, much less on the job. She had to be more careful. But for her to deny it now could make things worse. Saying nothing about his guess and letting him draw his own conclusions? That almost always worked.

"I'm just trying to establish if anyone, including the FDA, has looked into the possibility of a malfunction."

"One that would cause harm to the user?" Anders asked, his eyes wide. He didn't wait for her to answer. "That's impossible. It's a low voltage, low amperage system. Even if you ran the current through the heart muscle, it wouldn't cause fibrillation. Not even close."

"But what about ...."

Anders cut her off with a wave of his hand. "What you don't seem to understand is that biofeedback equipment is responding to changes in your body, not producing them. The equipment is passively reading, listening to your body if you will. Now, it is true that measuring something like skin conductance involves passing a very tiny charge between two points, usually two fingers of one hand. But the charge is so small, you feel nothing. And there is no amplification circuit in our equipment that would turn these minuscule charges into anything dangerous. That's why the FDA just wants to be informed of new products rather than testing them."

Again, Anders was very confident in his answers, suggesting that if their design was substantially different from others, they hadn't informed the FDA. That would be quite risky for a company their size ... and without any reason that Rebecca could see. They wouldn't skip the regulatory steps on a revolutionary design on the off chance that it malfunctioned and fried someone's brain later.

Though Anders was the strongest suspect so far, Rebecca's quick mental accounting of the evidence implicating him revealed how pathetic her case was. He had no motive, save possibly a secret, whirlwind affair with Cruz. The timing was also a problem, but again, if she could find even a single public sighting of them out on the town or a series of calls on Cruz's phone records, lust turned toxic became more likely. But as for the means—it remained a mystery. Healthtech putting a new wonder treatment at risk by not following the law was a stretch ... unless it was one madman taking advantage of their equipment.

"Were you involved in the design of this biofeedback equipment?"

"Hardly," he replied with a chuckle. "I've picked up the terminology for obvious reasons, but my background is marketing."

That was too easily verified for Anders to lie about it, but she'd check anyway.

Typically, at this point, Rebecca would have returned to some of the early questions and rephrase the issue or introduce a slight error into her summary of it. Unfortunately, there wasn't much to cover. Anders would know his company's procedures and FDA requirements chapter and verse, which left timing. But when she mentioned the date of Cruz's death and tried to subtract four weeks from it, Anders was quick to correct her. "Sorry, but I believe it was three weeks later, not a month."

What was left was the possibility that Anders was using his position to turn women's trust and appreciation into sexual favors, and Rebecca wasn't about to let that continue. But before she mentioned her suspicions to his superiors, she'd make sure he wasn't involved in Cruz's death and then collect a bit more evidence. She needed enough for his management to take her seriously and then have security escort him out the door. Hopefully, criminal proceedings would follow, but her objectives would be met either way.

With the interview at an end, Rebecca thanked Anders for his time, and he called reception to escort her out. But rather than waiting, they started the walk toward the front door, planning to meet the bodybuilder receptionist halfway. Before they got that far, however, Rebecca, on a whim, asked, "Do you happen to know Dr. Sam Price?"

It was fortunate that the hallway was straight and uncrowded because if she hadn't been watching his face out of the corner of her eye, she would have missed the most striking admission so far. In the matter of a few split seconds, Anders's expression went from eyes wide to mere slits before his public persona masked his feelings again.

"A researcher at Ruger-Phillips, if I remember right. He's been interested in testing some of our equipment for training use. How do you know him?"

Rebecca hadn't really expected Doc to drop the case. That wasn't in his DNA. But when and how he might approach Anders wasn't clear. Now, with the contact already made and Anders's earlier reaction to his name, she saw a chance to increase the pressure on her leading suspect. The only problem was, the ploy might increase the chance Doc got hurt. But then, he wanted to play PI. And besides, she would warn him to watch his back.

"I don't really know him. But strangely, he seems to be talking to the same people that I am about Cruz's death. He seems to be on something of a crusade to find out who or what got her so out of touch with reality."

Prepared this time, Anders did better, but Rebecca still caught a slight twitch in one eye.

Evening, Resterilli's Italian Restaurant

"Samantha Rowles?" asked Doc of the black-haired, brown-eyed woman seated at a table near the back of the restaurant's dining room. She looked up from her phone. Doc would have sworn she hadn't been looking at one when he started across the room. If true, this wasn't a promising start to an interview that, in his mind, had to go well.

"No, sorry," she said, hardly breaking eye contact with the screen.

Doc looked around the room, then back toward the woman. His brow wrinkled, not so much in displeasure as perplexity. He hadn't expected this much resistance when all he was asking was an audience, five minutes of her time. Of course, as attractive as she was, discouraging come-ons from strangers—even ones who had called in advance—was probably as common as brushing her teeth. And then, a slight smile crossed his lips. "I didn't know a blank screen could be so interesting."

She looked up, frowning.

"The screen's reflected in your wine glass."

She shoved the phone in a pocket, slowly shaking her head. "OK, I'm Samantha Rowles, but I was just trying to save us both some awkwardness. Sorry, but you're not my type. So, let's just say you never found me."

"And that might have been the case if you hadn't come. But you did, which makes me think you're at least a little bit interested in what I have to say."

"Damn little," she muttered. During the disapproving scowl that followed, Doc had a chance to look at Rowles more closely. First impression, he wasn't sure he'd ever seen anyone make elegance look so easy. Her lustrous black hair fell loosely onto her shoulders, yet every strand seemed perfectly placed. Her clothes looked comfortable, yet trendy at the same time. Even with her face scrunched up in displeasure, she couldn't hide a perfect complexion and deep brown eyes. And she was wearing tennis shoes.

"They're comfortable," she said, noticing the direction of his gaze.

"Sorry, I didn't mean to stare."

A slight smile came to her lips. "That's OK. At least you didn't spend all your time looking at ...." But rather than finish in words, she waved a hand over her chest.

"The logo on your shirt?"

"Very funny," she said without sounding at all amused, then rolled her shoulders. "You might as well sit down."

Doc quickly pulled out a chair and sat. He didn't want to give her a chance to reconsider.

"You know, your story's pretty unbelievable? You have a friend who developed these strange ideas shortly after going to Healthtech for some type of treatment?"

Since honesty with Anders's assistant had gotten him this far, Doc figured he give it another try. So, he had told Rowles everything … well, almost everything. He'd kept Cruz's and Barclay's name out of it, figuring that information might keep Rowles from talking. Who wanted to be involved with a political assassination attempt driven by insanity?

"Correct, except it's the cousin of a friend. And though it's probably just a coincidence, the cousin developed the symptoms shortly after a treatment that Scott Anders gave her."

"So, you said," replied Rowles, looking down at the table for a moment, then back up. "You do know that the industry that Scott works in is highly regulated. If anything unexpected happened after a treatment, it would raise all kinds of red flags."

"It would if it was reported, but it's not likely that it would be. Since their technology is mostly designed to help people relax, they only ask about how tense or anxious people feel before, during, and after treatment."

"You sound like you know something about their methods."

"A bit."

"But you won't tell me what the change was," continued Rowles, "because if it was that she became promiscuous, that's probably not their equipment. Scott has a way about him."

She'd asked about the change in behavior when Doc called to convince her to meet with him, but he'd decided that mentioning Martians mating with humans to take over the world would lead to the same rabbit hole he wanted to avoid. But if he didn't give her something, he was worried the talk would stall.

"It's a sensitive topic," he said, eliciting an expression from Rowles that said, I've heard it all. So, he added, "Basically, it was a very strange shift in her beliefs, sort of like believing that the Russian mafia is focusing deep space gamma radiation on the Capitol. It's nonsense, but she believes it."

Doc had used his *ad hoc* example enough now that it was starting to sound almost plausible to him but apparently not to his first-time audience.

"Weird," she muttered, then started slowly tilting her head side-to-side as if mentally tallying the pros and cons. "You know, I could be guilty of slander for anything I say to you about Scott."

"Only if it's communicated to a third party and I have no plans to talk to the media about this."

"Just going directly to the police, huh?"

That she was starting to give him a hard time was a good sign and Doc chuckled. "Not them, either. It'll take a lot more of a smoking gun than anything you've seen or heard to get even the media's attention. I'm just hoping for a starting point." That was almost true in Doc's mind, though if the name Violet Cruz was added, any reporter would jump at the story.

"So, is this amateur detective work for a cousin of a friend typical of researchers at Ruger-Phillips?"

That Rowles had done a search on him wasn't surprising, but it might spell trouble. "Helping a friend is probably not that rare in any company."

"But working at a company that you used to open the door to meet with Scott? That's not at all common, is it?" And there it was—the connection that might get him fired if Ruger-Phillips found out.

He was fairly sure he'd kept his expression bland, but apparently, Rowles didn't need any confirmation. "Don't worry, Dr. Price. I'm just using this information as a bit of leverage. So, who is this friend, and why the lengths to help her? And, no, you've never said that the friend of the cousin was a woman, but I'm betting it is."

Doc chuckled again. "You're good. Maybe we should trade places because you're right."

"Look, you can't sit there drooling while I have dinner. I'm getting the linguini with clams. You should, too."

And so, he did.

The next hour flew by, filled with Doc's stories of why he valued Gustafsson's help and the work he did. Rowles reciprocated with a few facts about her job—the company she worked for handled a lot of juvenile offenders and she was a paralegal who helped manage the voluminous paperwork in that area. She also insinuated that her knowledge of the juvenile justice system came from experience as much as education, but the references were vague. But every time he tried to shift the conversation to Healthtech and Anders, she'd come up with some new diversion.

When the check arrived—which she insisted on paying—Doc realized he'd divulged quite a bit about himself, received precise little about Rowles in return, while getting virtually nothing on Anders. So, as they stepped onto the sidewalk in front of the restaurant, he asked, "Any chance you can tell me anything about Scott Anders's work at Healthtech?"

Rowles sighed, looking up at the darkened sky, then back to his face. "Yeah, probably. But let me sleep on it, OK?"

"Breakfast is on me."

"And I thought we were going to make it through the entire evening without you propositioning me."

"No, that's not what—" Her laughter interrupted his denial.

"You're off the hook. I've rarely spent an evening dining with a man with fewer sexual overtones. So, is it a man or a woman?"

"The latter," Doc replied with a what-can-I-say shrug. He was grateful, however, that she hadn't come up with this insight earlier because he didn't know how to explain that he had been involved with a woman, and later, with her memory. But he also thought perhaps that needed to change. Though Rebecca's remarks had infuriated him and he had tried for several days to dismiss them out of hand, some had taken root. Perhaps, it was time to see if his obsession wasn't exactly what she said—self-inflicted pain for a story that could never end differently.

"Can you meet me here again next Monday night, same time? And I'll even let you pay since it'll be me spilling my guts this time."

"Absolutely," Doc replied. "Monday it is." She turned and left. Doc watched for a moment as she disappeared into the darkness, then headed home.

Same Time, Across the Street from Resterilli's

Kluge stepped out of the shadow of the alley as his eyes darted up and down the darkened street. No one was watching; no one was paying any attention, so he returned his gaze to the restaurant about a half-block away. He knew he shouldn't be skulking around this part of town—he didn't belong here—but he needed to verify that nothing had changed in the life of the woman the world knew as Samantha Rowles.

He, of course, understood that all the world saw was a physical container, a vessel more artificial than natural. He was more concerned with her psyche, her internal essence that had been, unfortunately, scarred by so many societal forces, he couldn't count them. And while he couldn't save her from these disfiguring influences that grew every moment—and that threatened to overwhelm the world—she would be his instrument to save others. Of that, he was now certain.

Kluge was sure because Rowles had accepted his invitation to meet. Unlike those who had declined his invitation before her, she realized, albeit unconsciously, the pinnacle to which he'd raise her, if only for an hour or two. But then, an hour of glory was sixty minutes more than most people received in a lifetime.

The door to the restaurant opened, and Kluge's breath caught in his throat. It was a couple; he could tell from the silhouette produced by the light streaming through the open door. Rowles had entered the eatery alone, but she could have easily planned to meet someone there. And the darkened outline of the woman was about the right height. It could be her. But when the door closed and they stepped onto the sidewalk, the dim rays of the streetlight a half-block away revealed a woman with light hair dressed in red. Rowles had been wearing black. His breathing returned to normal.

As he relaxed, Kluge realized his wrist was hurting. He looked down, only now realizing he had been digging the fingernails of one hand into the back of the other. A drop of brilliant red blood ran across his pale skin and dropped to the sidewalk. For an instant, he panicked. He was leaving his DNA outside the restaurant where she was dining. But after a moment's reflection, he laughed at his folly. He didn't yet know exactly where she would die, but it wouldn't be anywhere near here. All the same, he removed a handkerchief from his back pocket and wrapped it around his wrist. No reason to tempt fate.

It was getting late, and Kluge began to wonder if somehow, he had missed Rowles's departure. Perhaps the restaurant had a back door and she had slipped out that way? Kluge was thinking about leaving when the outline of another couple appeared at the entrance. Again, the woman appeared to be about the right height. And when the two shadows transitioned from black to muted color under the streetlight, he saw it was Rowles.

Apparently, she had planned a rendezvous at the restaurant or had made an impromptu connection. Kluge watched as the couple talked for a moment. She laughed about something, then reached out and placed a hand on the man's arm for a moment. They talked some more. Then, Rowles turned and headed in the direction of her apartment.

Kluge waited, watching the man. He was around six feet tall, seemed a little too thin, and had hair that was a dark brown or black. It was difficult to tell. He was watching Rowles. Was he about to go after her? But after a moment, he turned in the opposite direction and started walking away. Kluge smiled. If they'd left together, he couldn't have ignored her betrayal because her time was at hand. He turned toward the man and muttered into the night, "Lucky you."

Kluge raised an arm to check the time, wondering if he dared follow Rowles to her apartment. The later it got, the fewer the pedestrians on the street and the more he stood out. But before he could read his watch, his vision dimmed. The ground around him tilted. He looked up to see where Rowles was, only to find her looking across the street and into the darkness of his hiding spot. He stepped farther back into the shadows, but the movement drew her attention even more. Now, she was leaning forward, her back slightly hunched as she stared straight toward him. Was it possible she had seen him?

He looked down, only now remembering the white handkerchief he had tied around his wound. She must have seen it, so he drew the hand behind his back. It was, however, too late because, when he looked up, Rowles had stepped off the sidewalk and was coming across the street.

Kluge turned, wondering if he should try to navigate the alley in the dark. As he took his first hesitant step, the ground tipped again, more sharply this time. He reached out to place a steadying hand on the building next to him. His world didn't want him to leave, but what was it trying to tell him? Was it saying, "Take her now?" He turned back toward Rowles, righting the pavement below him.

When Rowles was about five feet away from the mouth of the alley, she stopped. "What are you doing here?"

It was a question that caused the beast within him to scream into his mind, "She's yours. Take her now."

But as he considered the demand, he knew it was all wrong. The ritual that had kept him safe wouldn't acquiesce to violence now. If he did, he would die, and his vision of the future would be lost. This newfound resolve calmed him, and eyesight that, unbeknownst to him, had dimmed with the dark image in his mind's eye now cleared. Rowles was not standing before him. She wasn't questioning his presence, but rather, she was casually strolling down the other side of the street, apparently oblivious to his presence.

Kluge sighed, allowing more of the tension to drain from his body. He could no longer do this. She was too important. Fortunately, he wouldn't need to hold the beast at bay much longer because, very soon, Samantha Rowles would be his.

MONDAY, AUGUST 8

Noon, Marte Investigative Services

"Samantha Rowles," Doc said loudly as he came through Rebecca's reception area and into her office.

Rebecca didn't stand from her seated position behind the desk but merely looked up in silence. Doc started toward a chair but stopped when she raised a hand. "We need to clear the air."

"OK," he said slowly. "And I am sorry that I lost my temper. It's your right to protect your livelihood however you think best."

"I'm sorry about my outburst, too," replied Rebecca. "But it wasn't the threat to my business that was the real problem. It's what you're doing to yourself, and my thoughts on that topic haven't changed in any way. It's horrible what happened to Nicole, but she's moved on. And so should you. And if you're not going to try to get on with your life, then get the hell out of my office. I don't have any more time to waste on you."

Rebecca knew her words were harsh, and she could see the muscles in Doc's jaw work as he chewed on her ultimatum. But she was beyond subtlety. And something about the excitement in his voice, a possible break in the case, had touched a nerve. If he thought they were just going to kiss and makeup, figuratively or literally, and go on with the case, she had to correct that misimpression.

Doc slowly shook his head, eyes downcast. "Yeah, I suppose I had that coming. I'm going to try."

If Rebecca had a mirror, she knew she'd be reading the doubt in her face. "I can understand your"— she struggled to find the right word—"your need to find Nicole when she was kidnapped. But in the last half-year or so, you've acted like you're still searching, even though you know exactly where she is. And now you're telling me, you're going to move on? Just like that? Frankly, I find that a bit hard to believe."

Rebecca half-expected him to try to defend his self-punishment when, as far as she could see, there was no justification. His path had been charted by his heart, and all his data and logic could do along the journey was inflict pain.

"Yeah, I suppose it seems sudden to you," said Doc. "But it isn't. There have been things that have happened, things that have left questions in my mind. But I kept putting those issues aside. That is, until Thursday after our ... difference of opinion."

Rebecca smiled to herself, realizing that Doc, too, was finding the right words elusive.

"Finally, over the weekend, I came up with a way to get to the bottom of my obsession. I spent most of Saturday listing everything that I did during the days leading up to Nicole's abduction. I ended up with something like a long string of dominos, each event and each thought that I had in a chain reaction to the end. But nowhere in that string did I find time that I'd simply wasted."

"I'm not surprised," said Rebecca. "While I wasn't with you for most of it, I know you kept coming back to the Crusaders' case, again and again. You had Gus and me on the phone a half-dozen times at least."

"Yeah," Doc replied, a bit of pain creeping into his voice with the memory. "So, Saturday night and all-day Sunday, I took my string of activities and asked the question, what if I'd branched out at some point to pursue a better line of investigation—and mind you, even after the fact, I don't know what that might have been, but what if I had? And invariably, the final outcome was either no different or was worse than where we ended up."

"So, you ran through those days in your head?" Rebecca asked slowly. "What if you had done X instead of Y at some specific point?" Doc nodded, but despite his agreement, she still wasn't sure she understood. "Can you give me an example?"

"Dozens of them, if you want. Let's see." Doc paused, looking off into space. "OK, the night we witnessed the executions on video. What if I'd declined your offer to stay at your office and had gone home before that happened? There's virtually no chance I would have learned anything back at my place. There was no suspicion that I was going to track down. There was nothing on the news that would have given me insight into the case. But because I was in your office, I witnessed the expression on the killer's face. That was only on the FBI feed, and without that ...."

"You would have never had the insight about the Crusaders," said Rebecca, finishing the thought. "And without that, Gus and I would have been busy with paperwork, while they completed their final act of terrorism, leaving Nicole as good as dead and at least one more body at the Biomedical Engineering building. Maybe a half-dozen more. I see what you mean."

"Yeah, playing out the possibilities in your mind isn't an exact science. Things might have veered off in a direction that I can't imagine. But I can't live my life waiting for the unpredictable and the unlikely to occur. And while it's an extremely bitter pill for me to swallow, I believe that what happened to us is about as good as it could have been. And clearly, things could have easily turned out much worse. So, I'm working on living my life consistent with that belief. As a first step, though it felt a bit sacrilegious, I burned all my kidnapper files yesterday."

"Sacrilegious?" Rebecca took a long breath. "Well, in any case, I think it's a great first step."

"So, are we OK?"

Rebecca got up from her desk, came around it, and placed a soft kiss on his cheek. "More than OK. We're friends. Now, no more kicking yourself while you're down. I don't want to have to yell at you again."

Doc nodded. "Me either. Oh, and one other thing." Rebecca drew back, her eyebrows knitting. "I don't have—nor have I ever had—anything for Dani Gustafsson except appreciation for all the help she's given me on the job."

"In that case, you're rehired ... or re-volunteered or whatever. Now, friend," she said with as much irony in her tone as she could manage, "why didn't you return my calls?"

"So you could tell me to stay away from your case? No thanks."

Rebecca shook her head, her eyes rolling up toward the ceiling. "It would be a waste of my breath to ask you to drop the case. What did you call yourself one time? A dog with a bone?"

"That's what others have said ... although I admit, it fits."

"Anyway, what I wanted to tell you is to watch your back. I brought your name up when I was talking to Anders, and by his reaction, he's none too happy about you poking around."

"Well, that's not surprising since he's—" started Doc.

"Using his electronic toys to get laid," finished Rebecca.

"How on earth did you figure that out?"

"Well, I am a PI, aren't I?"

Doc smirked in reply.

"The first piece of the puzzle," said Rebecca, now serious, "Dani thought her cousin and Anders might have dated. She wouldn't have thought that if Cruz hadn't said something to her, and Cruz wouldn't have said something if she was dozing in the back of the room. And when I asked Anders if he ever gave private lessons with their equipment, well, let's just say his reaction said more than his words. So, this person whose name you were shouting when you came in?"

"Samantha Rowles."

"She one of his conquests?" asked Rebecca.

"Most likely."

"Most likely? I thought you had something solid."

"I do," Doc shot back, then rubbed his forehead with a hand for a moment. "Look, it took a long time to get her to trust me. And it took even more time to convince her that this is something important enough to violate a confidence, even if she does consider Anders a sleaze now. She said she wanted to sleep on it, and we're meeting tonight at a restaurant at 5:30. I really believe I'll get all the facts then."

Rebecca didn't want to think about what Doc might have done to generate all this goodwill in a woman he had just met, but at least it sounded like he was close. "And you think Anders has something that could really do what we think it does?"

"Samantha didn't talk about whatever he has, but I'm pretty sure she's petrified of it. And when I met with Anders, he talked about having a part of a radical new technology being developed by a conglomerate of some of the biggest companies in the world. So, yeah, this could be the real deal."

"We're going up against the big boys in the commercial world?" That wasn't the type of case Rebecca thought she'd ever have and not one she particularly wanted, but she could hardly drop it now.

"The organizations aren't misusing the technology. It's Anders who has the bad intentions."

"And these companies aren't going to want to protect their investment?" Doc started to answer, but Rebecca interrupted. "I'm getting ahead of myself. Let's see what Ms. Rowles has to say and go from there. Now, unless you have something else, I'll give you a rundown on what I've learned."

Doc didn't have anything more, so Rebecca spent the next twenty minutes summarizing her interviews. Doc added a few more specifics from his meetings and they were finished.

When he was gone, Rebecca leaned back in her office chair, her thoughts immediately returning to one specific moment in their conversation—when Doc had mentioned the time he'd taken gaining Rowles's trust. She wondered why flirtation had leaped into her mind. And when she, Gustafsson, and he had met that first day, why did she keep thinking his unease was due to an affair with her client? Apparently, he'd been worried he was playing on her pity.

And then, it made sense.

Her initial attraction to Doc had developed under the most unlikely of circumstances. On a night that had ended with three gruesome executions, they had talked. She couldn't think about that evening without an image of the grisly killings, but she also remembered the warmth she felt confiding in him earlier in the evening. Then, unexpectedly, her feelings continued to grow under conditions that seemed toxic to any emotion, save perhaps hatred. When he was the apparent target of the kidnappers, his safety was always in her mind. When her partner had been killed saving her life, she wanted nothing more than to feel his arms around her. And when he'd turned his back on the rest of his life, including her, she could only think of helping him ... even though that might mean losing him forever to another woman.

She now saw that her emotions were stronger than she'd dared to admit to herself. And if she had to guess, she'd say it was the kiss tonight that had brought that fact to light. Though a mere peck on the cheek, the feeling couldn't have been stronger if they had been locked in a passionate embrace for the night. He wasn't ready for anything more—not yet—but at least, he was ready for a small step out of the darkness that had dominated his life. Perhaps they could be more. Perhaps not, but she was ready to find out.

Afternoon, The Ruger-Phillips Complex

Doc stood from his desk, walked to the window, and shoved his hands into his pockets. He watched as the traffic sped by on the freeway beyond his building's parking lot. Soon, the mere trickle of cars would become a deluge as they moved into rush hour. He could hardly wait. Tonight, he was certain Samantha Rowles would deliver everything he and Rebecca needed to nail Anders for his crimes.

Rebecca? He slowly shook his head. If her simple kiss on the cheek meant she liked him, he'd never seen that coming. And yet, perhaps he should have, as the emotion explained some things that had never made sense. It explained her calls when he'd abandoned his life. It gave their makeshift partnership a reason for being besides pity. It clarified the reasons behind her unwavering willingness to listen when his ideas felt unbelievable, even in his own mind. And though he thought accepting affection from anyone would release an avalanche of feelings of betrayal, it hadn't. The pain and guilt for what had happened remained—and he felt it always would—but now, anticipation of tomorrow claimed its own place in his world.

"Doc?"

He turned from the window. "Hi, Linda. What's up." Her cat-that-swallowed-the-canary grin said she thought she had news that would make his day. She held up a box.

"Hmm. What's that?" Doc asked.

"No idea. On the outside, it only says, 'From a Friend.' But from the handwriting and the slightly perfumed wrapping paper, I'd say it's a lady friend," Linda said, raising her eyebrows. "It was delivered up front. Some company called Same Day Delivery according to Liz ... not that that's going to tell you much."

Actually, it told Doc that someone had found or made something for him and then had used a general service to get it delivered. Maybe that wasn't much different than ordering a box of candy online and having the store deliver it, but it felt more thoughtful and considerably more involved.

Linda held the small box out, but when Doc reached for it, she pulled it back. "Only if you tell me who's the secret admirer when you find out." She did the eyebrow raise again.

"Of course," he replied, and she handed him the gift. Linda turned to leave. "Don't you want to see if there's a card inside?"

"Oh, no. It might be something … intimate." She'd lowered her voice for the last word as if she was saying something naughty. But then, as a somewhat grandmotherly, nearly sixty-year-old, maybe she thought she was.

Doc chuckled. "I'll let you know when I solve this mystery." Linda nodded and left, the smile still on her face.

Of course, Doc thought he already knew who had sent the package. Rebecca had used the word "friend" just a couple of hours ago. As he opened it, he half expected to find a gag gift, maybe something like a toy badge that said "PI" on it. But when he looked inside, he found a very delicate pastry. It looked like a small iced cupcake wrapped in a shell of geometric patterns in gold and brown. On top sat a butterfly that appeared to be gold leaf, while two thin wisps, most likely chocolate, were attached to the back of the cake.

Though not much more than two bites, Doc decided to share it with Rebecca after he met Rowles for dinner. It would be a nice gesture. And besides, he wasn't even sure if the golden butterfly was edible.

Evening, Resterilli's Italian Restaurant

Doc slowly stepped through the restaurant's front door and glanced up and down the street. The look was more of a precaution—he didn't want to run into anyone on the sidewalk—than a search for Rowles. As it was more than an hour after the time they'd agreed to meet, she obviously wasn't coming.

After the first half hour of waiting, he had tried her work phone, the only number he had, but it rolled to her voicemail where he left a message. A search for a home or cell number had proved fruitless; they were most likely unlisted, but he was able to find an address. It was close, so he walked over.

If he'd connected the address with the structure—an imposing building he'd driven by numerous times—he never would have made the trip. The architecture alone said that a tenant or realtor would be the only way inside, and if Rowles was avoiding him, she'd be no help. But surprisingly, security started just beyond the front door in the form of a doorman at a reception desk and a guard posted discreetly by a bank of locked elevators. The residents obviously took their privacy seriously.

In his feigned politeness, the doorman proved somewhat helpful, assuming his statement wasn't just a standard line designed to get rid of the riffraff. According to him, Rowles had left early that morning and had not yet returned. That piece of information left open the possibility that something pressing had come up at her work. If so, then her failure to answer the phone only meant that she was huddled with other lawyers and aides in a conference room working on the issue.

Then, in deference to his somewhat compulsive nature, Doc had returned to the restaurant for one final look. As she wasn't there, he had to admit failure, at least for today. Hopefully, she'd reschedule tomorrow.

Now, the only question was whether to give Rebecca the disappointing news first or get something to eat. The former, he would do in person—she was expecting him and she might have additional thoughts on this development. But he was also starving, having skipped lunch in anticipation of an elaborate dinner with Rowles at the restaurant.

Doc walked back and opened the door to his car, still pondering his options when the dome light illuminated the pastry box he'd left hidden in the shadow of the passenger footwell. Rebecca wasn't expecting him to be bringing food and eating the small cake now would mean he could deliver the bad news and then go home to get something more substantial for dinner. Decision made, Doc opened the box and took a small bite, immediately thankful for his caution.

"Yuck," he muttered to himself. This much sugar might kill his hunger now, but in an hour, he'd be exhausted and probably headachy. He tossed the uneaten portion back in the box and placed it back in the footwell. He could wait for something to fill his stomach before finishing the dessert.

When Doc got to her apartment, Rebecca answered her door in a white T-shirt and gray gym shorts. With her light blonde hair and fair complexion, she almost glowed.

"Getting ready for bed?" he asked, belatedly realizing that her radiant look wasn't the only thought lurking in his mind.

"Hardly. It's not even 7:30. But the power was off for some repairs, and it got pretty stuffy up here. The electricity's back on and the AC should catch up pretty soon, but we could go out for a short walk if you want. It's probably a little cooler outside than on this floor."

"That's OK," Doc said. "I'll just join you in your state of half-dress." With that, he peeled off his T-shirt. For an instant, he considered removing his jeans, too, but for reasons that had nothing to do with the temperature of the room. "Ah, that's better," he said lightly, hoping to slow his growing desire.

Rebecca, on the other hand, seemed more amused than aroused as she stood there smirking. "Fine, but I don't care if you're wearing gray boxers that match my gym shorts or not. The pants stay on." She turned, walked into her living room, and sat on the couch. "Now, tell me. What did Rowles have to say?"

"Change in plans," he said, the details of being stood up no longer feeling important to him as he looked down at her. "We're getting together tomorrow, so you'll just have to keep your pants on, too." Doc almost added, "Or not," because that was what he was thinking.

"Change in plans? Then, why didn't you come by earlier?"

"Between waiting at the restaurant, going by her place to see if she was there, and a final look at Resterilli's, this is earlier. The doorman at her building said she'd been gone all day, but that's all I know ... except for the fact that I'm here now."

"So, the reschedule for tomorrow is just a guess?" asked Rebecca

"She'll be there," Doc said with a certainty that felt misplaced. He shrugged, not trying to trace the emotion to its source. "I don't know how you women sit like that, with your feet tucked up underneath. Nicole used to sit that way."

Rebecca wasn't so quick with a comeback this time, as she looked up at him with a puzzled expression. "Thanks ... I guess."

"I didn't mean to offend you. I mean, with the comparison to Nicole."

"No, it's not that," said Rebecca quickly. "It's just that you've rarely said her name around me unless it's about the kidnapping. And comparing us?" She slowly shook her head. "Never."

"Getting over my unease in talking about her is a part of me getting on with my life, right?"

"Sure, but ...." Rebecca paused as if looking around the room for a reason. "I think it's great, but take the time you need."

Doc smiled. "I took a half year. You think I need more?" Rebecca started to answer, but Doc spoke first, the humor in his voice replaced with gravity. "No, I think I've wasted enough of our time."

Doc sat down on the couch beside her, their legs touching. He could feel the warmth of her body through his jeans. Rebecca drew back, although it appeared that she just wanted a little space to watch his face. If she intended to read his expression, Doc was certain she'd find desire there. As to why that was true at this moment, however, he couldn't say. She'd always been very attractive, of course, but then, so were many other women. Something had changed. Perhaps her admission of friendship had kindled something more? Whatever it was, Doc could feel his desire continuing to grow.

"You kissed me yesterday," he said, looking into her blue eyes. "I thought I'd return the favor."

"That was just a friendly peck on the cheek," Rebecca replied, her brow wrinkling again.

"And mine will be friendly, too, although I thought we could try a different place."

Doc leaned in, wondering if she would retreat. But as their faces neared, he saw a different ploy in his mind's eye. She'd wait until they were close, then rush in to brush his lips and withdraw quickly. So, at the last moment, he bent his head and placed a long soft kiss on the side of her neck. The warmth of her skin, the beat of her heart passed through his lips and ignited a heat deep within his body. Perhaps she felt something, too, as he sensed a slight shiver.

Rebecca placed her hands gently on the sides of his face, drew back slightly, and looked into his eyes. "Doc, are you sure about this?"

And with her question, Doc knew. Gone from her voice was the self-assurance she'd forged in the male-dominated world of the FBI and honed in the cruel realities of her profession. In its place was the hesitancy of vulnerability.

"Never more so," Doc replied and started to bend to place another caress on her neck. This time, however, her hands gently guided his lips to hers. The kiss was long and passionate, as their heat and desire grew in the embrace. When they parted, he stood from the couch and took off his jeans.

"They are gray ... your boxers, I mean."

Rebecca stood and grabbed the hem of her shirt, but before she could pull it over her head, Doc gently took her hands away. He knelt in front of her and carefully slid a thumb under her T-shirt on each side. Slowly, he raised his hands, his fingers softly caressing the bare skin of her back, his thumbs still hooked under the garment. He'd thought that the act was for her, but as the shirt inched skywards, he was mesmerized by her soft pale flesh and the steel of toned muscle just below its surface.

When Doc pulled the shirt over her head, they stood looking at each other for a moment. Then, Rebecca leaned forward and whispered in his ear. "Something tells me we're going to need more room than this couch." She took his hand and led him toward her bedroom.

Evening, Rebecca's Apartment

There was someone in the room with her.

It was one of those premonitions Rebecca sometimes got just as she awoke. Generally, they were just remnants of unfinished dreams; this one, however, was different, as if she could feel the weight of another's eyes on her. She sat up in bed, drawing the sheet up around her neck. Sure enough, a shadow lurked in the corner near her closet. Quickly, quietly, she reviewed the location of every form of weapon within easy reach.

And then, a wave of relief passed through her body as she remembered the events from earlier in the evening. "Jeez, Doc. What are you doing?" She glanced at the clock on the bedside table, then chuckled. "I must have dozed off. It's only a little before 10:00."

Doc said nothing, though she could see him raise an arm as if he was trying to grab something floating in the air. "What, no snide remarks about how you wore me out in only two hours?" Still no response from the shadow.

"Doc?" Nothing.

"Doc, this isn't funny. What are you doing?" She reached over and switched on a lamp, wondering if the shadow might not be Doc. But there stood the familiar figure ... well, familiar in shape if not appearance. It was the first time she'd seen him naked in the light.

Rebecca smiled to herself. "I never expected you to be an exhibitionist. Don't get me wrong, I like the view. But if you're going to walk around like that, you need to keep the lights off in the rest of my apartment. There's not a curtain drawn in the whole place." Still, silence. "Doc?" she said more loudly.

He turned, but when she saw his face, Rebecca almost wished he hadn't. It was as if his eyes were focused on someone or something far beyond the confines of her bedroom, leaving his expression distant, almost lifeless. She started to ask what was wrong again, but before a sound had left her lips Doc collapsed to the floor. The slap of his bare skin against the hardwood made her shudder. Rebecca jumped up, wrapped the sheet around herself, and rushed to where he lay. But in the few seconds it took her to reach him, he stood.

"No, lay back down," she said, putting a hand gently on one shoulder. He knocked it aside roughly. And then, as if seeing her for the first time, he said, "Rebecca?"

"Yes, what is it?" But his moment of lucidity passed as quickly as it had come. He fell forward, grabbing her arm tightly as he did. For an instant, she thought she had him, but then his body went limp. She laid him down as gently as she could only to see him start convulsing, violently one moment, mere twitches the next. She rolled him to his side so he could breathe freely, then took off the sheet and placed it under his head. After moving a small chair away, his surroundings were as safe as she could make them.

"Doc," she said quietly, "I need to get my phone, but I'll be right back. Just stay here."

She rushed into the living room and grabbed their clothes from the floor. When she returned, it appeared that the spasms had lessened, and she breathed a little easier. She pulled her phone from a pocket and called for an ambulance.

"Help's on the way," she said to him soothingly when the call ended. She tossed her phone on the bed and sat on the floor as she hurriedly pulled on her clothes. She even managed to get Doc's jeans on him before the twitching started again.

Doc turned his gaze in her direction. "What are we doing down ...." He didn't finish as his look again became distant. "Grandad? What are you doing here?"

"So, that's where you are," said Rebecca softly. "So, how is your grandfather?" She actually knew the answer—he was dead— but she wondered if Doc knew. Or even if it was wise to ask. But at least his spasms were mild for the moment.

Seizures, Rebecca knew, could take many different forms—loss of consciousness and falling, muscle spasms, confusion. But Doc's rapid and complete transitions between reality and hallucination, between standing and thrashing on the floor didn't seem characteristic. Neither did his behavior seem drug-induced for the same reason. That left the possibility that Anders had given him something. And if that was true, this episode wouldn't end with a couple of fainting spells.

Suddenly, Doc sat up and his arms shot out. His fingers closed around Rebecca's neck.

"Nine seconds." It was a strange thing to pop into her thoughts, but her training said that was all that was left of her life if she didn't act. She drew her arm back and slammed the heel of her hand into Doc's chin. He seemed unfazed, although perhaps it aroused some self-preservation instinct. He pulled her in closer, his labored breathing now seeming to claim the little air remaining for her.

Rebecca curled her legs between them, then pushed to gain some space. She drew her arm back again and put every ounce of strength and leverage she could find into a palm strike to his nose. His head banged against the floor in a sickening thud. His grip relaxed. Rebecca backed away, wheezing and coughing as she did.

After a few moments recovering—which strangely, she seemed to need more than he—she said, "You hear the siren?" He said nothing. "We're going to take you to the hospital, and the doctors will fix you up. But you have to tell me. What did you eat and drink before you got here?"

Doc raised his head slightly, and Rebecca wondered if he was going to answer. But instead, his eyes rolled back, and he dropped back to the floor.

Rebecca leaned forward and yelled to his face, "No, dammit! Open your eyes." Difficulty waking someone with a suspected concussion could signal problems, and as hard as Doc's head had hit the floor, Rebecca added that check to the first aid for seizures she was already providing. It was a hodge-podge of treatments, but without knowing more, it was the best she could do.

Fortunately, Doc's eyes opened, though his face still showed no recognition of anything around him. "Good. You can rest in the ambulance if you need to, but I'd like you to stay with me till they show up." Her voice had reverted to the soothing tone someone might use with a newborn.

With surprising speed and agility, Doc leapt to his feet and raced toward the back door of Rebecca's apartment. He nearly tore it off its hinges as he hit it at a dead run. Rebecca jumped to her feet and gave pursuit, shouting for him to stop. It was immediately clear, however, that she was wasting her breath.

Doc started down the stairs that connected the decks in the back of the building, taking the steps two or three at a time. But occasionally, he also lost his balance and crashed into a wall or a railing. She caught up with him on the first-floor landing.

Despite what's portrayed in the movies, tackling someone from behind is seldom a good idea if that person is a threat. Best case, she'd end up on the deck with Doc's hands, head, and feet unrestrained and dangerous. Worst case, she'd miss and hurt herself seriously. So, she planned to knock him off-balance with a push from behind. She didn't think it would take much with him being somewhat unstable already.

But just as she closed in to give him a shove, he spun around, grabbed the waistband of her jeans, yelled, "Here we are," and launched himself over the three-and-a-half-foot deck railing. Rebecca's right hand caught the top board, but her grip was no match for the momentum of Doc's free-falling weight. Over she went.

Doc's fall was broken by some bushes near the stairs. Hers was broken by Doc, as she landed on top. She was dazed and gently shook her head to clear some of the cobwebs. Doc, on the other hand, appeared to be unconscious. She grabbed him under the arms and managed to drag him a few feet to the edge of the parking lot. The emergency medical technicians were apparently seasoned veterans, barely giving the half-naked couple a second glance.

Soon, they had Doc loaded. Rebecca climbed in, using the "he's my fiancé" ruse and her background to gain a spot in the back.

She wasn't certain she'd need the little white lie when they got to the hospital—policy had changed frequently during the pandemic and she hadn't been there for some time. But it was insurance against being exiled to the hospital's front lobby because she was just a friend. The ambulance pulled out of the lot. Rebecca perched herself on the edge of the bench, forced to watch helplessly as Doc fought against the bindings. The fifteen-minute drive to the hospital had never felt so long.

Evening, St. Louis Regional Medical Center

Rebecca thought about taking back some of the credit she'd given the EMTs for their measured demeanor when she saw a policeman waiting by the ambulance entrance. But after a moment's reflection, she doubted the officer was there for them. Even if they were bruised, bloody, and half-dressed, poor grooming wasn't a crime. And the way he was dividing his attention among all of the comings and goings made her think he was probably off-duty and working security for the hospital to make a little extra cash. In any case, he didn't follow them inside.

After Doc was admitted—the process going smoothly after someone brought her the billfold from his jeans—she refused treatment and found a bathroom to clean up. Then, she made herself comfortable in a waiting room near the treatment area. It was nearly empty with only a few individuals sitting apart, one staring out the window, another checking her phone, another dozing until something only he could see or hear jerked him awake. She sat in a corner, rubbing an arm that had started to ache.

The police officer Rebecca had seen previously wandered in, perhaps making his rounds. She stood and walked toward him. He nodded in her direction. "Ma'am."

He was tall with light hair that looked like it would be gray by the time he was 30. She guessed he was about 28 now. She read his nameplate. "Working security this evening, Officer Bates?"

"Yes, ma'am. Can I help you?"

But as Rebecca considered what to say next, the door to the waiting room opened. A man in scrubs entered. He gazed around the room, then walked up to Rebecca. "Ms. Marte?"

"Yes."

"I'm Doctor Ravesh Gandhi. Your fiancé is showing some very unusual symptoms for a seizure. You're certain this is the first time he'd had one?"

"Yes, I'm almost certain." Rebecca found it somewhat uncomfortable sounding so sure about this conjecture, but she figured if Doc had a history, it would have come out sometime in the year or so she had known him. And he'd probably be wearing a medical bracelet; Doc tended to hold to scientific and medical prescriptions conscientiously. But it was her growing conviction that foul play was at the root of his problems that gave her the additional boost in confidence she needed to make this claim. She just needed his doctors to investigate that possibility since she couldn't.

"And you're checking him for a drug overdose like I suggested?"

"We're running broad panels of tests that will reveal most common types of drugs, but again, his symptoms aren't helping us narrow the search. It's like he's on something that's alternating unpredictably between a stimulant and a depressant. And you're sure you have no idea what he might have taken? No designer drug he's been talking about? Nothing like that?"

"No, not that he's ever mentioned to me. And frankly, he's not the type to mess with anything experimental. Like I mentioned before, he was probably drugged without his knowledge or consent."

Gandhi frowned, turning his gaze toward Officer Bates, then back to Rebecca. "OK, do whatever you can to find out what he's taken, if indeed, that is what has happened. His stomach was virtually empty, so whatever it was, it's in his bloodstream now."

What the doctor didn't say, but what Rebecca knew to be true, was that the chance they could pull Doc through without that information was moderate, at best. And if what he'd been given was as out of the norm, as she expected, that moderate chance became virtually nil.

"Finding out is exactly what I was going to talk to Officer Bates about," Rebecca said, nodding her head in the direction of the policeman.

"Good," replied Gandhi, and he hurried out of the room.

"My partner …," started Rebecca before she reconsidered. "My soon-to-be partner, Sam Price, had a falling out with a local businessman recently. I think that person did something to him to get him out of the way for a while. But it looks like it's gotten out of control, and now Sam's in a bad way." Actually, Rebecca was certain that if Anders was behind Doc's delirium, long-term incapacitation or even death was his objective. This story, however, was going to be difficult enough for Bates to accept without it being a murder plot.

"OK," said Bates slowly. "Why don't we sit down, and we'll take this a step at a time."

The sigh that left Rebecca's lips was just the tip of the scream that she held in. With what the doctor had said, she felt every second was precious. "I'll stand because we don't have time for a long talk. I need you to check out the individual I mentioned, Mr. Scott Anders at Healthtech, as soon as possible."

Bates hesitated a moment. "OK, just let me get a few facts first. You've been hurt. Did Sam Price do this to you, and before you answer, you should—"

"Domestic abuse? Is that what you think this is?" Rebecca asked in disbelief.

"I think I know nothing about what has happened to you or your fiancée. I'm just trying to fill in the details."

This line of questioning, Rebecca knew, served a purpose. Many battered women would make excuses for an abusive boyfriend or spouse—or worse, blame themselves. The admissions Office Bates might elicit could help break through that barrier. Unfortunately, not only was this process irrelevant in her case, it was deadly. Doc was going to die while she tried to explain to the officer the implausible hunches they were investigating. She was going to have to take matters into her own hands.

"Will you be here a while?"

"I usually leave sometime between 2:00 and 2:30 AM. It's usually quiet enough by then with the bars closing at 1:30. Why?"

"There are some things I need to do—calls I need to make. His parents don't even know what's going on. But by 2:00, I'll know a lot more, and I'll give you a complete statement."

Bates frowned, probably trying to make it look paternal, even if they were about the same age. "OK," he said finally. "Just don't wait forever to take care of whatever it is that's going on."

"Fair enough." Rebecca stood and turned away, thinking she'd take her phone to a quiet corner. The trouble was, her phone was at her apartment, along with her money and driver's license. She turned back to Bates. "Would you mind calling me a cab? And tell them the driver will need to wait at my apartment while I run inside to get some money."

Bates looked over her shoulder, then asked, "Where do you live?"

"Soulard, maybe twelve, fifteen minutes from here."

"Ride in a patrol car work for you?"

"Sure."

Officer Bates walked by, and Rebecca turned to find two other officers talking quietly on the other side of the room. After a few moments in discussion among the three of them, a couple of laughs, and a call to dispatch that Rebecca recognized as a personal-out-of-service request, Bates returned with one of the other men. "Officer Phillips here can give you a lift."

* * *

Twenty-five minutes later, Rebecca was back at the hospital, having broken every speed limit in her return. Then, over the next twenty minutes, she called everyone in law enforcement she knew who might do her a favor, explaining that a man had overdosed on a hallucinogenic substance believed to have been developed by Healthtech. Several agreed to look into the matter until they learned the timeframe—now if not sooner. She suspected that some of them pushed back in their recliner and turned up the TV after they hung up. But some went to their phones, their computers, their cars.

After calling out the cavalry, she started phoning Healthtech herself. It was wasted effort. They had some staff for after-hours emergencies, but they were maintenance technicians, not scientists who knew what Healthtech might be developing that had Doc talking to dead people. Fortunately, someone else was more successful, and around 11:30 PM, she received the text message naming the Brain-2-Brain Project as the probable source of the substance. When she found the project online, she knew they'd struck pay dirt.

B2B was a massive collaboration involving many of the biggest computer software, hardware, biomedical engineering, and social media companies in the world. Their objective was to develop a social network of brains by reading one person's thoughts and transmitting them to another. If successful, it could make everything from phones to the Internet virtually obsolete.

"That might even eliminate talking," Rebecca muttered to herself, then looked around the waiting room to make sure no one was listening. Surprisingly to her, B2B was already building on several proofs-of-concept developed in other labs and not just with rats or chimpanzees. In one, two people collaborated to solve a Tetris-like problem using only the thoughts of one transmitted to the brain of another. And the second person couldn't even see the game board. It was one of those projects both exciting and worrying in its potential.

While the B2B website didn't list the roles of the participating companies, Rebecca was virtually certain that Healthtech was involved in developing the devices that would record and generate brain activity; there was only one company described as having a

"Midwest location." And while several approaches were being tested for these devices—microscopic electrodes or a fine mesh that would be inserted through the skull, electrodes that could record and generate activity when placed on the scalp—the Midwest company was developing nanobots. These microscopic, man-made creations had been studied primarily for the precise delivery of medication to cancer cells. The ones Healthtech was developing, however, had the ability to pass through the blood-brain barrier and then both read and induce brain activity. The idea was that by both recording information while people performed specific tasks and by stimulating the brain and watching the reaction, the researchers could determine where on the cortex the nanobots had come to rest. Once perfected, setting up B2B communications would be as simple as two people receiving doses of the tiny creations and then going through a short period of calibration.

Rebecca's discovery of Healthtech's role in the project was enough to set off another round of phone calls and Internet searches, although checking the Healthtech website was all that proved necessary. The project wasn't mentioned by name—confidentiality being a paramount concern—but the vice president in charge of "Advanced Medical Applications" was the only option. After a visit from a police detective, the VP called the scientist in charge of the design and production of the nanobots, and soon, the researcher was talking to the doctors. That had been around 12:30, and Rebecca had breathed a sigh of relief, knowing the doctors now knew what they were facing.

But now, it was approaching 1:00, and Rebecca's calm had vanished, along with all the other visitors to the small waiting room. "What the hell are they doing in there?" Rebecca muttered to herself.

Then, almost as if in answer to her question, the door opened and Dr. Gandhi hurried in. He was only about halfway across the room when he said, "How sure are you that your fiancé ingested the Healthtech nanobots?"

"Virtually certain. Why?"

"And there is nothing else you know of that he might have taken?"

"We've been through this already." Rebecca could hear the impatience in her voice and paused for a long breath. "Sorry. He drinks beer and wine. And one time he mentioned trying marijuana in school. He may even drive over to Illinois once in a while, where recreational use is legal, and partake at a friend's house. But he stays away from synthetic drugs or even the more refined natural ones. And besides, we had things we were going to discuss tonight, so being stoned wouldn't make sense."

Gandhi nodded. "OK. Let's sit for a moment."

Rebecca hated the sound of that suggestion. If sitting meant the news was bad, didn't she bear much of the responsibility for their lack of progress? After all, she had pointed the finger at Anders. And every other word out of her mouth had been a guess about Doc's past health or his current inclinations. Did she really know him well enough to make these claims? She certainly hoped so because, otherwise, she might be sentencing him to death. She sat down with the doctor.

"Why are we still talking about what Sam took? You've talked to the Healthtech scientist. Don't his symptoms match what the scientist described?"

Gandhi rubbed his chin a moment. "The man from Healthtech has been very helpful in describing how the nanobots were developed and how they function. But as for symptoms from a massive dose of them? He has no idea." Gandhi took a long breath. "I'm sorry I have to say this, but frankly, things don't look good for your fiancé. I've talked to his parents. Apparently, he's not religious, but if you are, we have a chapel here in the building."

"You aren't giving up, are you?" Now, the impatience in her voice was even more apparent, but this time, Rebecca had no intention of swallowing it. "There has to be something you can do."

"We're doing everything we can, but this is something that no one has seen before. There's no pattern to the parts of his brain that are being stimulated, so there's no persistent set of symptoms we can treat. Take heart rate. One minute he'll be showing tachycardia. The next it'll drop below 20 beats per minute. About the only consistent pattern we're seeing is that blood flow and blood oxygen are dropping. Basically, he's suffocating even though he's on a ventilator. I'm sorry the news isn't better."

"How long does he have?"

Gandhi looked at her closely for a moment. "I don't know."

"But you have an opinion," said Rebecca.

Gandhi slowly shook his head. "If the rate his blood oxygen is dropping doesn't change, it's doubtful he'll make it through the next few hours. But we hope the rate of stimulation from the nanobots will drop and let his heart and lungs catch up."

"So ...." Rebecca paused, trying to think of the best way to ask this question. "You're trying to treat his symptoms, which are constantly changing. But are you doing anything to treat the cause? Anything that might kill or incapacitate the nanobots?"

"The Healthtech scientist was pessimistic about that option. Apparently, they are designed to function in a quite hostile environment."

Just from the inflection of his voice, Rebecca could tell there was more to this answer, so she waited.

"The best treatment option our team has come up with so far is to medically induce a coma. That won't stop the stimulation of his brain, but the suppression of brain activity should, in theory, dampen the transmission of the neural spikes the nanobots are creating. All the spasms and hallucinations should decrease in strength and frequency, and maybe that would let the rest of his body recover somewhat."

"So, why aren't you trying that?" asked Rebecca.

"Two reasons," he said slowly. "First, the treatment is somewhat counterintuitive. Medically induced comas are used to treat brain injury by reducing blood flow and his is already too low. But in his case, suppressing the random activity may let his heart and lungs return to a more normal pattern. The second reason is related to the first question I asked you when I came in — what are the chances his symptoms are from something other than nanobots? Just because Healthtech makes them and your fiancé had a disagreement with someone there doesn't mean that's what he's ingested. And if we treat him for the wrong thing ... well, that could make things worse. I'm sorry my news isn't more promising."

"I understand," replied Rebecca, although she wasn't sure she did. Wasn't trying anything better than sitting by and letting him die? Was there something she could do to break the impasse? Immediately, she recognized that this was the right question. "So, if I could find proof that he's eaten something laced with nanobots, you'd be willing to give this induced-coma treatment a try?"

"Without knowing more than we do now, the risk is just too great."

Rebecca came close to yelling, "Is that a yes or a no?" But she calmed herself and instead, asked, "And knowing he got a dose of nanobots is knowing more than we do now, right?"

"It is."

Finally, a simple answer, even if it wasn't the promise of action she'd hoped. "I'll call the hospital when I have the proof," she called over her shoulder as she ran for the door.

Rebecca had driven fast returning to the hospital from her apartment earlier in the evening, but that trip was at a snail's pace compared to the speed she reached going to Doc's apartment. Fortunately, at a little past 1:00 AM, there were few cars on the streets. She didn't have a key to Doc's place, so after checking all the obvious hiding spots for one—under a welcome mat, on the frame above the door—she picked the lock. It felt like it took forever, though it was probably less than two minutes before she was inside.

She went room-to-room, making piles of anything that looked like it might contain the microscopic killers. The collection grew rapidly—a half-empty bottle of water, a partially eaten bagel, an open box of cereal. But maybe the nanobots didn't have to be swallowed? Maybe they could be absorbed through the skin, which added cleaning products, polishes, and even the foot powder he put in his hiking boots to the growing heap. It was also possible that the nanobots could be inhaled, but that option seemed too complicated. How could Anders be sure Doc was near the source of the fumes unless he was using the product? And since she'd already collected any spray bottles that were not sealed, checking air vents for gas canisters felt like a waste of the extremely limited time she had.

About halfway through her frantic search, Rebecca paused to make a phone call. Her efforts would be wasted if there was no one to test the suspicious items, and since the Healthtech scientist was the only one who knew what to look for, she needed him in the lab. That meant another visit by the police detective who had spoken with him earlier. She had only just identified herself to the detective when he said, "Thought you might be calling. Let me guess. You need the Healthtech guy to go back into work?"

Rebecca wondered how he knew, although Officer Bates was a good guess. But rather than asking, and wasting valuable seconds she didn't have, she simply confirmed the need, thanked him, and went back to her search.

Normally, her focus on anything as time-critical as this hunt would have squeezed every other thought from her mind. But tonight wasn't normal, and Rebecca felt the self-recriminations forming at the edge of her consciousness as she tossed Doc's apartment. Why had she kicked the hornet's nest by telling Anders that Doc was looking into Cruz's death? Even if Anders had no part in that specific crime, Rebecca was sure he had plenty of secrets to keep—enough that he apparently decided to kill rather than face the consequences. Of course, Doc knew the risks, and she had told him to watch his back. But she also knew that his relentless search for a pattern in the case data could distract him from almost everything in his surroundings.

After one complete pass and a second, cursory review of Doc's apartment, Rebecca had piles of suspect items in every room. She retrieved several large trash bags from under the kitchen sink and started filling them. But after the second one, she paused and sat down on Doc's couch, putting her head in her hands. Who was she kidding? Even if it only took five minutes to test each item, she had enough loot to keep the Healthtech researcher busy for a day, perhaps two. And what if each test took twenty minutes ... or an hour?

Could she prioritize the items, putting the most likely culprits in one sack so they could be tested first? She thought not because she had no way to sort them. Was an open bottle of ketchup less likely than a half-finished bottle of wine? Could she put items that would generally be cooked—oils, flour—lower on the list than things that were eaten cold? She didn't know if heat would disable the nanobots but thought it might. Would Anders favor items that would be used frequently, like salt, rather than a bottle of hot sauce that looked like it hadn't been used in weeks? If she prioritized the items, she'd have to hope she got lucky.

There was, however, one more thought in her mind that was even more disquieting than any of these questions. For some reason that Rebecca couldn't explain, she felt the nanobots weren't in any of the items she'd collected so far. If so, even if the expert could test every item in mere moments, it wouldn't make any difference. Doc would be dead.

"To hell with the rules," Rebecca muttered to the room. Like Dr. Gandhi and his colleagues, she, too, wasn't absolutely certain Doc had been dosed with Healthtech nanobots. She was, however, sure enough to take the risk that the doctors wouldn't. She started to dial the hospital when her phone rang. It wasn't a number she recognized.

"Rebecca Marte, Marte Investigative Services."

"Hi, Ms. Marte. This is Lanie Price, Sam's mom. I'm at my wit's end. A doctor called us from St. Louis and said that Sam is in a bad way and that we should get there as soon as possible. But I just talked to Sam a couple of days ago, and everything was fine then. We're leaving here as soon as we're done talking, but I thought I'd see what you knew about his condition first."

There was a pause on the line, during which Rebecca was trying to decide what to say. There were certainly a number of options, but anything that might calm the frazzled woman jumped to the top of her list. But before she came to a decision, Lanie continued.

"I'm sorry. Where are my manners? I didn't even get to congratulate you. I guess you and Sam are engaged?"

"Sorry, but no, we aren't. We're just friends. I told the paramedics we were engaged so I could ride with him to the hospital. And I guess they told the hospital. I'll clear this all up immediately."

"No, no, don't do that," Lanie replied quickly. "Like I said, we're leaving in a few minutes to drive to St. Louis. I'd feel better knowing someone was there just in case the doctors can't get us on the phone." She paused. "Is that all right, Ms. Marte? I know I'm asking a lot."

It was, Rebecca knew, the perfect opportunity to shift some of the responsibility for Doc's treatment into the hands of the people who should have it—his parents. To do so, she'd have to explain Doc's suspicion of Anders, his meeting with Rowles and her disappearance, Anders's role in creating brain-stimulating nanobots, and finally, her belief that Anders had given their son a lethal dose of them.

That was a lot of detailed information to try to explain over the phone, but when Rebecca thought about it, the complexity of the story wasn't the reason she decided against it. The problem was, even if his parents believed everything she had to say, the doctors still wouldn't treat Doc without stronger evidence that he'd ingested nanobots. And if she had to fake that proof—which was what she was considering—then she would have involved his parents in her lies just as the house of cards might collapse. She couldn't do that.

"Please, call me Rebecca. And I'd be glad to stay around the hospital and pass on anything I hear. It's not like I'd be sleeping anyway. As for your son's condition, I believe the doctors are closing in on the cause of his problems, so hopefully, they'll know more very soon."

"Thanks, Rebecca. I hope you're right. And call us as soon as you hear anything. Sam thinks the world of you, talks about you all the time, and I understand why. Now, we have to get going. I'll probably see you in four hours or so."

"See you then."

Doc talks about me all the time? That felt more like something a parent would say than anything real, but Rebecca filed the comment away to think about later. Right now, she had more pressing concerns because she was no longer sure what she should do. She had just eliminated any chance at sharing responsibility for Doc's treatment. Could she alone roll the dice with Doc's life the wager? But if she didn't, she was almost certain his parents would arrive to find their son a corpse. She had to take the chance and then live with the consequences.

She dialed the hospital. After several pointed exchanges with the staff who were the gatekeepers to emergency services, Dr. Gandhi answered.

"This is Rebecca Marte. I have the proof," she said without preamble. "You can start your treatment of Sam Price."

There was a pause, making Rebecca wonder if Gandhi was going to require evidence, maybe ask to talk to the Healthtech scientist about what he'd found. But after a moment, he simply said, "I'll inform my team." He hung up.

Again, it wasn't the promise of action she'd hoped, but since Gandhi had proof, even if it was fake, from a fiancée, also fake, he would proceed. He would because it was their best chance to save Doc, and if everything went sideways, he'd have deniability while she got the blame.

She went back to loading the trash bags, trying to focus on saving Doc's life while she did a rough prioritization of the items. Soon, she had five bags full enough that she could carry only one at a time, partly because one of her arms had started aching. She'd strained muscles before and this felt similar, but whatever the cause, she'd just have to manage the rest of the night one-handed.

After loading her car, she left for Healthtech. About halfway there, her phone rang again. This time, she recognized the number. "Detective, I hope you have good news."

"Some good. Some, not so good. I'm escorting the Healthtech scientist to the lab now, so we'll be there when you arrive. His boss was a bit hesitant to call this guy earlier—said he couldn't believe Anders had made off with some of their research. But after that first call, he got someone else out of bed and had them check their supplies. And guess what?"

"They were short."

"By quite a bit," said the detective. "So, when I called back, he was all too happy to send his guy back to the lab for your samples. That's all the good news. As for the rest, with the missing inventory, we had enough evidence to pay a visit to Mr. Anders, but no one's home. We put out an alert and left a car at his house, but I'm guessing he's in the wind."

"You'll find him."

"Hope you're right. Anyway, thought you should know."

"Yeah, thanks. I owe you one." Rebecca disconnected. The missing inventory was consistent but unfortunately, not conclusive proof that Anders had drugged Doc. Maybe Anders had just used his take as an aphrodisiac for his sexual conquests. In small doses, it would definitely do the trick. But even this circumstantial evidence helped ease the knot in her stomach.

"Oh, crap." Rebecca skidded to the curb and stopped, checking her rearview mirror only after she'd completed the reckless maneuver. Perhaps it was the partial reprieve from the pressure—the first she'd had since waking up to a nanobot-controlled Doc in her bedroom—but whatever the reason, a rough timeline had formed in her thoughts. Doc wouldn't have gone home before going to the restaurant to meet Rowles. His place was out of the way, and he'd need all of the half-hour he had between the end of his workday and their appointment. And the idea that he'd ingested something in the morning before going to work that only showed up more than twelve hours later didn't seem possible. So, the contaminated item wasn't in one of the trash bags because he'd been exposed sometime later in the day.

He could have become infected from something he ate or drank at work, but even that scenario pushed the timeline. The nanobots hadn't taken full effect until around 9:30 or about four and a half hours after he would have left work. And while she didn't know how fast these man-made entities would get past the blood-brain barrier, that still seemed too long.

If his encounter with the nanobots occurred after work, it wouldn't have been at a restaurant—that would be too complicated and much too risky. Grocery stores and gas stations were also out. How could Anders know where Doc might stop for a snack? It had to be something he got from what he considered a trusted source. And he had most likely eaten it en route to her apartment, hopefully, in his car. All she needed was a sip of liquid in the bottom of a bottle, a crumb on a crumpled napkin. This time, she checked her mirror before speeding from the curb.

Rebecca found Doc's car easily, just a half-block from her apartment. The doors were unlocked, which made her wonder if the nanobots were affecting Doc's thinking even before he got to her place. Once inside, it only took her a moment to spot a small decorative box on the floor in front of the passenger seat. It even looked like the kind of formal gift that might disguise a threat, though Rebecca thought that might be her hope speaking more than her head.

Although the would-be killer had probably wiped off all the fingerprints—and Doc probably would have smeared any that had been missed—Rebecca still handled the box carefully. She found a pen in the glovebox and used it to carefully lift the lid. Inside, there was a pastry, a bit dried up but still elegant in appearance. But more importantly, it had a small bite missing.

"Gotcha," she muttered. She had some evidence bags in her car and after retrieving one, she carefully slid the box inside.

When she arrived at Healthtech, Rebecca took the evidence bag with the dessert box inside first. Right or wrong, she was going to give her theory about Doc's movements and the speed of nanobot infection priority. The police detective was still there, so she signed over the evidence bag, giving him the task of overseeing the examination by the Healthtech scientist. Then, she unloaded the five trash bags, let the men start on their work, and left for the hospital.

Though the streets were even emptier than before, she drove the speed limit. The weight of her actions and the constant rush had taken their toll. She was exhausted, leaving her head pounding and a throbbing ache in one arm. But at least, she'd done all she could. The test for nanobots in the dessert would either support her gamble with Doc's life or not. And if not, the scientist would move on to the rest of her haul, although she held little hope for success there. She didn't replay the consequences of failure again; she'd made her decisions and she'd live with them.

The walk from her car to the hospital waiting room felt surreal, partially from fatigue and partially from knowing that the direction of her life could reverse at any moment. She could be bathing in the warmth of saving a man she liked, or she could be in handcuffs in the back of a police car within hours. When she reached the waiting room, she found Officer Bates sitting in a chair. She nodded and started across the room as he stood. Her phone rang. She read the text before finishing her approach.

"Do you know how Sam Price is doing?"

"You know doctors," he said. "They always want to take a wait and see approach."

Rebecca released a long sigh, trying but failing to relieve some of the tension of the last four and a half hours. "Guess that's what I'll do then—wait and see. But, as promised, I have a statement for you."

He nodded.

"Healthtech is involved in the design of nanobots used to stimulate the brain for a large-scale project called Brain-2-Brain. The company has verified that some of its research supply is missing. Mr. Scott Anders of Healthtech had access to that inventory. Mr. Sam Price and I believe that Anders might have been stealing the nanobots for recreational use, but after a disagreement, Anders used them to try to silence Sam. Attempts by the St. Louis police to contact Mr. Anders have been unsuccessful, and it's believed he might be on the run. Earlier this evening I found a partially eaten dessert in Sam's car. I delivered it to one of your detectives and to a Healthtech scientist for testing. And a while ago, I received a text that said it tested positive for nanobots."

In this case, "a while ago" meant less than 30 seconds, but that was still the past.

Bates nodded again. "Thanks. I knew a lot of that already, but you've filled in some additional details. There is, however, one other fact that you failed to mention."

"Oh, what's that?" Some of Rebecca's progress in reducing the tension in her gut was lost with his words. Was it her fake relationship with Doc that they had discovered? They probably wouldn't care, but she didn't like the appearance. Could they have figured out she was bluffing when she said she had proof Doc had consumed nanobots? The timing would look bad, but now that she had the proof, it would probably blow over quickly.

"This disagreement with Mr. Anders, as you called it," said Bates, "also involves an individual named Samantha Rowles. She, too, seems to have gone missing, perhaps with Mr. Anders, but not likely since they haven't been in a relationship in a while. But one of Ms. Rowles's friends says there has been someone asking a lot of questions about her before she dropped out of sight. And that person was Sam Price."

WEDNESDAY, AUGUST 10

Afternoon, St. Louis Regional Medical Center

Unfortunately, Doc recognized the setting the moment his eyes opened—a hospital with its hushed murmuring in the halls broken by the occasional announcement and the beeping of equipment at his bedside. What was less recognizable, however, were the sensations from his body as his nerves awoke. Was it really possible for every muscle and joint to ache at the same time? Apparently, it was. But how the change in scenery from Rebecca's apartment and the shift from passion to pain had occurred, he had no clue. The last thing he remembered, he was in the bedroom with Rebecca. And though the emotional intensity and vision of their lovemaking felt as real as the room where he now lay, other parts of that night were vague and felt out of context. And still other images he recalled were clearly impossible. He wasn't sure what any of that meant.

When Doc felt he had summoned enough fortitude to stand the pain, he raised his head and looked around the room. It was mostly equipment he didn't recognize and a rolling table holding a plastic bottle with a straw. But as his gaze moved to the right, he saw Rebecca, her head down as she studied her phone. Though she was wearing a mask over her nose and mouth, her short blonde hair and pale skin were unmistakable.

What was equally clear was the fact she'd also been injured, and if the number of visible bandages and bruises was any indication, she had been hurt badly. There were numerous small dressings on one arm, with a larger covering on the forearm. The other arm was in a sling and her neck was bruised. He wouldn't have been surprised to find her leg in a cast, but he couldn't raise his head that far.

"What happened?" Doc managed to choke out through a parched throat.

Rebecca looked up. "Ah, you're awake. I didn't catch that, but your parents just stepped out. I'll send your mom a text."

Doc cleared his throat and tried again, only slightly stronger this time. "Just a second on the text. First, what happened to us?"

Rebecca gave a half shrug, then waved a hand over her bandages. "I suppose the best answer is, we did this to each other." Her voice was also hoarse, although less than his. She reached down to the floor, retrieved a drink, raised her mask for a moment, and took a sip.

It was but a single datum—"we did this to each other"—but it was more than enough for Doc's mind to start racing with the possibilities. Perhaps the most straightforward was that he'd made a mistake in bed, been too rough, gone too far. She'd asked him to stop, and when he didn't, she responded. Initially, she would have done so with restraint, hoping to avoid hurting him. But when he fought back against her half-measures and hurt her, she had been forced to subdue him. He just didn't know what self-defense maneuver she could have used that left every part of his body aching.

There was, however, a problem with this guess. Hurting any woman would be completely out of character for him. He'd never been into any type of rough sex, so why would he have started down that path with someone whose friendship he valued as much as Rebecca's?

But then, the animal attraction he'd felt when she'd answered her door also felt a bit unusual, not in its content, but in its suddenness and strength. And its peculiarity was nothing compared to his later thoughts. Hadn't he spoken to his long-dead grandfather at one point? Could whatever had affected his memory also be rewriting his character? Or was his personality intact, and he had dreamt up all these strange events to cover a memory he'd repressed—a memory of attacking a friend?

Doc didn't find this last conjecture particularly satisfying, however, partially because he wasn't sure repression could occur this quickly. All of this had happened only yesterday. And though psychoanalysis wasn't his specialty, if repressed experiences were replaced with wild and impossible beliefs, he felt he would have run across some of that research at school. He had never heard of anything like that.

Doc watched as Rebecca stood from her chair, picked up his drink from the table, and gave him a sip. That act of kindness, however, still fit his theory. She was upset because things had gotten so far out of hand. "Did I ...." Doc couldn't finish, the question being one he thought he'd never hear from his lips, but he had to know. He squeezed his eyes closed, only daring to open them after he'd summoned the determination he needed. "Did I rape you last night?"

"Whoa, not so loud," she said under her breath as she turned to look at the door. "There are people outside."

Doc momentarily forgot his state. The stabbing pain in his neck when he turned to follow her glance, however, was an immediate and unwelcome reminder.

"Just what do you remember from that night?" asked Rebecca. "And, for the record, it wasn't last night. It was two nights ago."

"Two nights?" he croaked. She nodded, so he continued. "I remember coming to your place. And, by the way, I didn't really cover everything that happened with Samantha Rowles. Or should I say, what didn't happen?"

"Probably irrelevant now, so go on."

People outside the door? A missing day? Samantha Rowles now irrelevant? What the heck was going on? But the mystery of what had happened to them was still the most pressing question in his thoughts, so he took a breath and continued. "I remember being blown away by the way you looked when you came to the door."

"You were blown away by my T-shirt and gym shorts?"

Doc shrugged—or tried before the pain stopped him. But he knew why he'd been so enthralled. Her attire looked like something she might sleep in, which, at the time, had generated all kinds of sexual fantasies. All of them now felt ridiculous. Other than a few platonic kisses and several handshakes, they'd hardly ever touched each other.

"Anyway, we talked for a little while, then we started making out on your couch. For me, it was really intense. Clothes came off and we ended up in the bedroom. After that, it all gets a bit fuzzy."

"That's fine," said Rebecca. "I just needed to know when the nanobots kicked in."

"Nanobots?" Doc blurted, again forgetting his state and suffering for the lapse.

The door to his hospital room swung open, and a police officer stepped in. "Ms. Marte?"

"I'm fine. I'm just starting to explain what's happened to him. Needless to say, it'll be a while."

"OK. I'll be outside if you need me." Rebecca nodded.

"Am I being held?" Doc asked when the officer had left.

"Yes, but...."

"And a policeman is taking orders from you?"

"Patience, Doc." Rebecca reached out and put her hand on his arm, and the turmoil in his mind abated. It was as if she'd said, "Stop trying to analyze the data before I give them to you."

That was an approach to life that Doc understood, and he nodded. "OK."

"First," Rebecca said, "let's clear up what happened two nights ago. Yes, you came over. And, yes, we made out, but that was it. It was all junior–high stuff, so please, no more talk of rape. There is way too much drama about this situation already and if that misinformation gets out? Well, you may get to kiss me again, but you can kiss your privacy goodbye. The reporters will be all over you."

"So, we didn't have sex?" Doc asked in a whisper, turning only his eyes toward the door.

"You don't consider kissing sex?" The frustrated look on Doc's face answered her question. "No, we didn't. Not like you're thinking anyway."

Doc felt a momentary pang of disappointment, discovering that one of the most emotionally intense experiences of his life was only a hallucination. "So, all these other things I think I remember? That's what the nanobots did to me?"

"Yes, apparently. When you started saying strange things and the seizures hit, I thought it might be drugs. But it didn't seem like any drug I had ever heard of. You were all over the place. And I didn't think you'd take something and then come over and try to seduce me."

Doc grimaced. He remembered some of his pushiness.

"It wasn't a big deal," said Rebecca, as if reading his face. "In fact, it was kinda sweet that you wanted to make out, although a come-on when you're not out of your head would be better."

Kinda sweet? It almost sounded like Rebecca was flirting with him, and if not for the mask over her face, he thought he might have been able to confirm it. Was there a slightly mischievous smile hidden there? Suddenly, the taste of her lips, the warmth of her body, the smell of her skin flooded his mind, although he wasn't certain if it was a memory or part of the work of the nanobots. And while he hoped to keep those thoughts to himself, the heartrate monitor gave him away.

Her eyebrows raised—something he could see over the mask—and she said, "You're going to get me kicked out of here. You need your rest."

"Yes, ma'am," he responded dutifully and pushed the sensations from his mind as best he could.

"And I need to send that text to your mom before I end up in her doghouse." After she did, Rebecca said, "Anyway, the doctors couldn't connect your behavior to any drug either, so I thought

Anders might be behind it. After all, he was none too happy with you nosing around, even if all of Healthtech's products are harmless. So, I called a couple of old friends in the FBI and a couple of police detectives I know. I'd say someone in that group put enough pressure on Healthtech to make them crack, but their involvement in the B2B Project is not really that hush-hush."

"The Brain-2-Brain Project? The big commercial collaboration on technology to share thoughts?"

"The same," said Rebecca, relieved that he knew about the project so she didn't have to explain it. "Apparently, Healthtech is working on nanobots as the means to read one person's brain waves and write them to someone else."

Doc chuckled, though even to his ears, the sound held no humor. "And Anders dosed me with a bunch of them and set them to fire off randomly. So, I ended up in a bizarre dreamworld of images, memories, muscle twitches, smells, pains, you name it. You're lucky I didn't kill you."

"Well, you tried," said Rebecca. "Although I have to admit, I got too close when I was trying to help you ride out what I thought was a seizure. But mostly, you just about scared me to death."

"Sorry. I guess it's sort of stupid to say I didn't mean to hurt you, but I didn't." As Doc considered his experience further, one other conclusion became clearer. "These nanobots aren't what caused Cruz's delusion, are they?"

Rebecca slowly shook her head, her eyes opening wide. "I didn't think you'd come to that conclusion so soon, but yeah, I can't see how. Those little devils produce uncontrolled hallucinations—a bizarre dream world as you just called it. I can't imagine Cruz typing one letter on her computer keyboard, much less writing her long involved posts under the influence of them. Anders's theft of some of them has been uncovered, and that makes him a thief, a sleaze, and guilty of assault, if not an attempted murderer. But I don't see how he had anything to do with Cruz's fate."

"That's disappointing. I thought we had the guy."

A chuckle escaped Rebecca's mask.

"What's so funny?"

"Well, two days ago, you alternated between not being able to stand and thinking you could fly. And now, you're worried about the case?"

Doc started to answer but realized that an insatiable need to understand wasn't a defense. So, he just shrugged, a gesture he now made without a groan. "I think I understand why I'm so sore. Getting all these cuts and bruises goes with the hallucination, I guess. But how did you get hurt?"

"Well, when you stopped making sense and the convulsions started, I called an ambulance. Mostly, we were just waiting for it to arrive, but when we heard the siren in the distance, you jumped up and ran out my back door. I caught up with you on the first-floor landing and then ... well, that was when you decided you could fly. You grabbed my jeans and over the railing you went. You got the worst of it since I landed on top, but I still got a lot of little scratches and what is probably a strained muscle in my shoulder."

"Mostly" they were waiting for the ambulance, thought Doc. What else had happened that she wasn't saying? "How'd you get the large bandage on your right arm?"

"It covers up a bruise. That's where you grabbed me when you fell, and, jeez, you have a grip like a vice."

"I'm sorry. And the bruise on your neck?"

"Enough, Doc. I'm not going over the reason for every little scratch and scrape. You were out of your head, so no reason to discuss each of my injuries or for you to apologize for them."

Her response was a little brusque, but Doc wasn't fooled. Diving off a balcony could be passed off with a quip—you thought you could fly—and the bruise on her arm—his instinctual reaction to falling. But her neck was probably bruised because he'd tried to choke her. That, and whatever else he had tried to do was no joking matter, but she wouldn't want to discuss them with the gravity they deserved. At least, not now.

"OK," he said. "But I'm still sorry for what I did to you, even if I didn't realize it was wrong."

"Thanks," said Rebecca after a moment, "but it's the nanobots who should be apologizing. Anyway, with what the doctors learned from Healthtech and the half-eaten cupcake in your car, they came up with a treatment plan. They put you in a medically induced coma. That's what happened to your yesterday."

"The nanobots were in the cupcake?" Rebecca nodded. "Well, that was really dumb of me, although Anders got lucky with the card and the timing. It was signed 'From a friend' just a couple of hours after we decided we were still friends."

Between the nanobots and the coma, Doc realized he couldn't trust anything he remembered of his night at Rebecca's apartment. But then—for him anyway—it had almost been too good to be real. And he still had the memories, even if they were imaginary. "So, why is Samantha Rowles's information irrelevant?" he asked.

"It might not be," Rebecca said slowly. Doc didn't need to see her face to know she was distraught; he could hear it in her voice. "Unfortunately, we'll never know. She took whatever she knew to the grave."

And now, Doc was upset, too. He knew Rowles well enough to know she enjoyed an adrenaline rush from time to time, but she didn't deserve to die. She loved life too much. "What happened?"

"We don't have all the details, but we know the basic timeline. She went missing two days ago. Her whereabouts that day are unknown, although she took a taxi downtown early that morning. Then yesterday, she resurfaced at the airport and took a flight into Washington, DC. There, she just happened to bump into a U.S. Congressman, Representative Kessner, whose wife just happened to be out of town. Presumably, Rowles got the man interested enough to share a toast at midnight, his being laced with poison. Then, she took her own life in the same way."

"So, someone planned this out very carefully," said Doc.

"If you believe her social media posts, she did. She felt extremely guilty about a ten-year affair with Kessner and planned the whole thing. But then, the posts were filled with things that could never have happened since he rarely came to Missouri, and she never traveled to Washington. I suppose law enforcement or the media may turn up something more about them later, but I'm doubting it."

"But how do posts like hers go unnoticed until someone dies?" asked Doc. Then, he started to slap his forehead but stopped with a grimace. "That was a dumb question, wasn't it? Without words like bomb or assassinate, no automatic system would flag them. So, someone would have to read them and recognize the implied threat. With millions of posts a day and hers being a long-winded tome about longing and guilt … well, no wonder we only see her posts after the fact."

"Or Cruz's, which fall into the conspiracy theory category," said Rebecca. "And since she was clear about the threat but not what she intended to do about it, hers were just more noise on the Internet. I suppose, eventually, calling a congressman a space alien might get someone's attention, but not any time soon. That's pretty bland, considering what they call each other." Rebecca was quiet a moment. "Why is it we get so many bizarre conspiracy theories anymore?"

Now it was Doc's turn to be silent for a moment. "I'm not sure. I've heard a few ideas, things like they give people a sense of control or make them feel like they're a part of something bigger than themselves. But those notions feel more like initial guesses than anything that's been studied in depth. Maybe it's just the way people are starting to think?"

"God, I hope not. Anyway, back to my … I mean, our client. I've started looking at the areas of overlap between Representatives Kessner and Barclay. And since it's data, I'm hoping you can help with that when you're up and around."

"Of course." Doc paused a minute, isolating the thought that was still bothering him. "Everything's starting to make sense, except for one thing. Why am I being held?"

"Apparently, Susy Wu … you remember her?"

"Sure, Anders's OA."

Rebecca nodded. "Again, I don't have all the details, but apparently, she and Rowles were friends ... maybe from a mutual dislike of Anders? In any case, she tried to call Rowles two days ago at work. When her company said she hadn't come in, Wu got worried, called the police, and gave them your name. They might not have done anything at that point because Rowles had only been missing a half-day, but when they got multiple reports from her work, client meetings she had missed, her doorman, and so on, they started looking for you. And, of course, you weren't hard to find, since I'd already told everyone I knew at the department where you were."

"But with Rowles getting on a plane yesterday, wouldn't they stop watching me? Obviously, I was here, and she was alive and well at that point, flying around the country."

"They know that now, but they didn't know it until the DC police contacted them about Kessner's death and her suicide. Until then, they were looking for Rowles in ditches and dumpsters, figuring you and she had experimented together until you dumped her to visit me. As for the officer watching you now? He's just waiting for the paperwork to catch up with the facts. But he knows what's going on, which is the only reason he stepped out when I asked. Any time now, it'll be official, and he'll disappear."

"So, where's Anders in all of this?"

"On the run," said Rebecca. "He was probably hoping you'd die in a fiery crash or in a nosedive from a 20-story building, but when you survived, he took off. Or maybe he split before that if he wanted a head start. I give him a day, three at most. With his name, picture, lists of friends and associates, they'll catch him. But even after that, it may be tricky linking him to the attempt on your life. He was one of only a few people who had access to the nanoparticles and his theft is known, but without something like a fingerprint on the pastry box, he might get off the attempted murder charge. Of course, he'll never work in the medical technology field again."

"Wow. I slept through a lot. But at least it's over."

Rebecca tilted her head to the side. "Not quite."

"You don't think Anders would be crazy enough to come after me again, do you?" asked Doc.

"No. But right now, you're something of a folk legend as the first nanobot-tripper in the world. It won't be over until you have your fifteen minutes of fame. Or is that, fifteen minutes of shame?"

"Just what I need," said Doc. But before he could say more, someone knocked on the door. A moment later, a woman in scrubs came in. Spotting Rebecca, she said, "Sorry, ma'am, but we need to run some more tests on your fiancé."

"No problem. I have to go back to work anyway." Then, Rebecca turned so the nurse could only see her back. Her eyebrows shot up, and she exaggerated a shrug with open hands in front of her.

Even without seeing her face, it wasn't difficult for Doc to guess the reason for her ruse; Rebecca wouldn't like being kept out of the information loop, and claiming soon-to-be-spouse status was an easy way around it. He thought about just letting it pass, but the temptation to rib her was a bit too strong. "Yeah, honey, you better get going. And later, you can tell me all the parts of the story that you left out."

"OK, but you asked for it," replied Rebecca, never one to back down from a little teasing. The nurse, on the other hand, gave them both a confused look while she unhooked Doc from all the instruments beside his bed. Just as she finished, Doc's parents returned.

"Sam," said his mother a bit too loudly for the small room. "You're awake. How do you feel? You've been in … well, I guess it was a coma for the last thirty-six hours. They said you might be able to hear us, so your father and I have been talking to you. Rebecca, too."

It hurt a bit, but Doc raised a hand to catch his mother's attention. "I'm a little sore, but I'll be fine, Mom. But now, I need to get some more tests run."

"Now?"

"Sorry, Ms. Price, but these won't take long," said the nurse. "Maybe twenty minutes. You can even walk along part of the way to the lab, and I'll push his bed slowly."

"OK. Let's go."

In the hall, the officer assigned to watch Doc stood and stretched his back. Doc nodded at him. "Still here, huh?"

"Someone needs to protect you from the paparazzi," he replied with a grin, dispelling Doc's hope that Rebecca had been joking about his fifteen minutes of shame while adding to his parent's confusion. When the entourage of nurse, patient in bed, and parents turned right, Rebecca said her goodbyes and continued straight ahead toward the elevators.

* * *

About halfway to the elevators, Rebecca stopped and took a seat in the hall. A hand came up to her head and she slowly massaged the tension in her forehead with her fingers. Why had she lied to Doc? Why had she called their tryst just junior-high stuff? It was more than that—at least it would be in the junior high she had attended. Doc wasn't close-minded. He wasn't a prude. And it wasn't like she'd drugged him and taken advantage ... although it almost felt that way. All of her thoughts about that night were confusing, almost as if she'd been the one with the foreign beings in her system.

Part of the problem was the possibility that, rather than turning a corner, Doc had cut one in his nanobot-induced rush to be with her. Would his passion be intact without those little devils swimming in his gray matter? When they were smooching on her couch, was he kissing the woman or the product of random electrical shocks to his brain?

But among the chaos of her feelings and memories, there was one certainty—had they both been thinking clearly, things wouldn't have gone as far as they had. But they weren't thinking clearly. The reasons for Doc's muddled thoughts became obvious as the night progressed. The nanobots became his puppet master, pulling invisible strings on his arms and legs. They created videos in his mind's eye that he couldn't understand and that he couldn't control.

And the reasons for her welcoming his advances? Though Rebecca didn't like admitting it, she knew. She didn't want to question Doc's desire. And every time that evening when she tried, though not often, he'd answered with the whisper of his breath on her neck, the warmth of his skin on hers, the taste of his lips. How could something that felt so right then feel so ... well, ill-timed and artificial now?

Rebecca heard her name being called. She turned around to find a familiar face. "Dr. Algar. What can I do for you?"

His eyes narrowed. "You don't have to wear that mask up on this wing. We had you checked out thoroughly when you were admitted for treatment. But if you're more comfortable that way ...."

"Just being careful around my fiancé," she replied, then pulled the mask from her face.

"Of course," replied the doctor. "It's in your patient portal, but I thought I'd share the good news. You can take off the sling whenever you want. Your arm will be fine. It's just a strained muscle. As you suspected, I might add."

Rebecca skipped the "I told you so" in favor of asking, "But?" She was certain there was more and almost as sure about the topic.

Algar chuckled. "Guess I can't fool a PI. We took care of all the minor cuts and contusions, but I'm still a little concerned about other possible internal injuries. You took a really hard fall and just because you landed on top of your fiancé, it doesn't mean you didn't sustain some internal injuries. Are you certain you want to discharge yourself without getting the additional tests that we discussed?"

"Yes, I'm sure. The last thing I need is more data about my condition in your records."

"But ...." Algar got no farther.

"I'm fine. And if anything develops, I'll be back." The last words, Rebecca had said over her shoulder as she headed for the elevator.

THURSDAY, AUGUST 11

Evening, Marte Investigative Services

Rebecca unlocked the door to her office, walked through to the back, and took a seat behind her desk. It had taken the doctors the rest of Wednesday afternoon, all of last night, and most of today to give Doc a clean bill of health. But as soon as he heard, he volunteered to bring dinner, and he wasn't interested in taking no for an answer.

The last time that had been the plan, the evening had ended without food and the two of them yelling at each other at the top of their lungs. Perhaps that was why he'd insisted on buying tonight. But then, five nights after the shouting match, they'd had no plans—dinner or otherwise—but Doc had appeared at her place and they'd ended up naked, entangled in each other's arms. Their single lunchtime encounter between those two trysts had been a respite of normalcy, she supposed, although now it felt nearly as surreal as the extremes.

So, what version of Doc would appear at her office tonight? Would he be the man who had succumbed to standards that no human could achieve? She didn't think so, but who knew what thoughts and memories the nanobots might have stirred? Or would he have started to believe his fragmented images from their night of passion and push for a repeat performance in the sack? She was sure her desk would be all right with him if his thoughts had gone in that direction. Or would he have come to say good-bye, his interest in her vanishing with the nanobots? Anything was possible.

All she wanted was for him to see her and not the past or a man-made apparition. After that, it would either work out or it wouldn't, though she hoped for the former. And so, she'd told herself to forget about the past—their argument, her little white lie, the unknown forces driving his passion. But the fact that she'd gone home before this meeting and had changed—twice—said she hadn't followed her own counsel.

"Whatever," Rebecca mumbled to the empty room. She didn't think it would come to it, but she had parted ways with Doc once, never expecting to see him again, and she had been all right, if not happy about it. She could do it again, if necessary. But in the meantime, she had a case to finish and a client who was becoming uneasy with her progress.

Rebecca couldn't blame Gustafsson for being concerned. Until about six hours ago, she had been worried herself. She'd found no likely suspects on Gustafsson's list, not even the people at the museum, the food pantry, or her doctor's office. She had looked into the politics of the two men who had been targeted by the delusional women, Representatives Kessner and Barclay, but they seemed like the same person. They had mouthed the same slogans and voted the same on nearly every bill. In effect, she knew little more now than when Barclay had been the only victim.

True, she had made some progress on other fronts. She'd uncovered Anders's unscrupulous behavior at Healthtech and had been instrumental in linking him with two crimes—his theft of the nanoparticles and his attempt to murder Doc—but Gustafsson wouldn't care. Well, she'd be glad Doc hadn't died, but these successes had nothing to do with her cousin. And worse, her part in putting Doc in danger might well outweigh any gratitude Gustafsson felt for saving him. Frankly, she would have felt the same—save a potential victim, plus ten; put that victim in a situation where he needed to be saved, minus twenty.

Then, to make exposing Anders even less sweet, it looked like he might have escaped, with the odds of his capture dwindling by the minute. And unfortunately, the likelihood he'd be apprehended hadn't been high for a while; someone who resembled Anders had used a forged passport to enter Mexico. By now, he could be sunbathing on a remote island in the Pacific or climbing a mountain in Tibet. Her original belief that he'd be lucky to last more than a few days on the lam had been replaced with guesses expressed in months or years. In fact, he might never be caught.

After considering her lack of progress, Rebecca had almost called Gustafsson to say the investigation was at a dead end. But about an hour before her self-imposed deadline, she stumbled on something that nearly took her breath away. Another government official had been murdered several months earlier with the killer, a woman named Tracy Linthecom, also perishing at the scene. And as before, she had posted about a connection to the man that was clearly delusional. At this high level—an obviously delusional woman kills a member of the U.S. Congress—the match to the Rowles and Cruz cases was undeniable. The details, however, made this new murder look like something completely different.

First, the man was a U.S. Senator from Iowa, rather than a representative. That alone wasn't much of a difference—all these men were in the business of legislating public policy—but it was still a change.

A second difference, although also minor, was that Linthecom looked nothing like Cruz and Rowles. There apparently wasn't a serial killer fixated on black-haired, brown-eyed, dark-complected beauties as Doc had speculated. What linked these women, if anything, wasn't their appearance.

Third, while Cruz and Rowles both resided in the St. Louis area, Linthecom lived some 550 miles away in Minneapolis, Minnesota. While again, this difference was small—any serial killer could have a car—it complicated Rebecca's theory that the cases were related.

Those three, however, completed the list of minor inconsistencies. Any one of the remaining two discrepancies between Linthecom on the one hand and Cruz and Rowles on the other would have most anyone in law enforcement responding to Rebecca's theory with an indulgent smile and an "I'll get back to you later" sendoff.

The fourth difference was that the women's delusions had absolutely no overlap. Linthecom believed that the senator was a Nazi in hiding who had, in fact, tortured her at a concentration camp in World War II Germany. There were no Martians. There was no guilt-ridden love affair. And the facts that neither the senator nor Linthecom was old enough to be in a concentration camp, that he wasn't German, and that she wasn't Jewish didn't affect her beliefs at all. It just made clear that she had lost all contact with reality.

And finally, there was absolutely no similarity in the women's *modi operandi*, the methods they had used in their assassination attempts. Rather than poison or a gun, Linthecom had rammed the senator's car with hers, pushing it off a bridge in rural Iowa and into a river where he had perished.

There was also a crucial difference in how Linthecom's death had been classified—one that had kept this case out of the murder-suicide category. Her car had followed the senator's into the river, but her death had been ruled an accident. That conclusion had been based largely on two factors.

First, two eyewitnesses in a car that was trailing the senator had stated for the media that the bumpers of his and Linthecom's car had become locked and that she had tried to brake before going over the side of the bridge. Skid marks on the pavement tended to support their statements. However, it wasn't clear to Rebecca that these witnesses could have detected the difference between burning tire tread because she was gunning the engine or because she was trying to stop. Most likely, they'd only observed smoking tires and the belief that Linthecom was trying to save herself was just common sense. And, at the time they'd made their statements, the witnesses hadn't known that common sense had fled Linthecom's mind.

Second, Linthecom's intent in the attack had been taken from her social media posts. In one place, for example, she'd written "I'll dance on your grave when the Maker takes you." But drawing any conclusion from materials that were filled with impossibilities and incongruities made any interpretation impossible, in Rebecca's opinion. For all she knew, Linthecom had meant her ghost would dance on the senator's grave.

With all these differences, Rebecca didn't think anyone besides she and Doc would believe the cases were related, but she called the police in both cities and the FBI anyway. The conversations went almost as she expected, except that no one told her directly that they couldn't waste the manpower on anything so farfetched. Rather, they listened for a while, then passed her onto another department, unit, or jurisdiction. Eventually, she couldn't take another minute on hold with elevator music in the background and disconnected. And during the whole sequence of calls, only an old friend at the FBI had been willing to level with her. "I think I could buy my two-year-old son saying he hadn't hit his little sister before I could get behind that story."

But for Rebecca, there was a good chance that Linthecom was the break she and Doc needed.

Rebecca heard the door to the reception area open and felt her stomach tense with the sound. All of her questions about who might come through her door raced through her thoughts one last time. But now, getting an answer was more important than what that answer was. She'd be OK whatever direction things took. She got up from her chair and came around the desk just as he entered the office with two bags of what appeared to be Mexican food.

"Wow, you have some big client today or something? You look great."

Her debate over wardrobe had finally ended with a dress—a dark gray tweed shift dress that fit her perfectly. It was a good middle ground between a sexless power suit, most of which she had discarded after leaving the FBI, and a T-shirt and gym shorts, although the dress was clearly closer to the former than the latter. "You've seen me in this before," Rebecca replied, not knowing if he had or not, but then, men never remembered things like that anyway.

"Must have been a while ago," he said as he dropped the food on the desk. Then, he gave her a quick kiss. "Just a friendly peck on the cheek," he said, repeating the words she'd used in her apartment.

"And that was perfect." Rebecca's concerns about the last couple of days vanished. She knew Doc would always feel guilty for what had happened to Nicole, but he appeared determined to move on. And if there was any carryover from what they'd done in the throes of the nanobots, it didn't show. In place of her unease, the feeling of promise returned. And it felt good.

"Now, how about I bring you up to date on the case while we eat," said Rebecca. "I'm starving."

Evening, Marte Investigative Services

"So," Doc said as he studied Rebecca's face, "you're assuming that these women—Cruz, Rowles, and now Tracy Linthecom—are merely the weapons being used in an attempt to change the direction of Congress? And you're assuming that someone has come up with a way to create an elaborate delusion in their minds and focus it on a specific congressman? You're also guessing that if we can find a pattern in the voting records of these men, we can identify the mastermind's political agenda? And finally, you're thinking that if we cross-reference this madman's political objective to the businesses and organizations in the area where Rowles took her taxi, we might find the perp ... which also assumes he or she needs a front to finance his or her plan? Is that everything?"

Doc was surprised and more than a little impressed that Rebecca's look of determination hadn't wavered as he'd listed all the assumptions in her theory. Most people would be backpedaling by now—"Well, it was just a thought." But not Rebecca.

"Exactly," she said, "but with one small correction. We won't be analyzing the voting records, and we won't be cross-referencing those results with the downtown businesses. I was hoping you would do that. I mean, it's data after all."

"That it is. And pretty messy data, as I recall."

"You've been in the GovTrack database?"

"Well, not recently enough to remember its name, but yeah. I got curious about how one of my senators had voted on a particular bill, but it took me forever to find the record. Back then, you could sort by date and things like the margin of victory, but not on anything like all the bills related to education or healthcare."

"I don't think the database has changed much, if any, since then, but wouldn't the margin of victory filter help?"

It only took him a moment to make a guess about her reasoning. "Are you thinking that the votes on the bills our killer opposes have to be close? Otherwise, there's no point killing just a few congressmen."

Rebecca pressed the tips of two fingers to her lips, partially covering a smile. He didn't even need to hear her affirmation to know he'd guessed right. "I was," she replied. "I'm just not sure how much filtering the database will reduce the number of cases because it seems like every vote is close these days. The Vice President has had to vote several times in the past year or so when the Senate was deadlocked in a 50–50 tie."

"I'll let you know the number of close races when I get those cases pulled out."

"While you're looking at that, I'm going to take a closer look at the women," said Rebecca. "You want to see a picture of Linthecom?" She held a print of a photograph that had probably been downloaded from the Internet.

"Hmm. Nothing like Cruz or Rowles," said Doc. "So, we're not after a serial killer who's picking victims based on a murderous fixation from his or her past. And the killer isn't picking these women because they're convenient, either. It's pretty much a day's drive to Minneapolis. Or a short flight, although I'm not sure our killer would want to leave that kind of digital trail."

"Agreed. If we could lock down a date and get law enforcement interested, they could get the passenger lists, but as you said, our killer probably didn't fly. Which is why I want to look at the women more closely. If we knew what made them the perfect instrument for the murderer's scheme, we'd be a heck of a lot closer to catching this perp ... if there is one."

"Yeah, if there is one," replied Doc. "So, I take it we have no other theories to check. It's a mastermind planting delusions or we have to tell Dani, sorry, but your cousin just went off the deep end?"

Rebecca held out her empty hands. "Not unless you have other ideas."

"Not really," Doc admitted. "Hey, if you want someone to talk to Suzy Wu to get background on Rowles, I could. She might feel like she owes me one after giving my name to the police, even though I would have done the same thing if I was in her place."

"Good idea. Can you handle that and the voting data?"

"I should be able to. After the doctors finished poking and prodding me around noon, I dropped by work and offloaded a bunch of the lower priority assignments I'd volunteered for." He thought about explaining why he had those jobs in the first place, but somehow, he suspected Rebecca already knew.

Rebecca nodded. "Good. I talked to Tracy Linthecom's husband this afternoon and have a flight tomorrow morning to

Minneapolis," said Rebecca. "She's obviously the largest hole in our knowledge of the women, so I wanted to start there. And it seems like something that should be done face-to-face. I won't be back until Saturday around noon, so can we get back together after the weekend?"

"Sure," said Doc. "Here? Say, six o'clock Monday night and I'll bring dinner again?"

"OK," Rebecca said after a beat. "That's it for me. You have anything else you want to talk about?"

"I'm good."

They both stood and headed for the door. In the hall, Rebecca pulled the keys to her office from a pocket, then turned to look at Doc. "How about six o'clock at my place, instead of here. And I'll cook. That is, if you think the couch won't be too much of a distraction."

Doc chuckled. Rebecca had been somewhat quiet all evening. Her bit of ribbing felt like a signal that she was returning to the woman he knew ... and was finding increasingly attractive. And he didn't think his developing feelings had anything to do with the "night of the nanobots," as he now privately called that evening at her place. Of course, the memories of her body, whether real or created, did nothing to slow their growth.

"I think I can resist," said Doc, as she locked her office door and they headed out of the building. "That is, as long as we readdress this couch-ban when the case is over."

Rebecca smiled. But rather than answering in words, she placed a kiss on his cheek and turned toward the parking lot. "It was my turn," she said over her shoulder.

Doc stood there on the sidewalk, grinning, as he watched her walk away. Just before she turned the corner to the parking lot, she cast a glance over her shoulder. Even in the pale rays of the streetlamp, he could see her smile.

FRIDAY, AUGUST 12

Morning, The Linthecom Home, Minneapolis, MN

It was a middle-class neighborhood on the outskirts of Minneapolis, built when speed and economy were necessitated by a rapidly growing population. The home belonging to George Linthecom, Tracy's husband, was a virtual carbon copy of his neighbors' houses—a one-story ranch with the entrance centered on the front and flanked by double windows on each side. The windows on the right were set back slightly to accommodate a shallow, concrete porch. Rebecca figured that three chairs would fill it to capacity. There was a one-car garage on the left, with a sidewalk branching from the garage's driveway and extending past a flower bed to the front door. Other than the choice of exterior paint colors, the houses in the neighborhood varied only in the number of children's toys lying about. George Linthecom's home had more than most.

From what Rebecca had been able to surmise from her short phone call with George, until three months ago, the Linthecom family had enjoyed a quiet and satisfying life. Tracy was the conscientious mother of four, doing all the things that stay-at-home moms did— making treats for the school bake sale, driving the team to their ball games, hosting birthday parties four times a year.

But now, in the eyes of the community, Tracy was a leper. She had lost all touch with reality, and in her insanity, she had taken the life of a well-respected politician from a neighboring state and, in the process, had lost hers. And while the attention span of the general public seldom lasted beyond the next big story, unless Rebecca had read the signals wrong, memories in this bedroom community were long.

Looking out on the physical remnants of the life that Tracy had lost, Rebecca realized that her belief that the trip would be difficult was a serious underestimate; it would be a gut-wrencher. She took a deep breath, grabbed her briefcase, and exited the rental car.

George had suggested they meet on a weekday morning after the children had gone to school. He didn't want to upset them again with another visitor who wanted to talk about their mother, so he had taken the morning off.

"Mr. Linthecom?" Rebecca asked when a man answered her knock. He nodded but said nothing as he stared through the screen door at her. "I'm Rebecca Marte from Marte Investigative Services in St. Louis. Thank you for meeting with me."

"You have ID?"

Rebecca pulled a badge holder from the briefcase and held it up for him.

"I suppose I didn't really need to see that," he said after a cursory glance. "I looked up your company online, and if you aren't the PI, you're her identical twin." Linthecom paused, continuing to look through the screen. "I know you covered this, but tell me again. Why are you interested in my wife?"

"I represent a client whose cousin developed irrational beliefs and tried to kill a U.S. representative. And since I took the case, we've had another woman who showed a similar pattern. I believe there may be some connection between your wife and these two other women."

"You know two other women who thought they'd found a Nazi who had tortured them back in World War II Germany?"

"The false beliefs have all been different, but they've all focused on a member of Congress. And each of the women documented a long, but clearly impossible, history with the man she attacked. I'm hoping, with your help, that I can fill in more of the details of your wife's delusion. It might be important in solving these cases."

"And you're not a reporter?"

It wasn't the first time Rebecca had been asked this question, but she still wasn't sure why people did. Would a reporter who had gone to the trouble of creating fake credentials and a bogus company online and who had flown over 500 miles to meet now admit to being a fraud? But Linthecom was undoubtedly struggling to raise his family alone, so it was more this stress speaking than his logic.

"No, I'm not a reporter. And I won't share anything we discuss with the media."

Linthecom released a long breath, then opened the screen door. "Come in. Let's talk in the living room." He led the way. "Sorry about the questions, but it was only a couple of weeks ago that a reporter tried to con me. Wanted a human-interest story about the man with the looney wife who got herself killed while murdering a senator. Who wants to hear about something like that?"

Unfortunately, Rebecca thought a lot of people would be interested. The demand for human tragedy stories seemed limitless, although she wasn't going to say that to this man. "Some reporters can be very insensitive. I'm sorry you had to go through that."

Linthecom nodded, then said, "Please, have a seat," as he gestured toward two overstuffed chairs and a couch centered around a television. There were a few light blankets, folded neatly and placed on a table in the corner. Rebecca was sure they were furniture coverings now removed for his guest. She sat in one of the chairs.

"Good choice," said Linthecom, as he sat in the other armchair. "You're tall like Tracy was."

Rebecca cringed internally, hoping that none of her unease showed in her face. That, too, was something she'd experienced before. If you walked into the home of someone with a deceased family member, sooner or later you'd sit in the dead person's favorite chair or pick up his or her last-read book or admire that person's favorite heirloom. Having been there before, however, didn't make it any easier.

"So, what can I tell you?" asked Linthecom.

"First, let me say how sorry I am for your loss. I know that doesn't sound like much since I never met your wife. But I've been around this business long enough to know the pain something like this can cause."

Linthecom's gaze dropped to the floor. "Thank you," he said softly without looking up. "It does mean something to me."

Rebecca gave him a moment, then said, "I understand from some of the newspaper accounts that your wife posted online about discovering the man she thought was a Nazi in hiding, but I couldn't find her posts. Do you have a copy?"

"No, I don't. I had copies, but I didn't want the kids to find them, so I burned them. Some of it was pretty graphic—the torture she thought she remembered and the like. The posts got taken down, of course, although there's got to be thousands of copies out there. But at least the kids don't have one, best I can tell."

"That's good," replied Rebecca, though she was hoping her search for the material would end here. She was about to move to her next question when Linthecom spoke.

"When I first downloaded Tracy's posts, I made several copies. I had this notion that there would be clues in there about what happened. And I thought there'd be people who would want to help, maybe a reporter or even a psychiatrist who wanted to look at why Tracy suddenly went off the deep end. But all anyone wants is the gory details of her hallucinations." Linthecom's volume had started increasing as he spoke. "I suppose if Tracy had been a movie star or a politician, everyone would be talking about the pressures of fame and the availability of drugs. But a homemaker? Obviously, she went off the deep end because of too many dirty diapers and all the driving for the soccer team."

By the end of his statement, Linthecom was leaning forward in his chair, his face a light shade of red as he bit off each word. But then, as if the reality of where he was caught up with his emotions, he took a deep breath and leaned back. "Sorry. It's been a rough few months."

"I understand," said Rebecca. "It's normal to be bitter when people are focusing on just two days of your wife's life rather than all the other years. But I would be interested in more of her background and especially, what was happening during the last few months and weeks before her death."

Linthecom nodded.

"First, were there any warning signs during that time? Not necessarily a full-blown delusion, but anything that seemed strange or out of place?"

"Looking back now, I'd have to say, yes. The day before she disappeared, she locked herself in our bedroom. She said she had to work on something while the kids were in school, but that she'd explain later. That was a bit unusual, but she'd done things like that before. Like one fall, she kept sneaking off to work on a sweater she was knitting for me for Christmas. Of course, now I know she was writing about something that never happened."

"So, you work from home?"

"I did sometimes, including that day. Now, it's nearly every day, so I can be here when the kids get home, or I can pick them up if they have activities after school. My boss has been very understanding."

"That's good. Not all employers are so supportive. The day before your wife went to Iowa, she was working on her story. How about in the days before that? Any confusion or forgetfulness or anything like that?"

"I'm not sure I would have noticed. We were both pretty busy, but I can't think of much out of the ordinary."

"But there were some things?"

"Well, yes, I suppose so." He rubbed his chin a moment, looking off into space. "A week or so before she disappeared, she got confused about the time volleyball practice ended. She was thinking it was 5:30, rather than 5:00, so our daughter had to wait with the coach for a half-hour. And she forgot she was having coffee with a neighbor maybe a week or two before that. But that's about all I can remember."

Two minor slips in memory in three weeks? That certainly didn't sound unusual to Rebecca, especially for a busy mother of four, but she made a note anyway. "Any health problems?"

"Not really. Just the normal colds and flu, an occasional upset stomach. Eventually, we both got COVID—hard to dodge forever with kids in school, but our cases were mild. And Tracy got migraines once in a while, but that goes with the territory, right?"

Perhaps, but Rebecca wondered if it could be something more. If nothing else, she and Cruz had migraines in common, and perhaps, Rowles got them, too. Hopefully, Doc would find out. "Did your wife take anything for her migraines?"

"She had something over the counter. Want me to check the medicine cabinet?"

"That's OK. But no prescription medications?

"No, no drugs for the migraines, but the doctors did put her on some pretty strong painkillers about a year ago. She was rear-ended in a car accident and suffered some whiplash, but that medicine couldn't be the problem."

"It couldn't be the problem because she took this medicine so long ago?" Rebecca's question came out slowly because she wasn't sure why he'd felt it necessary to mention this bit of history.

"No, not from before, but after what happened in Iowa, I started wondering if she was taking them again. See, she had an appointment with our doctor two days before she disappeared, so I started thinking he'd renewed the prescription. That might have done it because she was pretty out of it when she took that stuff. Anyway, I told the police, but I wasn't sure they did anything. So, I called the doctor's office. They said she hadn't shown up for her appointment."

Linthecom paused, seeming unsure if he wanted to go on or not. But after a moment, he said, "I was pretty upset at the time and started wondering if the girl I'd talked to was trying to cover up something. Maybe Tracy had shown up and they gave her something. Maybe something even worse than the painkiller. So, I checked our credit cards and bills. There wasn't any charge for medicine, but they probably wouldn't charge if they knew they'd screwed up. Then later, I did get a bill in the mail. They charge you half if you don't show up for an appointment and don't cancel it and that's what it was. The postmarks on the envelope showed it had been mailed the day she died. So, unless the Post Office and half the doctor's office was involved in a coverup, there wasn't one."

"That seems like a reasonable conclusion," said Rebecca, although she was thinking the evidence wasn't quite as strong as Linthecom believed. If the doctor had made a mistake and knew he couldn't correct it, he could have marked Tracy as a no-show. With six in the family, the office probably knew her, but the doctor could have given the receptionist who had checked Tracy in a few days off. Then, the woman Linthecom had talked to only knew what was in the falsified record. The bill would go out automatically, also the result of the fabrication. It was still unlikely that the doctor had gone to these lengths rather than trying to help Tracy, but it wasn't impossible. "Can you give me the name and address of your doctor's office?"

Linthecom looked perplexed but got the information from a bill in his desk. After Rebecca had written it down, she asked, "Did your wife take any medical treatments for her migraines or even for her health in general? Anything like relaxation exercises, biofeedback, anything like that?"

Rebecca was hoping there might be an unexpected connection among the women—they'd all received introductions to biofeedback, for example—rather than believing anything like these treatments could be the cause of his wife's delusions.

"No," replied Linthecom with a shrug. "She didn't do anything like that."

"Ever hear of a company named Healthtech?" For the same reason that their B2B research probably wasn't the source of Rowles's or Cruz's delusions, they probably had nothing to do with his wife's mental deterioration either. But it didn't hurt to ask.

Linthecom's eyes narrowed. "No, I haven't. Is there a reason I should have?"

Rebecca needed to defuse his suspicion. Linthecom didn't seem like the type of man who would take justice into his own hands, but a specific focus for his pain might be enough to push him over the edge.

"No, not at all. One of the women in St. Louis briefly dated an executive at the company several months ago. And the other considered but never used one of their products. This is just the nature of my work. We check out dozens of possibilities that turn out to be nothing more than coincidences."

Linthecom leaned back in his chair and nodded. "Sure, makes sense."

"Has anyone besides your family doctor treated your wife in the last year?"

"No, not since the car accident."

"Other than it, has your wife been injured in any way in the last year?"

"No, nothing I can think of."

"No falls? No bumps on the head?"

Linthecom frowned. "Tracy had a mild case of REM Sleep Behavior Disorder. That's when people act out what they're dreaming, and when it's bad, the person might kick and scream. Tracy never did anything like that, but sometimes she would fall out of bed. I don't think she ever hurt her head, though."

"I've never heard of that disorder. Is it common?"

"Not really," replied Linthecom. "Maybe one percent of the population has it. But it's also more common for older men, so for her to have it is pretty unusual. At least, that's what they told us."

"Did she take anything for it?"

"She took something ...." Linthecom massaged his forehead with his fingertips. "Melatonin, that's it. She took melatonin for a while, but not for a long time now. Mostly, we just put some blankets on the floor on her side of the bed and removed anything sharp. That helped her relax. As for any episodes right around the time she disappeared, I'm not sure. I didn't always wake up when it happened, but I don't remember one."

Rebecca had no idea what to make of this information, but she duly recorded it in her notebook. It was worth some research. "Did your wife make any new friends in the month or so before her disappearance? Or develop any new interests with the ones she had?"

"Minneapolis is a good-sized city, but Tracy stuck with a relatively small group of other women, mostly other mothers at our kids' school. I can't think of anyone new or any change in what they did, but Tracy and the woman next door, Linda Jackson, were close. She might know something."

"The house to the right or the left?"

"The one straight across the street."

"OK." Rebecca glanced at her notes, more to disguise her mental review of her agenda than to read what was there. After a moment, she said, "That's the last of my questions. Here's my card, if you think of anything else. Is there anything you'd like to ask me?"

Linthecom didn't hesitate. "Do you have any idea what happened to Tracy?"

Rebecca wasn't feeling like they were very close to solving Cruz's case, and in turn, possibly that of Rowles and Tracy Linthecom. But George needed hope more than brutal candor.

"I think with all you've told me today, we're closer. And when we compare this information with what we have for the other women, there's a chance we'll find a pattern."

Linthecom still looked grim but nodded. "I guess that's the only question I have." They stood and started for the door. "Call me any time if you have other questions or if you find out anything about Tracy's death."

"I will," Rebecca said as they parted at the front door.

Before crossing the street to see Linda Jackson, Rebecca went to her rental car and got in. First, she composed a text for Doc, asking him to find out if Rowles had a history of migraines or any sleep disorders, the REM one in particular, when he talked to Wu. Without more background, she knew that would send him off on a fact-finding mission on the Internet, but ultimately, what he learned might be a help. Then, she spent a moment consolidating what she'd heard and what she made of it.

Tracy Linthecom had some health issues including injuries from a car accident, migraines, and a somewhat rare sleep disorder. But they appeared to be relatively mild, and at least in the case of the accident, quite some time ago. Her family doctor had provided most, if not all, of her care during this period, giving him opportunity. And if he had made an error in her treatment, a coverup could be his motivation.

The problem with suspecting the family doctor, of course, was means. How had the man created a delusion focused on a politician that looked, at least on the surface, much like the ones developed by two women in St. Louis? True, the content of the women's delusions was different, but the fact that the targets were politicians, that the women had documented their strange beliefs in social media posts, and that they had died in their attempts to kill was too much to ignore. If you were a serial killer, with or without a political agenda, what better way to hide from the law than to have someone else do your bidding in plain sight?

Unfortunately, Rebecca didn't immediately see any good suspects coming out of the interview. George Linthecom's emotions felt real to her, and his candor, even when the topics of conversation were painful, suggested he desperately wanted to understand what had happened to his wife. As for other individuals, the doctor was a long shot and Tracy had no new friends or interests. Rebecca would verify these observations as best she could, of course, but if they were accurate, then there was little in her immediate past to suggest how she had developed a fantasy of such compelling realism.

She and Doc needed to find the link between these women. That commonality was where the killer had found them, and it was what would lead them to him or her. Rebecca exited her rental, ready to see if Ms. Jackson could confirm the stable personal life of one Tracy Linthecom—stable, at least, until it had all shattered.

Late Morning, The Basement of Kluge's Home

Kluge stared at the black rotary phone in his basement office. It was practically an antique, but in his domain, he wanted only the minimum in a phone—just enough to dial, talk, and listen. All it would take was one phone number stored in memory, one text saved to an external server for him to end up strapped to a table, a needle stuck in his vein, waiting for the end.

But he wasn't admiring the beautiful simplicity of the phone; he was wondering why it was ringing. He'd only given this number to three people, and two of them were dead. And the third? He'd never expected to hear from her. She was the alarm he'd set and left at the scene of his second conquest. She was the failsafe device he'd built before he knew how flawlessly his scheme would work. And now that he had that history of victories, he wondered why she would call. Surely, there was no reason for her concern. But since this was the third call in the last half-hour—suggesting it wasn't simply a wrong number—something must have spooked her.

"Yes," Kluge said when he lifted the receiver.

"Kluge, it's Linda. Linda Jackson."

"Yes."

"You told me to call if anyone came snooping around the Linthecom house. Well, today a PI from St. Louis came by. Stopped here, too. She was asking all kinds of questions about Tracy's health, whether she had made any new friends before she disappeared, stuff like that."

"She?"

"Yes," replied Jackson. "The PI was a woman."

"And what did you tell her?"

"Just what we agreed. That Tracy had become unhinged completely out of the blue. And this PI? She bought it. It was like she couldn't see the truth, even when Tracy identified her captor and when she described in detail what he'd done to her and so many others. But at least he got what was coming to him."

"Indeed," replied Kluge.

"What's wrong with people, anyway? I mean, it's so obvious what happened, but this PI just believes all the media lies—that Tracy was never in Germany. That this man who murdered so many wasn't a Nazi. Why can't people like her recognize the truth when it's staring them in the face?"

"Some people can be blind that way," said Kluge. "And do you remember what else you were supposed to do if anyone came nosing around?"

"Oh, I got her name all right. She even gave me a business card. It's Rebecca Marte of Marte Investigative Services. That's M-A-R-T-E. She's got a web address. It's ...."

"That's OK. I can find it. You did well, Linda."

"I remembered, but do you? Do you remember what you promised me if this ever happened and I came through?"

"Give me a moment. I need to check something, and then we can discuss your reward."

Kluge hadn't thought about this woman for months, so he wasn't going to grant her wish without considering the risk. Could she be enlisted in his cause? Even the slowest police detective or FBI agent would notice if two neighbors became delusional and killed a congressman within months of one another. And finding the link between them might increase the chance that they connected these two to the women in St. Louis. Then, they'd be looking in his backyard.

And yet, he could see a way to make it work if she was a good enough candidate. He booted his computer and opened his special database. When the image of Linda Jackson came on the screen, he nearly gasped. He'd forgotten how flawless she was. He even wondered why he had bothered with Tracy Linthecom when this creature was begging to become his.

"Yes, Linda, I'll help you. I'll help you put a face to those hands you feel in the night. Those rough, callous hands that tear at your clothes and abrade your skin. I'll give you the face of the man who violated you in the darkness of his prison and who now invades your sleep."

"When? Please, it has to be soon. Now that I've fulfilled my promise, I cannot wait another minute."

"And yet, you must. Now, remember this because you cannot write any of it down. Understood?"

"Yes, of course," replied Jackson.

"I'll come to Minneapolis today. Do you remember the hotel where we met before?"

"I remember."

"Good. I'll meet you in the lobby, Saturday morning, at 9:00 AM. By the end of the day, you'll have that face ... and a name and address to go with it."

"Thank you, Kluge. Thank you. I don't know how I'll ever repay you."

"Until Saturday, 9:00 AM," replied Kluge and he hung up. After a moment staring at the phone, he said, "Actually, Linda, I know exactly how you'll repay me."

Noon, Resterilli's Italian Restaurant

"You didn't ask me to lunch so you could yell at me, did you?"

Doc recognized the voice, looked up from the menu, and stood. "No, Ms. Wu. I asked you because I thought you might be hungry." Doc thought the statement a bit funny; Wu, however, just frowned.

Though Doc knew the pitfalls of stereotypes—people often saw what they expected rather than what was before them—during their two phone calls, he had pictured a woman with dark slightly almond-shaped eyes, long black hair, and a pale complexion. That was exactly what he saw before him, and he didn't believe it was all expectation. In fact, the only thing that surprised him was her attire. Torn jeans and a baggy T-shirt weren't exactly the Healthtech company uniform. She must have noticed his glance.

"I have the day off, with Mr. Anders out of the office."

That was a very diplomatic way to put it when her boss was running from the law. But then, Wu still worked at Healthtech and she hardly knew Doc. He started around the table to pull her chair out. A little extra politeness might reassure her that he held no hard feelings about her calling the police—something that she seemed hesitant to accept on the phone. But before he could reach her, she sat down. Maybe she was worried he'd yank it out from under her at the last second? More likely, however, she felt it was degrading, as if she couldn't manage a chair on her own. Perhaps that was part of his upbringing that he should drop.

"About you calling the police on me? Frankly, I would have done the same. I'd shown an unusual interest in your friend just days before she vanished, and that's too suspicious to ignore."

"Thanks," replied Wu. "But talk about irony. I thought you'd done something to Samantha when in fact, Anders was out for both of you."

Doc wasn't sure that was irony, but there was a more fundamental issue in his mind. "I don't think your old boss had anything to do with what happened to Samantha. As someone who's experienced his brand of nanobot-induced hallucinations, she wouldn't have been able to write anything coherent once those things got into her head."

"Well, that's what they're saying," said Wu, referencing the omnipresent, mysterious "they." This time, however, Doc knew exactly who "they" were, as he, too, had seen a couple of news articles that laid the blame at Anders's feet. In this case, they were just a couple of reporters who hadn't done their homework, in his opinion.

"Well, I suppose it's possible," Doc replied, more to move the conversation forward than because he agreed. But getting to his questions too quickly wasn't a winning idea either. "So, I've only been here once before. What's good, Ms. Wu?"

"If you're really not mad at me, it's Suzy."

"So, what's good here, Suzy?"

She smiled … finally.

"I love the fettuccine Alfredo, but I guess that shows."

"Nonsense. You look great," replied Doc, wondering if she'd been fishing for a compliment because she didn't appear overweight. The slight blush and demure smile that followed said, perhaps so.

That moment when Wu was somewhat self-effacing, however, didn't return over the next twenty minutes of small talk. She was confident and assertive. Her ideas were well reasoned and articulately expressed, despite the impression she'd initially made with her appeal to the ubiquitous "they." Doc liked her and almost hated to get into his questions about Rowles, but he would hate failing to advance the investigation even more.

"I mentioned on the phone I had a few questions about Samantha Rowles."

"And I said, she was beyond harm, so ask away."

Doc chuckled. "I recall. Anyway, do you know if Samantha suffered from migraines?"

"I hope you're not going to tell me migraines lead to delusions because I get them sometimes."

"Not as far as I know. Mostly, we're looking for patterns between her and a couple of other women who may have had similar experiences."

"Similar? You mean, right down to killing a representative?"

"Or a senator, in one case."

"Jeez," said Wu. "This is deadly serious stuff, isn't it?"

"It's far from certain that anyone is causing these women to become delusional. But if someone is, then, yes, it's deadly serious. This person is basically declaring war on the government and letting these women die in the process." Doc knew those words might cause some alarm, but he wasn't going to be less than completely frank with Wu. She deserved to know.

"What's the risk this murderous traitor learns about me? Or more to the point, decides to come after me?"

"Slight, I'd say. But I'd understand if you decided to walk away."

"I'm pretty hungry for that," she said with a smile. "But I'll keep that option in mind."

"Good. I mentioned the woman private investigator that I work with?" Wu nodded. "Well, she's just one of dozens of police detectives and investigative reporters looking into these incidents. And probably, the FBI, too. True, she's the only one who believes the cases are related—at least as far as we know. And if they are related, that pushes her a little further into the killer's spotlight."

Doc paused, realizing the implications of his words only after they were out of his mouth. Rebecca was always careful, but he wondered how much thought she'd given to the stakes of this game. Depending on the killer's political objective, the potential rewards were incredibly high. The country could become more socialistic, more dictatorial, more isolationist. It could be anything. And when Doc considered those outcomes, who was to say there was only one person involved? The possibilities could tempt any number of political figures and powerful businessmen. Could there be a conspiracy to remake the country in a new image?

Damn, he and Rebecca had to get the FBI or some organization with a lot more clout than Marte Investigative Services looking into these possibilities. It might well be, as Wu had put it, deadly serious stuff.

"Doc?"

"Sorry, Suzy. I lost my train of thought for a moment." Doc paused a moment to rewind the conversation in his mind. "Anyway, the PI I'm working with might be in some danger, if the killer finds out she's asking questions about two or more of these women, but that shouldn't translate to you. Why would it? You've witnessed nothing. You're just one of these three women's friends and family. So, like I said, I think you're OK."

"The crowd might not be that big if these other women were like Samantha."

Doc had gotten the impression that Rowles didn't have a lot of close, long-term friends. Wu appeared to be confirming it. And Cruz didn't have a big network of friends, either. Could that factor be related to their suitability as a political weapon? He didn't see how but made a mental note to ask Rebecca if Linthecom was also somewhat reclusive.

"Yeah, you're right. I'm probably worried about nothing," Wu admitted. "So, migraines? She might have gotten them, but I can't say I remember her talking about it."

"OK. How about sleep disturbances?"

Wu looked perplexed. "You're not thinking we were a couple, are you?"

"No. I wasn't thinking that. I just thought the topic might have come up."

"And the guys you work with," Wu said. "How well do they sleep?"

Doc chuckled. "OK, I get it. She didn't get into a lot of personal stuff with you."

"You had dinner with her. She spill her guts around you?"

"No, just the opposite. She asked me a million questions about what I do but hardly said anything about herself. Are you saying it was the same for you?"

"I kinda think that was the way she was with everyone. I know she had a rough time growing up and got into quite a bit of trouble, especially with her father. She said that's why she got along so well with the kids she worked with. But details? Not in front of me. Hey, that's an idea. Maybe you can find some of the girls she worked with and see what they know."

"Girls? She only worked with females?"

"Yeah. You didn't know that?"

"No, although it stands to reason. I guess my PI friend gets the job of talking to some of them. I could always ask these young women if Samantha ever showed up with bandages all over her head, but the last thing I should do is question an underaged female about Samantha's choice of birth control."

Doc knew his reference to birth control was obscure. It was one of the hundreds of random facts about Cruz that were probably irrelevant to the case—her prescription gave her headaches, not delusions—but it was still running around in his head, and it made his point perfectly. But by the surprised look on Wu's face, he wondered if he'd hit on something by accident.

"Samantha Rowles had problems with her birth control prescription?" he asked.

"Jeez, Doc. How the heck do you think that would come up in conversation when we've both said she kept things close to the vest?"

Doc held out his empty hands, ready to claim complete ignorance when Wu continued.

"What got me was the bandaged head comment. The first time I met Samantha, her head was bandaged. She said something about a fall from a ladder, but that was shortly after she started going out with Mr. Anders." Wu released an ironic laugh. "Guess I don't need to address that scumbag like that anymore, do I? Anyway, I wondered if the scumbag known as Mr. Anders had caused her injuries, and now, I suspect he did, giving her a dose of those nanobots."

"When did you see her bandaged up?"

"Hmm, maybe six months ago. It was about a month before the opening ceremony that I suggested you look at. I even wondered if he took her there because of the injury. He didn't take dates to public functions very often. He didn't even want to give the appearance he might not be available."

"Six months? That seems too long between the injury and the delusions for them to be related, but I'll have to see if I can find someone more knowledgeable to ask. Anyway, in the week or so before Samantha disappeared, did she start any new medications?"

"Not that I know of."

"Did she try any new medical treatments, maybe something like what you have at Healthtech?"

"Not that I know of."

"How about any new friends? Or old ones that she started spending more time with?"

"Not that I know of."

"New interests or pastimes?" asked Doc. "No, let me guess. Not that you know of."

"Like I said, she didn't talk much about herself. And if your investigator friend can't find one of her clients who knows some of these answers, you may have trouble getting them. I think her parents died when she was in her early teens, but I say that only because the alternative—that they abandoned her at that age—is pretty tough to swallow. I know she ended up in foster care, but whether that was because she didn't have other kin or none that would take her in, I don't know. I doubt she was close to anyone at work. At least, she never mentioned a friend there. Basically, she was a woman with hundreds of acquaintances but no real friends. And that seemed to be OK with her."

"Even so, that's a rough way to live," Doc said, thinking of his own experiences when he'd left his life behind. But at least he had turned the page on that chapter. Or better yet, maybe he should tear it out of his book and burn it after this case is over. After this case is over ....

"Enough on Samantha Rowles," Doc said after a moment. "What's on the horizon for you, now that your boss is on the run from the law?"

Wu grinned. "And I thought this whole conversation was going to be a downer." The rest of lunch was spent in small talk about work and hobbies and kin and planned vacations—anything but murder and political motivations. It was nice and ended too soon for Doc, but they both needed to get back to their jobs.

As they left and the restaurant's door closed behind them, a lone diner in a corner booth rose to leave. He, too, had much to do because the purge of Congress was far from complete.

MONDAY, AUGUST 15

Evening, Rebecca's Apartment

"Where were you all day?" Doc asked as he rushed past Rebecca, waving a sheaf of papers in the air.

"Hello to you, too," she replied. What she was thinking, however, was, what happened to my kiss on the cheek? She felt she needed it. But then, when Doc put his mind to something, there wasn't much left for anything else. And his mind was definitely churning on something. "I took the day off. I needed a break and had other things that needed to be done."

That brought Doc up short and his hand with the papers dropped to his side. He turned to look at her. "Tough trip to Minneapolis?"

Rebecca released a long breath. "It wasn't like I was breaking the news to George Linthecom that his wife was dead, but yeah, those visits to families that have lost someone recently are never fun. So, what is it that's got you so worked up?"

But as she asked, she saw his mood had swung as completely as the conversation. She led the way to her living room, and they sat on the couch.

"I'm sorry you needed to make that trip," said Doc. "When the husband of one of my best friends at Ruger-Phillips died, I felt awful. But it seemed to help her to talk about anything other than his death." Doc tilted his head to the side. "But there's something else on your mind, isn't there?"

Rebecca frowned. "Why do you say that?"

"Well, there's something on my mind, and I think it should be on yours, too. When I was talking to Suzy Wu, I started thinking that if we are right—and I know, the chances of that aren't the greatest—but if we are, this is nothing less than an attempt to overthrow the government. Or at least, violently alter the direction of public policy. No one else is pushing a single-mastermind theory—at least that I know about—so the questions you're asking are bringing you a lot of unwanted attention. That's been running through your head, hasn't it?"

"Yeah, it has, although don't you mean, our questions are bringing unwanted attention to us?" Rebecca said.

"All I've done is have lunch with a friend of Rowles."

"You're joking, aren't you?"

Doc's eyebrows shot up, but he said nothing.

"Look, when I was in Minneapolis, I had some of the same thoughts as you about the possible stakes in this case. It was easy to believe we were wrong about a mastermind weaponizing Cruz when it was only her. When Rowles was added to the list, it got a lot harder for me to discount that possibility. And after hearing more about Linthecom, there's little doubt left in my mind that something like that is going on. But whether it's one mad genius with a political agenda or some large well-funded group that's been researching mind control for decades, I couldn't say."

"So, time to call in the cavalry?" And then, Doc's eyes narrowed. "They're already in, aren't they?"

"I'm sure they are," replied Rebecca. "While the local police are willing to close cases with the obvious explanation of a sudden mental breakdown and the media are happy with their dramatic headlines, federal agencies won't be so quick to shut down an investigation when you're talking about attempts to kill sitting politicians. It's just too rare and too much of a threat to democracy. Maybe the FBI closed down the Linthecom case after a couple of months with nothing, but after Cruz and then, Rowles, I wouldn't be surprised if the task force is approaching fifty or more agents, spread among Washington, St. Louis, and Minneapolis."

Doc was quiet for a moment. "I haven't heard a thing about it," he said, "but I suppose the call between the public's right to know and the Bureau's need for secrecy to catch a perp has to be a tough one in almost every case."

Rebecca nodded.

"And in this one, the most they could say—unless they know a lot more than we do—is 'watch out for anyone with a beef with the government because they could be preparing you to be a martyr in their political war.' That should start a nice panic."

Rebecca paused a moment. "Would it? Start a panic, I mean."

"The FBI says a serial killer is on the loose and you think it will be business as usual?" asked Doc.

"Even in cases where the action needed to secure the public's safety seems relatively clear, getting the majority to act on a government warning has been tricky in recent years. And in a case like this one, there's no smoking gun. There's no wanted poster. There are only vague, shadowy figures wielding who the hell knows what kind of capability to make innocents do their bidding. I wonder if a warning like that would do anything besides bring out the conspiracy theorists."

"Great," said Doc. "An FBI warning about a killer who uses conspiracy theories to cover his crimes generates more conspiracy theories? I'm not sure if that's a brilliant insight or fatigue talking. But either way, what are we going to do about it? Is it time we tell Dani that this case will be solved but by federal law enforcement, not us?"

"I think so," replied Rebecca. "I'm giving myself until the end of the week to tie up the loose ends, but it's time you distance yourself now. If this is some secret society chipping away at the government, I'd guess they'd probably ignore us. They have bigger fish to fry. But something tells me this is the work of one deluded individual, and who knows what he or she might do when cornered. And, yeah, I'm betting we're getting to that point, even if the FBI isn't publicizing the threat yet."

"If you're working till Friday, so am I."

"God, Doc, why are you so stubborn?" He started to say something, but Rebecca held up a hand. "Look, I didn't shut my phone off for a mental health day. I shut it off so I could get my firearm out of the safe and clean it. And to check my security at work and here at my apartment. I can't necessarily stop a lone killer with nothing to lose—no one can. But I can make it damn hard for him. What I can't do is protect both of us."

"And I'm not asking you to," said Doc. "I can hole up in a place more secure than you could ever make your apartment—Ruger-Phillips. You can't even get within fifty yards of my office without a security badge. The whole place is locked down with keypad and biometric door locks and is patrolled 24/7 by armed guards. And there, I have a couch, there are showers, and I can get food delivered ... from known sources. No more pastries from just some delivery service."

"And just how are you getting to this fortress?" asked Rebecca.

"I have a plan there, too. You remember the officer who was watching me at the hospital?"

"Sure."

"Well, normally, he patrols nights in my neighborhood, and we've been talking. I'm sure when we get done tonight, he can meet me at my place long enough for me to run in and grab a few things."

"What about the parking at Ruger-Phillips?" asked Rebecca.

"On the grounds, also secured."

Rebecca stood from the couch and paced her living room a moment. "Well, that doesn't sound half bad. If you're sure."

"Never more so," Doc replied. "You can't have all the fun for the next four days."

"Yeah, right," Rebecca replied, then returned to the couch and sat. "OK. That's decided. So, what's with all the papers you were waving when you came in?"

"There's been another attempt on the life of a congressman."

"You're not serious?"

"I tried to contact you. But anyway, you'll never guess where the would-be assassin lived."

After a moment, Rebecca said, "Minneapolis." Doc looked disappointed. "It could have been St. Louis or D.C., but the real irony would be Minneapolis. So, is this definite? How good's the match with the other cases?"

"Too good for one of them," Doc replied. "It's almost an exact match of the Linthecom case, at least until the end. The woman in this new case described the same Nazi-in-hiding delusion with similar stories of torture and sexual abuse. She also tried to kill a U.S. Representative in the same way, but the congressman's car got hung up on a guard rail. Hers, on the other hand, went over the side and she drowned."

"And the attempt was in Minneapolis, not D.C.?" asked Rebecca.

"Right. He was home for a long weekend to do a little campaigning. Say, do you think it means anything that the two women in St. Louis both went to Washington to confront their targets, while the two Minneapolis women both attacked the congressmen in their home states—Iowa in one case, Minnesota in the other?"

Rebecca couldn't see the relevance, and apparently, neither could Doc after he gave it some thought. He chuckled.

"Brainstorming is one thing, but that's pretty off the wall for even unconstrained thinking. Anyway, the attack occurred this morning, after a groundbreaking ceremony for a new school. The congressman was going to fly back to Washington right after that."

Doc paused a moment, perhaps making sure his imagination wasn't running wild again.

"There is one thing in the attack that may suggest something new about these delusions. It looks like the woman rammed the congressman's car at least three times, trying to get it off the guard rail. And since all the damage to her car is on the front end, by that time, her car should have been spewing water all over the highway and overheating. She had to have known that she'd failed."

"And she committed suicide anyway?"

"She did," replied Doc. "Which makes me wonder if a key element of these implanted delusions is that they must end in the assassin's death. That way, kill a congressman or not, there is nothing to link these women to the real murderer. The obvious alternative is that the woman was so despondent over her failure that she took her life, but that doesn't make as much sense to me. If she'd waited a lifetime to take revenge on this man, I'd guess she would have crawled on her hands and knees to get to him if there was no other way."

"Could be," said Rebecca after a moment. "Or maybe she was injured or knocked unconscious, and the car simply rolled into the water."

"That's possible," admitted Doc.

"You know, the fact that this woman has similar stories of torture and abuse makes it sound like a copycat crime."

"Which is ... what did you call it ... the obvious explanation?" She nodded. "It's the obvious explanation that the local police are trying to use to close the case. And it certainly helps that this woman had a long-standing, hostile relationship with the local congressman. So, I guess when I called this one almost an exact match to Linthecom, that's a big difference."

"It is," said Rebecca. "In fact, it's huge. It makes it fit a copycat crime almost perfectly. She hated the congressman, so when she saw a way to disguise her crime as someone else's, she took it. The fit would have been perfect had she not died during the attempt while he escaped."

"There's another theory running around in the papers, and you're gonna love this one. Some are saying it's a case of folie à deux, a delusional disorder shared by two. And while they explained the term, it was new to me. So, I did a little research. Apparently, it's extremely rare, but there are documented cases."

"You're not buying that, are you?"

"You think I might because it's based on psychological theory?" Doc chuckled. "No, I'm not buying it. It does nothing to explain the two other cases."

Rebecca paused a moment. "You know, this killer is a real pro at disguising the serial nature of this spree. Kill a senator after an illicit affair using poison? Unfortunately, both the romance and the payback don't seem that strange in a setting like Washington. Or start raving about a Martian takeover and go after a congressman with a gun? You blend in with all the other conspiracy theorists out there. Share the same MO between two hits, it looks like a rare mental illness or a copycat. That raises doubt, especially about whether these crimes are connected to the St. Louis cases. About the only thing consistent is the women's penchant for posting about their delusions on social media. And that, of course, isn't all that unusual."

"Well, if the social media posts are the link among the cases," said Doc, reaching over and picking up the sheaf of pages he had brought with him, "then here's the complete text of the latest online fantasy. If we compare this one to the one that Linthecom wrote, we can look for patterns. Did our latest woman assassin change any of the script to fit her particular gripe with the congressman? Or is it virtually identical?"

"That might tell us something," said Rebecca slowly, "if we had Linthecom's posts. Unfortunately, we don't. George didn't have them. Neither did the next-door neighbor. And the Minneapolis police either don't have them or they couldn't be bothered to find them for a PI when Iowa has closed the case anyway. Of course, I probably didn't do myself any good when I said we were looking for a link between Linthecom's case and two in St. Louis. Let's just say, no one was ready to jump on that bandwagon. Anyway, I'm sure there are thousands of people who have copies of those posts hidden on their hard drives, but I couldn't find one. So, we'll just have to see what we can get from the excerpts included in the news reports."

"OK, maybe we'll get lucky using that. Now, how about the posts from Cruz and Rowles? We have those, don't we?"

Rebecca nodded.

"Good. Then, we can compare them to the one I have."

"So, we can find out there's no overlap between a space invasion, a romance turned deadly, and Nazi torture?" But the second Rebecca said it, she saw the logic behind Doc's idea and snapped her fingers. "Of course. With those delusions being so different, similarities, if there are any, may reflect what was constant among the cases. Say the mastermind is left-handed and, somehow, that fact made it into all of the women's posts, then we'll have a solid piece of information on this killer."

"Exactly," said Doc. "The mastermind and the delusion-inducing procedure would be the same for each of the women. The place where the delusion was implanted may or may not be the same, but we can watch for it. In any case, we're looking for common terms that might reflect something about the three Ps—person, procedure, and place."

"The three Ps? You spend long coming up with that?" Rebecca asked with a grin.

"No. It's a gift," Doc replied. "I figured we could start with simple word searches. For example, in these posts"—Doc raised the sheaf of pages again—"I noticed the woman mentioned she was sweating, even though this happened in the winter in Minnesota. Of course, recalling extreme trauma can also make a person sweat, so it might be nothing. Or it might tell us something about the conditions of her confinement or how the delusion was produced."

"Worth a try," said Rebecca. "Is the reason you keep waving those pages because you don't have them in electronic format?"

"Yeah, unfortunately. I was at lunch when I heard about this and only had my phone. Copy and paste on it is really clunky, so I did a bunch of screenshots. By the time I got back to work, the posts had been taken down. But I've seen you type. You can do eight of these pages while I do the other two."

"Sounds like a plan," said Rebecca. "But let's get something to eat first."

"That's right," said Doc, rubbing his hands together melodramatically. "You were going to cook. I can hardly wait."

"You're gonna have to," Rebecca replied. "I ran out of time, but I did pick up something on the way home."

It wasn't a total fib. After she'd looked up recipes and changed menus four times—who knew that stew took so long or that spaghetti needed so many ingredients she didn't have—she barely had time to get takeout.

"Let's see those pages," she said as they walked toward her kitchen. Doc handed them over. "You never said. What's the name of the woman who wrote this?"

"Linda Jackson."

"No way," replied Rebecca, staring at Doc in disbelief.

Evening, Rebecca's Apartment

"Didn't you notice where Linda Jackson lived?" asked Rebecca, frowning at Doc as they reached her kitchen.

Doc wasn't certain why Rebecca was so surprised by the name. Was Jackson an old friend? Maybe someone she knew from school? Or .... "Did you meet her on your trip to Minneapolis?"

"Not only did I meet her, but she was Linthecom's across-the-street neighbor. And, according to George Linthecom, Jackson and his wife were very close. In all the stuff you've seen and read about Jackson, that never came up?"

"Mostly the news talked about the similarity of the cases—same delusion, same assassination method. And I remember one reporter who talked about the folie à deux theory saying that the delusion was usually shared by people who were very close emotionally. But that they also lived physically close to each other? That fact was almost undoubtedly mentioned in some of the stories, but I missed it."

Rebecca sighed. "No problem. We've got a few days to become intimately familiar with both Linthecom and Jackson." She opened the door to her refrigerator and removed a sack. "Pesto pasta with sliced chicken and a Caesar salad." When she turned around, Doc was removing plates from a cabinet and silverware from a drawer. But after placing them on the island, he paused, looking around the room.

"I have an image from that night," Doc said, knowing that Rebecca would know which night he meant. "We came in here for a snack ...." He was going to add, "all hot and sweaty," but then thought better of it. It was a hallucination, after all, and Rebecca might not like the implications. Or maybe, the mental picture came from earlier, before the little devils had taken complete control of his mind, and only their state of undress and the timing was imagined. "Apparently, a little kissing makes you very hungry."

He looked at Rebecca, wondering if she'd confirm the timing or the food.

She had, however, turned back to her refrigerator and was looking for something inside. "Apparently," she said without turning around. "As I recall, you wanted a bagel, then complained nonstop because I didn't have any cream cheese. And speaking of no cheese, I thought I had some parmesan for the salad, but I don't see it."

She shrugged, then closed the refrigerator and opened the pasta container. She added some to a plate and put it in the microwave to warm it up.

Doc, however, hardly noticed what she was doing. He was still wondering about what she'd said because he'd never cared for cream cheese on a bagel. But then, he somewhat recalled—and Rebecca had confirmed—he had talked to his grandfather who had been dead for five years. Maybe he'd hallucinated a liking of cream cheese? The trouble with that was he didn't remember a bagel but rather ....

"Unless you're going to watch me eat," said Rebecca, breaking into his thoughts, "you need to fix yourself a plate. About a minute in the microwave for the pasta should do it." She tore two paper towels from a roll and slid one across the island to him. Then, she added some salad to the plate of pasta and started nibbling on it as he prepared his meal.

"Weren't you going to compare our three congressmen's voting records?" asked Rebecca. "See where they agreed, especially on the closely contested bills?"

"And after that, I was going to find the downtown St. Louis businesses that were related to these common voting areas because Rowles made a trip down there before she flew to Washington. Unfortunately, I haven't gotten that far."

He removed his plate from the microwave and added a helping of salad.

"Even limiting the search to narrow margins of victory or defeat left anywhere from 500 to over a thousand votes a year, and then, I had to check how each man had voted. Just getting those data was time-consuming, but it's done."

Doc sat down next to Rebecca and shoveled in a mouthful of pasta. He hadn't thought he was hungry until he smelled the food, and now, he was famished.

"And the data wizard can't make sense of it?" asked Rebecca with a grin.

"Not yet," said Doc, wiping his mouth with the paper towel. "The problem is that yea or nay votes alone aren't data at the level I need.

A bill isn't just pro or con law enforcement. It's pro local law enforcement when funded through federal sources aimed at curbing human trafficking, for example. So, one of our three congressmen may have voted against a bill because he thinks the local police need to be reorganized. Or because he wants to conserve those funds for other anti-trafficking programs. Or because he believes that this crime is generally a state responsibility, and so on. I can't pinpoint areas of agreement based on bills that have dozens of different elements to them."

"So, nothing yet?"

"Almost nothing," Doc replied, setting a forkful of salad back on his plate. "At a very, very high level, our three appear to agree on increased funding for cybersecurity, law enforcement reform, countering terrorism, beefing up education, stronger immigration laws, overhauling healthcare, and improving voting procedures. And their support seems the strongest when these changes are aimed at state-level programs versus federal or local. They don't agree at all on defense spending or infrastructure. So, if there were defense contractors located downtown, we could eliminate them."

"So, are you saying this is a dead-end?"

Doc picked up the forkful of salad he'd abandoned earlier and ate it. "Maybe, but I haven't given up yet. I'm working on law enforcement bills now, looking at things like the source of funding, the recipient of the money, how the funds would be spent, and so on. Maybe our mastermind wants to rid Congress of anyone who opposes funding for local police training. To know that, I'd need to know what bills included training for the locals."

"I see what you mean," said Rebecca. "Timeframe?"

Doc knew that was the nearly impossible question it seemed and again rested a bite of food on his plate while he thought. "In a word, long. Let's say I get all the law enforcement-related bills broken down into their parts next week. Then, the analysis—what elements did these three congressmen vote for consistently—that's just a matter of a few hours of work. With only three datapoints .... Or are we going to add the fourth congressman to the list?"

Rebecca dabbed at her mouth before answering. "That probably depends on the rest of your answer."

"Makes sense. I was going to say that with only three data points on dozens of elements in each bill, I won't be able to isolate the key factor in a lot of cases. Let's say, all three voted for more local training when there was federal oversight and the money was a reallocation. If there was no federal oversight, would I still get agreement? If it was a bill for equipment, would the result change? Then, matching the interest in local police training to downtown organizations adds more guesswork. How many organizations from religious to civil rights want to see better training for the local police? And we also have to consider the fact that opinion within these organizations will not be uniform. Everyone in a given company or organization may not want to fund better training even if that's the public position of the group. Basically, our killer could be an outlier."

"In the movies, this approach would have worked a lot better," said Rebecca shaking her head.

"Or if we had the resources of the FBI and a couple of supercomputers."

"If you had the resources of the FBI, then you would have a couple of supercomputers," replied Rebecca, drawing a smile from Doc. She folded her napkin over her empty plate. "Sounds like evaluating the women's posts would be faster and possibly more informative. Shall we switch to that for the duration of the evening?"

Doc paused, a bite of his dinner inches from his mouth. "Sure, as soon as I finish eating."

"What have you been doing? Time's a wastin'."

Doc's surprise lasted only a moment before he realized she was teasing. But before he could reply, her phone rang. "Looks like you've been saved by the bell," Rebecca said. She stepped into another room to answer the call.

Doc turned his attention to his half-eaten meal, figuring if the call went long enough, he could be typing up Jackson's posts before she returned. Then, he'd hit her with the time's a wastin' comment. But as he was finishing his last bite, she returned.

"You'll never guess."

"Hmm. Representative Barclay hated Representative Kessner, so he duped Rowles into killing him. The ineffectual attempt on him by Cruz was a distraction designed to make him look innocent, as well as the other attacks."

Rebecca just stared at him a moment, then smirked, "Yeah, that would have been my first guess, too, but it's wrong. It looks like the Minneapolis police want to talk to me. I'm supposed to go to the South Patrol building tomorrow for an interview."

"What about?"

"I'm not sure. Maybe they reconsidered the theory that these four attacks are related, although that would be quite a turnaround. They didn't exactly laugh in my face, but there was plenty of eye-rolling. So, shall we get to typing?"

Late Evening, Rebecca's Apartment

The screenshots weren't as clear as Doc would have liked, but an hour later, they were finished. After reviewing the news articles on the Linthecom attack, they decided to omit the quotes from her posts that they contained; it was clear that these excerpts had been picked for their ability to sell papers, rather than being anything like a general sample.

With the three remaining sets of posts—one each from Jackson, Cruz, and Rowles—Doc and Rebecca set out to find words that each of the women had used despite the wildly differing natures of their delusions. And based on the typing they'd just finished, they had plenty of candidates to consider.

Doc's guess that words and phrases related to sweating might be in each of the three sets of posts proved true. Each of the women had used some form of this word multiple times. Unfortunately, there was often a good reason why it was there that had nothing to do with the three Ps. Who wouldn't sweat if they were about to kill a congressman or if they were being held in a concentration camp? They were about to drop the term from their list when Rebecca noticed that sweat was often used with words related to darkness and cold: sweating in a cold, empty void; a freezing blackness made worse by my sweating; and the like. The trio of sweat, cold, and dark was common among the women's posts, and it might relate to place or procedure.

There were, as well, words they both thought would be common among the posts but weren't. Hatred, for example, was one, but that was because Rowles had depicted her relationship with the congressman not as loathing, but as if they were star-crossed lovers. Not only would their spouses never forgive them, but neither would the rest of the world. That comment was made all the more inexplicable because Rowles wasn't married. Congressman was another term that failed to make the list though they had expected otherwise. Apparently, Rowles was the only one who recognized that the man she was about to kill was a member of Congress.

When they finished around midnight, they had a set of thirteen concepts that were common among the posts, though the connection to any of the three P's was somewhat tenuous for most. The terms included the triple of cold, dark, and sweat; shooting stars; tingling, usually of the skin but sometimes a hand, ear, or arm; a plan or scheme that had been thrown together; clouds or cloudy; cars, autos, or trucks; hoarseness; death or killing; a weapon, although rarely described; precise steps as in a plan or procedure; clothes; perfume; and a nutty or almond-like smell.

Since her kitchen was the only room big enough to accommodate them working together, they'd set up on the island. Now finished, Doc tried to push back, nearly tipping over the stool in the process. Rebecca poorly hid a snicker behind a hand. "Tired?"

"You have no idea," Doc replied, stifling a yawn. "Like I mentioned, extracting the data I need from the voting records took me forever, and it took a serious bite out of my sleep. At least we got through this a lot faster. So, a quick summary, and then I'm off to pack for holing up at the office. So, what did you think of the posts?"

"Well, first, nearly all of the content of each is unique. I mean, all that stuff about NASA's secret missions to Mars in the mid-1970s that opened the way for the aliens to infiltrate the earth? That's only in Cruz's posts. Same for the concentration camp descriptions in Jackson's and the love story of Rowles and Representative Kessner. I'd say 90 percent or more of these individual fantasies are unique."

Doc didn't think he frowned, but maybe he had because Rebecca quickly added, "I didn't actually compile the numbers, but I'd guess that's close."

Doc yawned, unable to control the impulse this time. "No problem, since I was thinking it was at least 90 percent. Funny, I never thought I'd get this familiar with each of these stories, but every time I thought I had a word match, I had to look at the context. Rowles killing time waiting for her lover is nothing like Linthecom's stories of killing in a concentration camp. I think I've read all of this material at least five times."

"Same here," said Rebecca. "The second thing I noticed was that each of these stories is written with a unique voice. If we're right, someone gave them the idea behind the delusion, but each woman composed the posts using her own vocabulary and way of expressing herself."

"I hadn't thought about that, but you're right." Doc rubbed his eyes before looking over his list again. "Did you pick up on anything that you thought was about the person creating these delusions? Because I'm seeing terms that might be about the procedure or place, but not really the person."

"Maybe, but this is on pretty thin ice. There's quite a bit about how the women should dress for these attacks, right down to the fact that they should wear perfume. You can call me sexist if you want, but that strikes me like something a man believes he needs to tell a woman. Any woman who wants to get close enough to a man to kill him wouldn't need to be told what to wear."

"But what about Linthecom and Jackson? What difference does it make what they were wearing inside their cars?"

"I'm not sure," replied Rebecca, "but clothes are mentioned in Jackson's posts. Maybe they played a well-heeled damsel in distress, and after the congressman stopped to help, they rammed his car before he got out. After all, hitting a moving car on a bridge isn't going to be all that easy."

"That could be," admitted Doc, rubbing a hand over the back of his neck. "Did the witnesses to the Linthecom killing mention anything like that?"

"Not that I recall but let me see." She picked up a stack of pages and began leafing through them. After a moment, she said, "Nothing's jumping off the page at me, but a lot of these articles are background on the senator, mental disturbances, or Linthecom's delusion. I wasn't able to get a copy of the incident report from the Iowa crime scene, so I asked George Linthecom to request a copy. And if that doesn't work, we can go the Freedom of Information Act route."

"Sounds like a plan," responded Doc. "Any other observations?"

"If you include gut feelings in that category, then, yeah. Jackson feels different than the other three women to me."

"In ways other than the fact that she is the first to repeat a delusion?" asked Doc.

"That's part of it. If you look at the first three women, there's very little overlap among them that we can find. Nothing's common in their lifestyles. Other than getting colds and the flu, their medical histories are distinct. The same with their work, social organizations, political views, and so on. They even posted on different social media. And then, we have Linthecom and Jackson. They almost share the same life except Jackson was divorced. They were neighbors and best friends. They had children the same age who went to the same school. They traveled in the same circles, belonged to the same clubs, had the same taste in books and music. They even preferred paperbacks and CDs over eBooks and streaming."

"You pick that up from seeing their homes?" asked Doc.

"Yeah. I even sent George Linthecom a text to make sure the country-western CDs belonged to his wife. After the first three women were distinct in everything from personality to pastimes, those two are like peas in a pod. What does that mean? Hell, if I know, but somehow, it seems like it might be important."

"Then, hold on to it. Sometimes, the reason for those gut feelings comes to me a day or two later." Doc stretched his neck and heard a pop.

"Ouch," Rebecca replied to the sound that must have been louder than Doc thought.

"Just stiff," he replied. "Too much sitting, not enough jogging and hiking."

"You'll have to take me on your favorite trail when this case is over."

"Absolutely," Doc replied, grinning. "Right after we do the couch thing that's on hold till then."

Rebecca took an ineffectual swing at Doc's shoulder. "Get your head back on business," she said. But if Rebecca's smile was any indication, she hadn't forgotten the promise they'd made each other either.

"You're tired," said Rebecca after watching his face a moment. "Why don't you give me a quick rundown on your thoughts, and then, let's call it a night."

"Well … I'm not sure this is going to be helpful, but I tried to sort the words into the person, place, or procedure categories. My only guess on person is also that our mastermind is male. Other than Rowles who poisoned the man she believed to be her lover, the means of execution—guns and car accidents—seem more typical of a man. Slim, I admit, but it might be something."

"It's probably a stronger inference than you're saying," said Rebecca. "Why would Cruz decide to shoot Barclay when she hardly knew which was the business end of a handgun? I find it easy to believe that the weapons three of the women used were picked for them. What about words for place and procedure?"

"The words that fit one seem to fit the other as well. Their hands tingled? Is that part of being tied up or some side effect of implanting the delusion? And the same can be said about the almond scent or the shooting stars. But frankly, there's another set of common words—things like clouds and cars—that just seems like coincidence. I mean, clouds are everywhere, so it probably means nothing that each woman mentioned them."

"That a wrap?" asked Rebecca.

Her tone said she hoped it was, probably because between the yawns and the ones he stifled, he was becoming less intelligible by the minute. But there was one other thing on his mind. And though he hadn't worked through the implications, it was worth mentioning.

"There may be some contradiction between a couple of the sets of common words we've found. On one hand, the posts mention clear, precise steps, like their attacks were fully choreographed. And that also fits with the detail in each of the delusions. But on the other hand, we have references to things being haphazard, like everything was just thrown together. I'm not sure what, if anything, it means, but it felt odd to me." The last few words came out distorted by another yawn.

"Good," she replied. "Lots of things to sleep on. And I mean that literally. You have videoconferencing apps at work, right?"

"Who doesn't, what with ...." He couldn't finish until he yawned again. "What with the pandemic making them almost a business necessity."

"OK. You may be dying to get out of your building by tomorrow night, but let's meet that way for the next few evenings. No reason to take unnecessary risks until this guy gets caught or the Bureau starts making public appeals for information. That should take the spotlight off us." She paused a beat. "And maybe we should call it an evening a bit earlier this next week? I don't want your real boss calling to chew me out because you keep falling asleep at your desk."

"No worries. I have an office door." Rebecca returned his grin with a roll of her eyes. "Tomorrow's good," said Doc, "but I have a late meeting. Is 6:00 OK for a virtual meet?"

It was a simple question—hardly a question at all—but Rebecca hesitated. Doc was about to ask her what was wrong when she said, "I'm not feeling good about sending you home half asleep. Maybe you don't realize it, but every time you blink, I wonder if your eyes are going to open again." She paused a moment, staring at his face. "You've been thinking about taking a nap in your car before you go home, haven't you?"

The question was clearly a guess, and it would have been easy for Doc to say, "No way." But in fact, the thought had crossed his mind. "I think about a lot of things I don't do."

Rebecca laughed. "Everything but an answer. Crash on my couch. Whenever you wake up, you can head home. And if you sleep until morning and your friend on the force is off duty, I'll follow you to your place. I don't want to lose a second partner in the first year of my business."

Partner? In a manner of speaking, it was true, but he couldn't remember either of them ever using the word before without qualification. Sometimes, he was a volunteer partner. Or when she was angry with him, a fake partner, but never just a partner.

"That's very thoughtful," said Doc, meaning the offer of the couch, although he liked the way she had addressed him, too. "I accept."

Rebecca left the room, returning a moment later with a pillow, sheet, and blanket. They walked into the living room, where she tossed them on the couch. "This should keep you warm. And here's a spare key." She put it on an end table. "Lock up when you leave and slide the key under the door. I'll put the lodging charge on your tab."

Doc leaned in, but just before he reached her cheek, he brushed his lips softly against hers. The kiss wasn't any longer or harder than the pecks on the cheek they had been sharing, but the difference in its effect on him had nothing to do with time or pressure. Doc was sure his body temperature had climbed at least five degrees in an instant.

Rebecca smiled. "And I didn't even have to mention that my rates had gone up." She left for her bedroom.

TUESDAY, AUGUST 16

Early Morning, Rebecca's Apartment

Rebecca had dozed off. She wouldn't have known for sure except the clock beside her bed said 2:28 AM. But now, she was awake, listening as Doc moved quietly around her living room. She hadn't been sure if she'd be dragging him off her couch at 6:00 AM so she could follow him home and start her day, or if it would be more like this—he'd rest just long enough to take the edge off his fatigue and then he'd be up. Now, the only question was, what had awoken him? Unfamiliar surroundings? A restless mind? Desire?

If the latter, she wasn't sure what she would do. She'd downplayed their previous night together to reset their relationship, to make the water disappear before it ran under the bridge. And three days and just the second night they'd been in the same town wasn't the do-over she thought they needed.

On the other hand, letting nature take its course was a possibility, and the thought made her face warm. But if she took that path, shouldn't she clear the air first, tell him what had really happened? That question had been in her mind more and more recently but never at a time when she could ponder it fully. She needed to make time for it soon, or she'd be making that call on the fly.

Tonight, however, wasn't going to require that impromptu decision because she heard the front door of her apartment open. To her, the sound was both a relief and a disappointment. After a moment, she got up to make sure the door was locked. It was and she retrieved the key from the floor and turned on the alarm. As she turned to go back to bed, she noticed a small slip of paper on the coffee table near the couch. She turned on a light and sat down on one of the armchairs to read it.

Rebecca –

Just had a thought about the women's posts, and in my current sleepy state, I think it might be something important. But I want to check it out first. Talk tomorrow – no, make that this evening.

The note was typical Doc, and it brought a smile to her face. He'd woken up not because of the setting or lust but because some of the data swirling in his head had suddenly come together in a way that gave them new meaning. He'd told her that happened from time to time, that sleep let the insights form. Hopefully, that process didn't result in him sitting up in bed in the middle of the night and shouting "Eureka" several times a week. That would be tough if they ever got together.

Then, she noticed there was something written on the back and turned the paper over.

And since I won't be here when you wake up in the morning, this is for you.

X

On the cheek? On the lips? That's your call, although I'd use it wisely. That might be it for a while.

Doc

Rebecca leaned back in the chair, her smile widening as she stared at the couch across the room. A week ago, they'd explored each other's bodies there. Four days ago, Doc had said he could ignore the lure of the couch as long as they readdressed that decision when the case was over. That timing had felt right to Rebecca then. Now, it felt perfect.

Well, that was unless the case dragged on. And if that happened, the schedule might need to be accelerated.

Morning, St. Louis South Patrol Building

Rebecca parked her car and watched a moment as the remnants of a morning shower left a fine mist on her windshield. She glanced in the driver's side mirror toward the St. Louis Police Department, South Patrol building behind her. A radio antenna that had to be close to fifty feet tall rose into the gray sky and towered over the simple one-story brick structure.

Other than knowing that a police detective from Minneapolis wanted to speak with her, Rebecca had learned nothing more about this meeting. The fact they wanted to talk, however, was quite the reversal from when she had been in their city earlier. At that time, no one was interested in a possible serial killer with a political motive when it involved a case that had been closed by the police department of the city where the crime had occurred. True, this call was mostly about Jackson, which was closer to their home, but she suspected they'd see it as equally unequivocal. It was just a copycat crime. And if something had changed in either of those cases, word hadn't traveled the 500 plus miles south to St. Louis yet.

Rebecca grabbed her notebook and a light jacket from the seat beside her, exited the car, and walked to the building. She pushed through the first door into a vestibule, designed more for security than to hold winter's cold winds at bay, and then through a second door. Just inside it sat an officer, graying around the temples and probably approaching retirement. But before she could read his name tag and introduce herself, he said, "Ms. Marte, Sergeant Jackson Beal. I know it's been almost a year, but I told myself if you ever came in my building, I'd tell you how much I thought of your old partner, Gus Clements. One of the finest investigators I ever worked with. And while the big boys might get their panties in a bunch when the Feds come in, as a working detective in those days, I felt the opposite. I'd take his help over anyone I've known."

"Thanks," said Rebecca. "Gus was a great teacher, too, though I can't say I mastered all his lessons. And an even better partner."

"I can imagine. They have you in that conference room right over there, Ms. Marte," said Beal, nodding his head toward a closed door across the room. "I think they're all set up."

"Oh, not in back?"

"Guess not."

It was somewhat strange that they'd want a visiting detective discussing an active case in what was basically a public area. But then, Rebecca had no idea what else might be going on in the building. Maybe this was all they had available? She walked across the space and entered the conference room. There was only one person inside, and if he was the detective from Minneapolis, his last assignment must have been undercover in a high school. Both in appearance and grooming, he fit the part to a T.

He was sitting at the conference room table working on a computer but turned when Rebecca entered. "You lost?"

"No, I'm here for a meeting. Rebecca Marte, Marte Investigative Services."

"No way."

"Way," said Rebecca in reply. "And you are?" If he said he was the detective, she was going to re-use his line.

"Oh, sorry. I'm IT. That's Information Technology." He delivered the definition of the acronym without hesitation, obviously figuring she wouldn't know otherwise. And his failure to give his name? She had to chalk that up to social awkwardness unless she wanted to take it as further evidence that he thought her little more than a ditzy blonde.

He turned back to the computer and started an application that opened a window on the desktop. "That'll do it," he said. "Just sit here in front of the computer. Everything else will happen automatically. Then, close the window when you're done. OK?"

"Sure, but won't everyone need to be sitting in front of the computer? This is to record the conversation, right?"

Mr. IT frowned. "As far as I know, you are everyone, at least at this location. And as for recording, I have no idea what they'll do on their end, but this app is just to set up a video link between here and Minneapolis."

That could mean that the Minneapolis Police had changed their mind about her theory but not enough to cover travel expenses for a face-to-face working session with her and the St. Louis PD. That is, unless the kid was right, and she was the only participant on this end. In that case, the whole arrangement was starting to stink. It smelled like someone up the chain of command from the Minneapolis detective had told him to make it happen for the sake of appearances. And if that was true, it also explained why she'd be discussing the details of her case in a setting where anyone from the Chief of Police to the cleaning crew might barge in at any moment.

"OK," Rebecca replied, as Mr. IT stood, hitched up his jeans, and left.

Rebecca sat at the table. It was about ten minutes after the appointed meeting time when the computer window came to life. "Ms. Marte, I'm Detective Angelo Verdelli. We met briefly a few days ago."

"Yes, Detective. I remember. What can I do for you?"

"To the point. I like that," said Verdelli. "I had a pressing case the last time we talked, and with it resolved, I wanted to discuss your ideas about the Linthecom and Jackson cases further. And I appreciate you taking the time to do it."

Despite the claim he'd been occupied with other matters, Rebecca felt his excuse was hollow. After all, Verdelli hadn't been too busy to say he didn't buy her theory. But maybe she was wrong. She simply nodded, then launched into a summary of Doc's and her thoughts to date. She covered everything including their earlier suspicion of Anders and their recent efforts to analyze the women's posts. And though looking at the congressmen's political leanings and voting records was a longer-term task, she described it, too. If Verdelli was interested, Minneapolis might contribute some manpower toward that end.

When she was finished, Verdelli said, "Looks like you've been busy. But it seems to me that once you eliminated the possibility of brainwashing, you removed the only thing that gives the single-mastermind theory any credibility—a method to create these delusions. Without that, it can't be done."

"It can't be done or you just don't know how?" asked Rebecca.

Verdelli's eyes narrowed. "Look, I could ask some academic types, but they're going to tell me the same thing. But if you find someone with credentials who believes it's possible, let me know. We can ...."

His brush-off ended mid-sentence as someone knocked on the conference room door where she was seated. Officer Beal appeared when the door cracked open, saying, "There's someone here to join the meeting."

Verdelli looked as surprised as Rebecca felt ... at least until she saw the familiar face. But rather than greet the newcomer, she turned to watch Verdelli's reaction.

"Sorry to interrupt, but it took me a while to find this meeting. I really expected it to be downtown. I'm FBI Special Agent Randall Blewitt."

Rebecca had to give Verdelli credit—his frown was hardly noticeable. But then, if the FBI had suggested that Minneapolis take another look at the Linthecom and Jackson cases and he, in turn, had been directed to do so, he may have halfway expected this interruption.

"I'm surprised the FBI can spare an agent to look into a closed case and another that'll soon be closed," said Verdelli. "And while there's an obvious connection between the two involving Minneapolis residents, any link to the St. Louis cases seems like serious overreach to us."

Agent Blewitt sat down beside Rebecca, turning the monitor slightly to get a good look at Verdelli. "The last U.S. congressman to be assassinated was Allard Lowenstein, Representative from New York," said Blewitt. "That was in 1980 after he left office. The last congressman to be killed while in office was Leo Ryan in 1978 when he was investigating allegations of human rights abuses at the People's Temple in Jonestown, Guyana. Now, we've had two assassinations and two attempts in the United States in less than a half-year. That warrants investigating every possibility. Don't you agree?"

"The FBI was involved in the original investigation of Linthecom," said Verdelli. "Those agents didn't have any problem with the Iowa police closing the case."

"They didn't have the benefit of the broader perspective we have now," replied Blewitt. "And with it, we've recommended that the Linthecom case be reopened. As for the Jackson case, I think you'll find the agents working with Minneapolis law enforcement on it will want to turn over every stone before it gets shut down."

It took a moment for Verdelli to remove the scowl from his features, but when he did, he said, "I think we've heard all we need to from Ms. Marte. Unless you have questions for me, Agent Blewitt, we'll get back to work."

"Sure," replied Blewitt. "I believe my concerns have been addressed."

Verdelli disconnected without another word.

Rebecca leaned over and gave Blewitt a hug. "How's the wife and the baby, Randy? Or should I say, Randall?"

He shrugged. "I was advised that Randy might be too informal for a special agent. And Rhonda and the baby are great, although he could let me get a little more sleep."

"So, I take it someone talked to Detective Verdelli's superiors about holding this meeting since he was as disinterested as ever."

"That would have been the mayor who called the Chief of Police who gave the detective his marching orders. But while they can make him place the call, they can't change his mind. Don't get me wrong. A lot rides on clearance rates for those guys, so when the governor of Minnesota implied that Linthecom's delusions had their source in the liberal leanings of Iowa politics, Verdelli was all too happy to wash his hands of the case."

"You're kidding," said Rebecca.

"Not really," replied Blewitt. "The governor didn't say Iowa politics causes insanity, but pretty close. There's not a whole lot of love lost between those two governors."

"But I don't get it," said Rebecca. "Why are you riding Minneapolis about Linthecom? The crime occurred in Iowa. It's not Verdelli's case to close. And probably not Jackson either, since the crime occurred outside city limits."

"You're right," said Blewitt. "But by a strange coincidence—and believe me, we checked—it is a coincidence. But one of the eyewitnesses to the car crash in Iowa was a Minneapolis resident. And when he contacted the local police about leaving the country for a couple of weeks on vacation, they kicked him lose ... much to the chagrin of the Iowa authorities and us. So, most of this back and forth is to make sure they don't try the same stunt with Jackson ... or worse."

"Say, you don't have a copy of the incident report from Iowa, do you? I haven't been able to get a copy."

Blewitt sighed. "Sorry, but you know I can't hand over their report. I'd say, get it through an official channel, but actually, that's not my recommendation. My recommendation is to let it go, both the report and the case."

"Excuse me," said Rebecca, "but I thought you could believe your two-year-old hadn't hit his sister before you could believe the single mastermind theory? Why should I let it go if I'm chasing a pipe dream?"

Blewitt said nothing and Rebecca knew that waiting in silence wouldn't loosen his tongue. So, she voiced the concern that he was probably withholding. "The psychological profile makes our mastermind look a bit unstable and extremely dangerous, huh?" But before Blewitt could offer a meaningless platitude, she said, "Never mind. I know you can't say. And besides, we'd come to that conclusion already. We're finishing up the current inquiries by the end of the week, and then, we're shutting down the case and leaving it in your hands."

"Good call," said Blewitt. "Look, I was supposed to sit in on your call with Minneapolis, see where your investigation stands, but I have another meeting. I need to get going. Is there any chance I can come by your office, say 9:00 AM tomorrow morning?"

"Yeah, that should be fine. Shall we get out of here?"

Rebecca and Blewitt left the conference room and said their goodbyes to Beal as they headed to the front entrance. But when they reached it, Rebecca turned to the agent and said, "If you're free, you could drop by my office tonight, any time after 7:00 PM, and get Doc's take on the case as well. I'll just have to drop by Ruger-Phillips and collect him. He's holed up there until things settle a bit more."

"Smart guy," said Blewitt as they left the building. "Yeah, I can do that. Rhonda took the baby to visit her mom for a few days. So, you and Doc are working together on this case?"

"Doc brought it to me. His coworker is my client and he's stayed involved." She paused a moment, thinking about what she'd just said. "Yeah, we're working on it together."

"OK. I'll drop by tonight," Blewitt said, as he turned toward his car and waved goodbye over his shoulder.

When Rebecca got to her car, she paused to send a text to Doc about the change in plans. After hitting send, she wondered, had Doc seen Agent Blewitt since that fateful afternoon when he had unwittingly delivered his fiancé to the kidnappers?

Maybe she hadn't thought this through as completely as she should have.

Evening, Marte Investigative Services

Rebecca's frown morphed into a smile when she saw Doc walking through the front gate of the Ruger-Phillips complex, his hands full of sacks. "Guess I forgot part of the replan," she said when he reached her car, "like who picks up dinner. Chinese?"

"Yep."

"Same here," she said as she waved a hand over a collection of bags on the floorboard of the back seat. "Hope you're hungry. And hope you want to eat fast. You're late."

"Didn't you get my text? The delivery guy got lost ... or hungry. Anyway, I just got my order five minutes ago." Doc placed his sacks next to hers in the back, nearly filling the floorboard, and got in.

Rebecca had pulled her phone out of a pocket, and after a few presses and swipes said, "And there's your message, waiting in silence for me because the sound's off. Must have forgotten to turn it back on after the meeting. Anyway, let me give you a quick rundown on today since Randy Blewitt will be at my office in" — she checked her phone — "less than thirty minutes." She pulled out of the parking lot, heading for her office.

"So, what did the Minneapolis detective have to say?" asked Doc. "Anything like they have a hot lead on our killer and they're starting to close in?"

"Hardly. They're still skeptical anything is going on except a once-in-a-billion-years coincidence that two of their citizens went after politicians within a few months of each other." Rebecca then spent a few minutes summarizing the rest of her call with Minneapolis and Agent Blewitt showing up at its end.

When she was finished, Doc asked. "The whole meeting location snafu—bureaucratic infighting or simple miscommunication?"

"Who knows? I'll stick with the simple mysteries, like who's behind these delusion-driven assassinations. So, what's the deal on this hunch that you mentioned in your note? You on to something?"

"Hard to say," replied Doc. "Mostly, it's just really odd, but let me start at the beginning. I began last night's work with Jackson's posts. Toward the end, she talks about some very detailed and precise steps she's going to follow—wear this, drive there at this time, and so on. But then, only a few sentences later, she mentions other actions as being part of a 'kludge plan'. Although it seems like it should have been spelled 'kludged plan' with the D at the end, I figured the word was misspelled. After all, without spell-check, the posts were riddled with them."

"Detailed planning vs. a hodge-podge?" Rebecca said slowly. "Well, you mentioned you thought there was some contradiction among the words. And that also suggests that these posts were first hand-written and only later typed into a computer, most likely with spell-check off. I'm not sure what that means, if anything."

"Me either, but something to keep in mind. Anyway, with the seeming contradiction, I started thinking that maybe our mastermind had implanted two types of plans—one carefully thought out and very detailed if everything went right and a second that was just the basics in case the women had to improvise. And if suicide is a crucial piece of each delusion, I figured it might be emphasized in the latter one."

"You found evidence of that because I don't remember anything like it?"

"No, neither did I, but the thought got me watching for it and what I found was even weirder. First, the only word any of the women used that implied thrown-together was kludged—never anything like makeshift or approximate. But the word kludge, although spelled in different ways, was used by all of them."

"Whoa. Seriously? How did they spell it?"

Doc grinned. "Wondering if my need to find something has me force-fitting things?"

"Just wondering how wide a net you cast."

"I counted a word as a hit whether there was the 'D' in the middle or not and whether there was one at the end or not. Cruz, I believe it was, actually used the phrase 'kludged plan', but that was the only place where the grammar and the spelling both indicated a plan that had been or could be cobbled together. Most of the other times, kludge was used as a noun. Rowles, for example, said 'kludge had everything in there'. And that, of course, sounds like kludge is something or someone. But the clincher for me was that across all the women's posts, kludge was always capitalized."

"I'd say I missed something obvious, but the grammar was almost as inconsistent as spelling. I'm sure you noticed, but Jackson kept writing Germany and Nazi without capitalizing them, but I figured that was to show her hatred. And even though I ran the posts through spell-check, it wouldn't have flagged kludge, however it was spelled, if it was always capitalized. It would just consider it a proper noun ... which I guess is where you're going with this, right?"

"It is," said Doc. "If it's the name of something, then there is probably a reference to it someplace online—a user account on social media, a name in a phone directory, a town on an online map. So, I started .... Is that an FBI car in front of your office?"

"Some government agency, I'd guess," said Rebecca.

"I'll finish this later," Doc said when he saw Agent Blewitt getting out of his car. They got out to meet him.

Rebecca nodded. "Special Agent Randall Blewitt. Welcome to the offices of Marte Investigative Services."

"Rebecca, Doc," said Blewitt as he approached them. "And it's still Randy to you two."

"In that case, make yourself useful." Rebecca handed him a couple of the sacks of Chinese food. "You did come with an appetite, didn't you?"

"You didn't say anything about dinner."

"And that's not an answer."

"Well, I had my usual to tide me over till I get home—a package of stale peanut butter crackers from a gas station down the street. So, if you're sure?"

"You don't think we got all this just for the two of us, do you?" Rebecca turned toward Doc and, when Blewitt wasn't looking, winked.

The threesome entered the building and climbed the stairs to Rebecca's second-floor office. Blewitt started to put his packages on the desk in the reception area, when Rebecca said, "Not here. Back in my office."

When they'd deposited their dinner on Rebecca's desk, Blewitt said, "Why not in reception? There's certainly enough room out there. Not so much as a phone on the desk, much less a plant or a picture?"

"Nonsense. The receptionist's phone is right here," Rebecca said, pointing at the one on her desk. "Someday I'll have someone out there. But no time soon if I don't get some easier cases. Unlike this one, which is turning out to be a bitch. But in the meantime, I'm saving big on cleaning expenses."

Doc extended a hand to the FBI agent. "Good to see you again, Randy."

"You, too, Doc. I wasn't sure you'd feel that way, given what happened the last time we were together."

"I'm pretty sure that I and everyone else in that building owe our lives to you, the FBI, and the local police. Yeah, things went sideways later—and it took me a while to admit this even to myself—but no one could have seen that coming."

Blewitt drew his lips together in a tight line and nodded once. "Thanks."

The talk over dinner was anything and everything but the case. Rebecca extolled the virtues of being in business for herself while Randy countered with the vast resources the FBI could bring to bear on an investigation. Doc just enjoyed the good-natured bickering between the two old friends. Then, each took their turn on hobbies—coin collecting for Blewitt, movies and books for Rebecca, and hiking for Doc. But when they were done with dinner, the conversation turned serious. Rebecca started by giving Blewitt the summary he would have heard had there been no confusion about the location of the morning meeting.

"So, the FBI is seriously considering the single, politically motivated killer theory?" asked Rebecca when she was finished.

"This is going to sound like the same line we often give reporters, but in this case, it's true. We're considering a lot of possibilities, including a serial killer."

"What kinds of possibilities?" asked Doc. "That is, if you can tell us."

Blewitt paused a long moment. "Not in any detail, but I doubt the list is much different than what you've already considered—brainwashing, drugs, injury, nervous system problems like Parkinson's or epilepsy, and so on. Across the cases, time and opportunity for brainwashing are limited. Linthecom, Jackson, and Rowles all had head injuries—two in car accidents and one from a fall from a ladder—but their MRIs showed that the traumas were minor, not enough to cause delusions according to the experts. And we have no evidence for drugs for any of the women. And then there's the old fallback position—that three of the attacks are pure coincidence and the fourth is a copycat."

"Linthecom had REM Sleep Behavior Disorder," said Rebecca, "which, as I understand it, can lead to Parkinson's and delusions. But, according to her husband, her case was relatively mild and didn't require medication. And at least in his mind, it hadn't produced any waking delusions, unless her attack on the congressman was one."

"Seems about right to me," said Blewitt. Rebecca knew that was about as close to a confirmation as she was likely to get from the agent and so, she merely nodded.

"If I have the evidence right," said Doc, "we have three women with possibly different, undiagnosed conditions all of which manifest themselves in similar ways. It seems like to me that your old fallback position would be a coincidence of gigantic proportions."

"Similar ways?" said Blewitt, his hand tipping side-to-side in a gesture that said, sort of. "So, in your experience, how does the likelihood of undiagnosed physical or mental conditions producing focused delusions compare to the likelihood of someone developing a way to produce those same types of confusions?"

"Other than the focused part, I'd say Healthtech has already done it," replied Doc.

"That's right. I'd almost forgotten about your run-in with the nanobots. Other than a few minor scrapes that are still healing, you don't show any ill effects. So, what was it like?"

"Disjointed and oftentimes, illogical, like a dream, but with a real feel, like a memory. To this day, I'd swear some of the things I remember from that night actually happened while others could have only happened in a dream. But it was all shoved together in a stream of utter bizarreness."

Rebecca felt as much as saw Doc glance at her, producing an instant of disquiet until she realized he was deferring to her. "I can vouch for that. Just by chance, you'd expect some of Doc's statements and actions to be related. But if there was any connection between any two, I missed it. And even less between my questions and his answers."

"That must have been one hell of a conversation," said Blewitt. "And battle to get him to the hospital, for that matter."

"It was, but we survived," said Rebecca. "Doc, did you want to get back to what you were saying earlier about the women's posts?"

"Sure."

But before Doc had even finished describing what had caught his attention in Jackson's posts, Blewitt asked, "Are you talking about the fact that the word kludge is always capitalized?"

"I should have known the FBI would spot that."

"We did, although .... It's an interesting oddity," said Blewitt.

Rebecca smiled to herself. Blewitt had apparently run up against the limit of what he could divulge, but there were only so many ways his unfinished sentence might have ended. And they all amounted to the same thing. They'd found the capitalization, but that fact hadn't led to anything yet. She doubted she needed to mention this guess to Doc, but even that slight uncertainty disappeared when he spoke.

"Yeah, I wasn't sure where to go with it either, so I just started searching online. Surprising to me, the name Kluge—spelled without the D in the middle—is fairly common, including a billionaire or two. So, there were a lot of social media accounts and entries in phone directories and the like. I could only make a rough cut at the ones that might be of interest, but I didn't turn up anything."

Doc paused. Rebecca figured he was hoping that Blewitt would volunteer something about what the FBI had found, but he kept quiet. Of course, information about intelligence sources and methods was tightly held by the Bureau, so she wasn't surprised.

"The spelling with the D in the middle, Kludge, has been used less frequently as a proper noun, often as a parody. Like naming an armadillo Kludge because it's part armored tank and part rodent, basically a hodge-podge of parts. But I didn't find anything that seemed particularly relevant to the case. So, even though I couldn't eliminate every living human in the St. Louis or Minneapolis areas with one of the relevant spellings as a name, I expanded the search to history and literature. I thought the killer might be using the name symbolically."

"It wouldn't be the first time," said Blewitt, "although it's often the press or the police that come up with the name rather than the killer. The Killer Clown for John Wayne Gacy, for example. But then, the Zodiac killer picked his own name."

Rebecca was a bit surprised by Doc's reaction to the supportive comment from the agent; his eyes narrowed slightly. She wasn't sure what to make of it.

"After I opened my search up to history and literature—and I even checked character's names in movies and in some of Greek and Roman mythology—I had a lot of hits. The spelling with the "D" in the middle contributed some, but like for real people, most of the hits were without it. Of course, the problem with opening the search this wide is that if you look long enough and hard enough, sooner or later, you'll find it, or something that looks enough like ...."

"Doc, you're killing me," said Rebecca, the reason for his slight frown now apparent. Whatever he'd found was a stretch and a half, and he wasn't in any hurry to expose that fact. "Just tell us."

Doc chuckled. "Sorry. The most interesting match I've found so far is a World War II German Army Officer named Günther von Kluge. He didn't actively participate in the July 20th plot to assassinate Hitler, but he supported it behind the scenes. He knew some of the conspirators, even kept some of them under his command. In a way, he weaponized others in the German army to do his bidding, just like our killer has weaponized these women who attacked the congressmen."

Blewitt was quiet a moment, and Rebecca wasn't sure if he was thinking about the possibilities or the ways he might tell Doc he'd gone overboard. But for her part, she thought the idea worth considering.

"You're right, Doc, it's a bit of a stretch. But on the other hand, this madman—assuming it is a man—wouldn't be using his real name around these women, so finding a kindred spirit in history makes some sense. It also fits with the Nazi-in-hiding delusion of two of the women. If there is a single person behind these attacks, he or she might be of German ancestry or be a student of World War II. How about it, Randy?"

"Well, it certainly wouldn't hurt to add those descriptors to our database searches. But let me make sure I understand. You're suggesting that our serial killer, if there is one, is working behind the scenes to remove the president from office?" asked Blewitt.

"I'm not sure that adds up, since none of the congressmen who were attacked were staunch supporters of the current administration."

"And that matches what I found, too," said Doc. "They didn't generally side with the president. Rather, what I'm saying is that our killer might have a political objective that's not specifically the removal of the president. As to what it might be? Well, that's turning out to be a tough nut to crack. The general areas where these four mostly agreed were cybersecurity, law enforcement, terrorism, healthcare, immigration, voting, and education. Removing those four men might tip the scales in any one of those areas, assuming they aren't being replaced with someone with the same views."

"You've got the list of general areas of agreement memorized?" asked Rebecca.

"Yeah, they are THE CVILE."

"The what?" asked Rebecca.

Blewitt tilted his head to one side. "A mnemonic?"

"Right," replied Doc. "The first letters of terrorism, healthcare, education, and so on. Probably sounds like overkill to you two, but you try looking up the list over and over when you're checking voting records. It gets old fast. Of course, by now, I've got them memorized anyway."

"Leave it to the training guy to know the shortcuts," Blewitt said. "So, let me see if I have your thoughts correctly. If these attacks are being instigated by one person, it's more likely a male than female, based on the advice that was being given on attire and the choice of weapons. He may have a political agenda in one of the"—Blewitt paused to check his notes—"seven broad areas you mentioned. He may be going by the name Kluge or Kludge. And he may be of German descent or have a background in German history. Anything else to add?"

After Doc and Rebecca exchanged a glance, Rebecca said, "No, I think that's it. And knowing FBI policy, I doubt there's more you can tell us, unless …."

Blewitt chuckled. "You're going to have to finish that sentence for me because in my boss's mind, and therefore, in mine, there's nothing that fits after 'unless.' Sorry."

"Well, it was worth a try."

"Nothing ventured, as they say," replied Blewitt. "But now, I need to get going. I've got an early morning meeting. Thanks for the dinner and the excellent conversation. Both were infinitely better than stale crackers and the radio. We'll have to do this again sometime—maybe a double date with Rhonda and me?"

Rebecca and Doc looked at each other, Rebecca thinking he didn't look nearly as surprised as she felt. Did Doc think of the two of them as a couple? She didn't have any longer to ponder his reaction, however, as Blewitt said, "Did I misread the situation? The way you two have been communicating all evening with just a look or some cryptic comment, I figured you were dating."

"It's the long hours on the case," said Rebecca. "You know how it is. After a while, you can almost read each other's minds."

"And as you know, we've planned a final week-long push on the case," said Doc. "But, hopefully, soon after that, we can take you up on the offer." He turned to Rebecca. "After all, it would be a chance for us to hone some of our nonverbal communications skills on topics other than serial murder and voting records."

Rebecca smiled. While Doc might not think of them as together, he was looking for ways to make that closer to reality. And frankly, she found that a very pleasant thought. "Sure, Randy, let's plan on it."

WEDNESDAY, AUGUST 17

Evening, Rebecca's Apartment

Doc quietly closed the door to Rebecca's bedroom after checking that she wasn't napping inside. After all, she couldn't have forgotten. She'd only called him about this working session at her place this morning, telling him in a cryptic reference where she was hiding a key so he could let himself in. But as for being overtaken by fatigue? That was a possibility. He knew he'd been running on fumes for days.

So, he had checked her bedroom, planning on only taking a peek inside. But that glance had led to ten minutes standing in the middle of the floor, wondering why it felt so familiar. He walked slowly into the living room and took a seat on the couch.

Doc knew that déjà vu, that feeling of having experienced a situation previously, wasn't uncommon. He had felt it several times before but never this strong. And never this specific because he could swear that he and Rebecca had been in there the night he'd been overcome by the nanobots. Maybe some of the "junior-high stuff," as Rebecca had called it, had taken place there? Something must have because he'd even tested himself, picturing the inside of her closet before he opened the door. And while things weren't exactly where he remembered them, they were close.

But even if he recalled the room and its contents somewhat accurately, the rest of his memories couldn't possibly bear any resemblance to reality. Those images of sweaty, naked bodies locked in a passionate embrace obviously belonged with the ones where he was talking to his long-dead grandfather. They were a total fabrication of those minuscule creations zapping the neurons in his brain. If he and Rebecca had done what he recalled, they would have ... well, if it was up to him, they would have reprised those roles every night. And Rebecca would have at least wanted to talk about it, right? He'd just have to ask her what had brought him into her bedroom on that night because there was too much accuracy in his recollections to be only déjà vu.

His decision to ask came at the perfect moment as he heard the front door open.

"Running a bit late, aren't we?" he called when he saw the darkened figure coming down the hall.

But when Rebecca entered the room, Doc could only stare. Rebecca was a very attractive woman. Even in his darkest days searching for Nicole, he had known that. But today, she was exquisite in a long black gown that would have been completely at home on the red carpet in Hollywood. A slit on one side exposed a leg to mid-thigh, while the neckline plunged just enough to hold the interest of any male who wasn't blind. She even wore a pale-red shade of lipstick, something that to the best of his knowledge, she had never done before in his presence.

"If you tell me I've seen you in that dress before, I'm going to have to disagree. There's absolutely no way I could have forgotten. You are stunning. More than worth the wait."

She smiled, but unless he was completely befuddled by her appearance—and that, he admitted, was possible—her expression held no warmth.

"Sorry to keep you waiting," she said. But again, Doc sensed a disconnect, this time between the words and the emotion. There was no "sorry" in her tone.

"I'm sorry," she said again, "but I didn't think you'd be in a hurry to meet your maker."

What was going on, he wondered. But before he could ask, a man stepped from behind her and into the living room. He was holding a gun leveled at Doc's chest. He looked familiar, but Doc couldn't place him.

"Ah, Dr. Price. What a rotten soul you're hiding under your façade of civility. But soon, as your partner said, you'll have to answer for your atrocities."

All uncertainty about the man's identity disappeared when Doc heard the voice. "Anders. I thought you'd be hiding in some hole far from here by now. Or should I call you Kluge?"

"Very good. My birth certificate says Anders, but I am Kluge. And with all the money that my alter ego has made for me, I'll never be hiding in holes. No, I'll be carrying on my mission, albeit from a safe distance. Let's see what the FBI makes of it when foreign visitors and Americans returning from abroad start exhibiting anti-government delusions. After my envoys remove a few more of the troglodytes from Congress, we'll be back in step with the natural order of humanity."

Though Doc was listening to the man, his gaze never left the woman because he knew—Rebecca was to be the instrument of his death. Whatever Kluge had done to the other women, he had done to her, because her eyes were now filled with murderous hatred.

"What did I do to you, Rebecca?" It wasn't only a question to stall for time. It was also a search for some crack in the fantasy Kluge had implanted, a weakness in her delusion that he could exploit to save his life.

"Well, isn't that rich," Rebecca replied, her tone dripping contempt. "Kluge told me you'd deny everything. But you know what? Once he helped me remember, the images will never leave my thoughts again. So, don't pretend you don't know."

"But I don't. Maybe I've repressed those memories, too."

Rebecca laughed, the sound chilling Doc to the core.

"Spare me the psychological crap. You reveled in our baby son's agony as you slowly tightened your grip on his neck. And when he passed out, you stopped so you could do it again. And then a third time, before you let him die. And you made me watch. At first, I didn't understand that, but you wanted to teach me a lesson."

"A lesson?"

"That this is what happens when I get pregnant. You can't imagine what it's like, wanting more than life itself to be barren, to hope with all your being that each time you rape me that I'll die rather than give you another child."

Tears started running down Rebecca's cheeks. Doc hated to continue, hated to put Rebecca through the mental hell Kluge had constructed for her, but if he had any hope of finding a flaw, it would be in the details.

"I'm sorry, but I still don't remember. Where did we bury our son?"

"Enough," hissed Kluge. "You're wasting my time. Her memory is fully restored—names, dates, locations, everything."

Was this concern speaking, Doc asked himself? Was Kluge worried that with enough digging he'd find a gap in her story or uncover an inconsistency that would free Rebecca from his spell? But, no, that wasn't right, was it? Doc had seen the detailed accounts of torture and space aliens and an unpardonable affair that Jackson, Cruz, and Rowles had written. Kluge would have prepared Rebecca for her mission just as well. And if mere suggestions or subtle changes in wording could create false memories in the psychology laboratory—memories that stood firm in the face of definitive proof to the contrary—what chance did he have of finding a flaw in the rich texture of a nanobot-created delusion? None.

He had to try something different.

"You know, the police and FBI are on to you," said Doc, turning to Kluge. This time, he was stalling for time, hoping to come up with a gambit that would overcome the man. But Kluge was being careful; his hand was steady as his eyes probed his surroundings. And the distance he kept was perfect—close enough he could hardly miss yet far enough away that rushing him was foolhardy. "That disguise isn't going to fool anyone for long. And that cheesy wig you're wearing? They'll spot it a mile away. It's just a question of time before you're spending your days in a prison, waiting to be executed for murder and treason."

"Hardly," Kluge replied with the arrogance of someone who believed he was smarter than everyone else. "The locals are chasing Scott Anders for theft and your attempted murder. And I have to say, I'm impressed you survived, but this look will be enough to confuse them until my business here is done. And as for the feds, they know nothing of Kluge. They're still thinking the crimes are coincidences and a copycat. By the time they figure out these cases are the work of a single man, I'll be long gone. And speaking of being gone, it's time I conclude my business with you and be on my way."

Kluge pulled a knife in a sheath out of his waistband. Rebecca held out a hand, but her murderous glare never left Doc's face. "She selected the weapon," Kluge said. "Perhaps she wants you to suffer like she has suffered?"

"Do I get to know why I'm about to die?"

"Ah, but you've already been told," Kluge said as he pulled the knife back from Rebecca. "But I suspect you actually want to know about the congressmen, yes?"

"As if the reason is different."

"Ah, but it is," said Kluge. "Those in the government believed they could trifle with the natural rights of being human and do so without repercussion. I'm merely showing them the error of their ways. You, on the other hand, are nothing to me, an inconsequential irritant. But even a grain of sand in the shoe can become more than one wants to endure. And to Ms. Marte, your death is her reason for breathing. So, I must, unfortunately, live with the memory of the fury I've unleashed by restoring her memory."

Kluge's taunts were becoming hard for Doc to ignore, but he had no choice. Once he broke, charging Kluge in desperation or pleading for his life, the man would have won and the end would follow quickly ... or at least, as quick as Rebecca made it. So, Doc continued to stall and probe.

"I don't get it. By drafting laws, Congress is changing the rights of humanity? Laws don't even keep people from driving over the speed limit."

"The only thing that Congress does well," said Kluge, "is to ride herd on the money. Send the dollars one way and people clumsily and ignorantly intervene. Send it another and natural forces retain control. Oftentimes, our interventions aren't a problem, but with the money and technology being considered to counter terrorism, it's a recipe for Armageddon. The men who have died and who will die would have funneled billions into technology to spy and enslave humanity. And that's an act from which we'd never recover."

Doc walked over to the couch and sat, both because it gave him a moment to think and because it put him closer to Kluge. Unfortunately, he made no progress on either front. Kluge backed away, maintaining his distance, while no new tactics to overcome the man came to mind.

"So, how does fighting terrorism interfere with the natural order of life? Other than the terrorists, who's affected?"

Kluge handed the knife to Rebecca, then took another step backward and sat in one of the armchairs. He might be farther away, but he still could hardly miss. He also might be slower to react from a seated position, but since all he had to do was pull the trigger, the difference was immaterial. Rebecca, on the other hand, would need her freedom of movement, a fact she apparently understood. Not only did she remain standing, but she took the knife from its sheath. Doc found it difficult to pull his attention from the gleaming blade but did so when Kluge spoke.

"If Congress was just considering ramping up COMINT for the National Security Agency, no problem."

"COMINT?" asked Doc.

"Communications intelligence—intercepting and analyzing communications between probable terrorist cells. But what constitutes communications is rapidly changing."

"As in the Brain-2-Brain project?"

"Exactly," replied Kluge. "Why wait for one terrorist cell to call another on the phone when you can read their minds before they dial? And before you tell me that Congress will never approve that kind of espionage, we tap phones, don't we? If all the goliaths involved in B2B—the computer hardware and software giants, the biomedical engineering companies, the behemoths of social media, the venture capitalists—have their way, brains talking to other brains will make the smartphone as obsolete as the buggy whip in short order."

Doc's assessment of his situation hadn't changed in any significant way. Kluge was resting his left hand on one of the chair's armrests and his right elbow on the other, the latter serving to steady his aim. Rebecca was shifting her weight between her feet, probably to stay loose and ready for action. And neither of them had so much as looked away for an instant.

"That day will never come," said Doc. "It takes a lot of evidence to authorize a wiretap. The regulations surrounding reading someone's thoughts will be even more rigorous."

Kluge chuckled. "Perhaps initially, but with that kind of power within the government's grasp, good intentions in the form of public laws will never stop them. First, groups will be declared our enemies, and nanobots will be introduced into their food and drink. Then, we'll tap the brains of entire nation–states and even that might be acceptable, but it won't stop there. Soon those minute mind readers will be dumped into the water and introduced to the food supplies of every city and rural area in the United States, all so we can be safe from the evil intentions of others. And safe from freedom, as well."

Doc knew he was running out of time. Kluge wouldn't keep up his diatribe much longer, but the only ploy he could see was to provoke the man. Perhaps in anger, Kluge would make a mistake, venture too close. Doc also knew he had to disarm him. Otherwise, Rebecca would just move in to finish what he'd started. But in her deluded state, would she stop even if he had the gun? There were too many unknowns, too little data.

"It's clear why you adopted the identity of a cowardly Nazi commander," said Doc. "He couldn't face Hitler himself, so he got others to do it. And when he failed, he committed suicide."

Kluge merely smiled indulgently. "Bravo, Dr. Price. You've done your homework. And I, too, might take my life if the government ever sets up housekeeping inside my head. But I have no intention of letting that happen."

"Well, the real Kluge was probably a decent shot. I'm not sure you could hit the roof of your mouth if you were sucking on the barrel."

Kluge frowned a moment before his grin of superiority returned. "Ah, you're speaking of the inept Ms. Cruz. True, I'm not a marksman and didn't realize she could miss standing in Barclay's shadow. Obviously, poison works better."

Kluge was proving difficult to anger, but without another option, Doc continued. "And from what I hear, poison didn't work that well either. All it got you is closer to making brain-to-brain communications a reality because Representative Kessner's widow will be taking his place. And she's an even bigger proponent of technology than he was."

Kluge slowly shook his head. "I said before that you're just a minor irritant to me, but you're actually something more. You're symbolic of the sightless masses who will wait until the sanctity of their innermost dreams and desires is laid bare by our government. Then, it's too late. So, whether you can see it or not, what Ms. Marte is about to do is nothing less than patriotism. And since you're apparently down to feeble attempts to manipulate my emotions, it's time we conclude our business. Ms. Marte, he's all yours."

"Don't you want to tell me how you did it? How you implanted the delusions in those women so they'd do your bidding?"

"No. Why should I?"

Because every mass murderer is a megalomaniac wasn't an appropriate retort, since Kluge apparently felt no need to boast. And unfortunately, that was his final ploy. Doc stood. He doubted that the FBI trained knife-fighting skills ... although perhaps they did. But even if Rebecca's only instruction had been in hand-to-hand combat, he was still doomed. Every punch of her fist or chop of her hand would become a killing slice from an eight-inch blade. He would fight back, but only because it increased the chance that she would miscalculate and his life would end quickly.

Rebecca passed the knife from hand to hand as if testing its balance, getting its feel. Then, she looked down at Kluge and smiled. She appeared to be enjoying her moment of retaliation. She took a step forward, and then, in a move that caught Doc completely off-guard, she turned and drove the blade into Kluge's left hand as it rested on the arm of the chair.

Kluge screamed in agony, reflexively pulling the trigger of the handgun, but the slug buried itself in the wall three feet from where Doc stood. In a smooth, quick motion, Rebecca stepped back until she was again directly beside the man. She took her right hand from the hilt of the knife and reached across Kluge's body to grab the wrist of his gun hand. Putting her weight behind the action, she lunged forward, pulling his hand and the gun away and down. Kluge fired again, this round safely lodging in the floor a dozen feet from where Doc stood.

As Kluge was wasting his second shot, Rebecca raised a bent left arm and twisted at the waist. Then, she reversed her previous motion, launching herself backward while driving her left elbow into Kluge's nose with a sickening crunch. His head hit the back of the armchair, then fell forward onto his chest. Rebecca twisted the gun from Kluge's hand, then backed away slowly.

Though Doc still felt a bit dazed by the speed and violence of Rebecca's attack, he was aware enough to notice that she hadn't joined him on the other side of the room. Rather, she stood apart from both men, her gaze tracking back and forth. "I don't know what to say," said Doc, "except thank you for not killing me."

"We'll ...." But she didn't finish as she turned toward where Kluge had been sitting.

When Doc turned to see what had caught her attention, he saw that Kluge had pulled the knife from his hand and was now rushing toward Rebecca, the weapon raised in the air. Before Doc could turn back to the PI, a third shot rang out. And then, a fourth. Two pinpoints of red blossomed on Kluge's chest as he crumpled to the ground. Calmly, she retrieved some shells from one of the dead man's pockets and began reloading the gun.

Doc's legs were trembling and were no longer able to support him. He dropped onto the couch and looked at Rebecca, amazed that she looked almost unfazed by the events. "I guess it's stating the obvious," Doc stammered, "but Kluge tried to implant a delusion about me in you."

"Did he?" she asked.

Doc wasn't sure what to make of her response—the words seemed rhetorical, the tone didn't—but it wasn't the time to ask. "Yes, none of what he told you was true." She remained silent, staring at him. "I suspect one of your neighbors has already called, but to be sure, one of us should phone the police."

"You can."

Doc placed the call, and when he was done, he said, "They're already on the way." Both of them turned toward the window when they heard a siren. "Like I said." Doc sat down on the couch again. Rebecca, however, just stood there holding the gun down at her side. "Are you OK? Do you want to sit down?"

"I'm OK." But then, she stepped around Kluge's body and sat in the second armchair. Both of them turned toward the window again when the first police car pulled up outside her building and turned off its siren. There was the sound of at least one more in the distance.

It took Doc a moment to process the scene in front of him—smoke and the metallic smell of the shots hung in the air over a corpse lying in a slowly expanding pool of blood. But there was something else that was demanding his attention, and she was sitting in a chair as if nothing had happened. If the would-be assassin's suicide was an irrevocable part of Kluge's implanted delusions, as he and Rebecca had speculated, she would be next. And she was still holding the handgun.

"Do you want to put the gun down?" Rebecca looked at him a moment, then placed it on an end table. "Good. I wouldn't want the police to get the wrong idea."

But that was too easy. Perhaps Kluge had something else in mind for her suicide. The knife? It was still in Kluge's hand, and Rebecca didn't appear to be looking at it. Or maybe she had a vial of poison in a pocket? But, no, that didn't seem right. It would be something more violent, more dramatic. After venting her rage by stabbing him, as Doc was certain the delusion was designed to play out, a leap to her death from her fourth-story window felt more appropriate. But then, so did a dozen other methods of taking her life. He couldn't afford to guess wrong.

"You're not thinking of hurting yourself, are you?"

Rebecca said nothing.

"Other than the lies about me killing our child, what did Kluge tell you? Anything about what you needed to do?"

Rebecca stared at him for a long moment. "He didn't have to tell me. I remembered and knew what needed to be done."

"But he didn't say anything else?"

"He said he was sorry, but that I had to remember. He said you'd do anything to try to stop me. And he kept talking about the PCS."

Doc slowly shook his head. "The PCS?" But saying it aloud didn't help; he still had no idea what the acronym meant. "What else?"

Rebecca just stared.

Knowing the police would be there any moment, Doc stood and started toward the door but stopped and turned back. Rebecca was still sitting on the chair although she seemed to have slid forward to the edge of the cushion. The scene was wrong, and now, he knew why. He went into the kitchen and got a plastic sandwich bag from a drawer. Placing his hand inside, he walked over to the end table.

"May I?" he asked, pointing at the gun. Doc wasn't sure what he would do if she declined, but she just nodded. He carefully lifted the gun by the tip of the barrel and moved it to the floor near the front door.

His timing was perfect as someone knocked loudly and yelled, "Police. We have a report of shots fired at this location."

"I'm opening the door," Doc called. "We have an injured man down, but the woman on the couch and I are both unarmed. Don't shoot."

Doc reached for the doorknob but paused when Rebecca spoke softly behind him. "I guess I can't protect myself now. Will you?"

Doc nodded at her. "Yes, of course I will. You'll be fine. I promise," and he opened the door.

SATURDAY, AUGUST 20

Afternoon, Marte Investigative Services

Rebecca took another lap around her office, wondering how she could have so much nervous energy when she'd hardly slept for three days. But she knew why; it was because of Doc.

Having been checked out at the hospital and then involved in untangling the criminal and political aspects of the Scott Anders/Kluge plot for the last three days, she'd had no opportunity to talk to him save a single text inviting him to her office this afternoon. And it was hard to deduce much from his one-line reply, "See you then." Did he want to look her in the eye to say he didn't appreciate being a step away from death at her hands? Not likely. Doc knew what the nanobots could do. If anyone would understand the nightmare world she had been trapped in, he would.

More likely, he just wanted to say he couldn't be with someone who couldn't be truthful with him. Yes, she knew he had been in her bedroom. Nothing much had been moved, but it was enough for her to know. She could, of course, claim it was just part of his hallucinations. He'd largely accepted that before, but she'd decided to handle the issue differently. She was going to tell him the truth, even if he didn't ask. Their life together, if there was to be one, had launched under a cloud, but there was nothing she could do about that now except admit it and go on. And again, if anyone would understand the need for a second chance, it was Doc.

When she heard the outer door open, she knew she'd have her answers soon enough.

Doc walked into her office, and though she started to say hello, he didn't stop until he was toe-to-toe with her. He put his arms around her. She couldn't help herself. A soft laugh escaped her lips as much of her edginess fled her body with the feel of his arms.

"I'm not sure I've gotten that reaction from one of my hugs before," he said as he pulled back to look into her eyes.

"And you have a lot of experience hugging women who wanted to kill you but then saved you so you could save them?"

"Is that what happened?" he asked, feigning confusion. "I just know that I couldn't be happier that you escaped that madman, Kluge. Or Anders. Or whatever we're going to call him."

"I think Kluge," Rebecca said after a moment. "We both met Anders, and he was shallow and a sexual predator. Kluge was ... different."

"Wow," Doc said, his head pulling back as if he needed to see her whole face. "Is this the Stockholm Syndrome or something?"

"That's the one where hostages start to take the side of the captors after a while?" she asked.

Doc nodded.

"No, it's not that," Rebecca replied. "I know he was deluded, perhaps not about the threat of brain-to-brain communications, but certainly about how to influence public policy and the value of human life. But in the twelve or so hours he held me captive, he treated me like I was something special. He provided the clothes and makeup. He called me a goddess. And he kept saying that my brain was beautiful. That's not something I've heard often—or ever—having grown up with blonde jokes my entire life."

"Even a broken clock is right twice a day," said Doc. "But I think your brain's beautiful, too."

Rebecca couldn't help herself and laughed. "Don't you dare go corny on me," she said. "I know all Kluge's deference was because I was to be a sacrifice in his grand vision for the future, but a girl doesn't get to be a goddess every day."

Doc nodded. "I can see goddess, but I was thinking you were more like Houdini. When I think about the night I was under the nanobots' influence, I can't imagine escaping their spell, seeing through the delusion that my grandfather was alive or ... well, any of the other stuff I dreamt up."

Doc's words were the perfect segue to her admission. That discussion, however, might take them down a rabbit hole or end in another shouting match. There was even a slight chance that it might rekindle their passion ... or hers at least, since she still wasn't sure what had moved Doc before. But she still had questions that needed answering. She took a seat in one of the chairs on the visitor side of her desk and turned it toward the other. Doc got the message and sat in front of her.

"I didn't really beat the delusion," said Rebecca. "At first, Kluge's lies were my reality. But slowly, I started to question them. It was sort of like waking up from a really vivid dream and needing a while to realize it wasn't real. But in this case, waking up was taking hours, not a few minutes."

"So, when you stabbed Kluge, you were still unsure?"

"Yeah. All your questions about his political agenda and the women with the delusions—they didn't fit in the world Kluge had created for me. I kept thinking that we needed to stop for a minute so I could work things out, but Kluge kept pushing the plan forward. And when you took the gun away from me? That was another huge disconnect. You weren't supposed to be alive, of course, and when the police saw your body, they were going to open fire. Not exactly standard police procedure, but I suppose Kluge wanted me to feel threatened and vulnerable. I'm sure if the gun had been within reach, I would have opened fire on them.

"What a nightmare," Doc sighed.

"So, my turn for a question. How did you know to take the gun away from me?"

"And my turn for an admission. I didn't know—not for sure, anyway. The theme of your delusion was extreme grief over the loss of a child, which opened the door for all types of self-destructive behavior. I considered a few different possibilities, but when I looked at you on the armchair with the gun at your elbow? Kluge wanted to recreate the same endgame he used with Cruz, and you'd die in return fire from the police."

"There were three officers who came in when you opened the door, right?"

Doc paused a beat as if replaying the scene in his mind. "Yeah, that's right."

"So, the risk Kluge was taking was that I wouldn't shoot all three of them before they got me."

Doc grimaced a bit too dramatically to be real. "Now, I'm going to lay awake at night, working out all the scenarios with you surviving the first assault. How long are we going to be trapped in the standoff with SWAT? Although the way you were dressed ...." Then, his expression became serious, and it was easy for Rebecca to tell he was wrestling with a question. "If I'm invading your life too much, just say so. But I was wondering what it was like when Kluge put that story about me into your head."

Rebecca chuckled. "If that's personal, then there are about two dozen officers and federal agents and doctors who've already heard this story. Kluge knocked me out with something in my car when I was leaving for work that morning. Maybe something on the steering wheel or a gas inside the car, but when I woke up, I was lying in a bed in the basement of a house he had down south. He forced me to drink something—remember the almond-tasting liquid in the women's posts?"

"I do."

"That was it. It must have had the nanobots in it. After that, it was storytelling time. But even the first time I heard it, everything he said made sense. And after a while, it was my ground truth."

"And you're completely recovered from the delusion? It's just a bad dream now?"

Rather than answering, Rebecca stood, walked to the other side of her desk, and opened a drawer. "That gun's in here, somewhere."

"I'm not sure that's funny," said Doc.

"Yeah, a little sick, I suppose. But what I have in here is this." She held up a key. "My firearm is locked in a safe at home. I feel fine, and the doctors don't think I'll have anything like a flashback but no reason to take chances for the next few weeks."

"I really, really like that precaution," said Doc with a grin. "So, after you took care of Kluge and the police arrived, they took a statement from me, and I went back downtown for about an hour of questioning the next day. But I have no clue what happened to you for almost three days. A lot of time with law enforcement or at the hospital?"

"If I'd been at the hospital for that long, you would have gotten a call ... or ten. But the doctors must have learned a lot from your episode; it only took them about five hours to give me a clean bill of health. From there, it was police headquarters for the rest of the time."

"They locked you up?"

"No, but let's just say that goodwill from local law enforcement is pretty important to a PI. After a half-day or so being interviewed, they took me to a hotel and asked that I not talk to anyone, including you. I'm pretty sure they had someone on the door, but since I was not going anywhere, I didn't look.

"Then, on the second day, it was time for a field trip, and fortunately, I remembered the location of Kluge's little one-story down south. Not nearly as grand as Anders's semi-mansion farther north, but it had everything he needed. I led them to the basement, where they found his computer. After some computer whiz broke into it, they found a gigantic database. At first, no one was sure what we were looking at, but then, they got someone with a medical background who said they were MRIs. After that, they figured they knew everything I did and sent me home with the same instructions to contact no one. Early today, they said ... I believe their exact words were, 'resume normal daily activities.' That's when I texted you."

"The discovery of the MRI database got leaked to the press," said Doc, "as well as the fact that Kluge's search history focused on a dozen or so women, including our four victims. And I understand they've talked to some of the others who confirmed they had been contacted by Anders but refused his offer to meet. Apparently, he had some line about abnormalities he'd discovered in their MRIs."

"But how did he get all those images?" asked Rebecca.

"Patients can donate their MRIs to an organization that maintains them for research purposes. Apparently, Anders requested large numbers of them under the guise that the women were possible participants in Healthtech's research. So, Anders took care of the money and got the brain scans, while Kluge carried out the cleansing of Congress."

"I think Anders took care of their romantic needs as well."

Doc's eyebrows shot up. "Oh?"

"I could be wrong, but even though there are only two people involved, I think Kluge, Anders, and Rowles were something of a love triangle. Anders lusted after Rowles, the physical woman. Kluge was in love with her brain. He, Kluge, said something about breaking his own rules by enlisting her when she'd been with Anders, but he just couldn't resist because of her PCS ... whatever the heck that is."

Doc sat forward in his chair. "No one told you?"

"Just give me the highlights," said Rebecca, "because I'm getting the impression you've spent the last three days researching the PCS."

"Not every minute of them," Doc said with a grin. "Well, I'm no expert, but as I understand the research, people tell the difference between what they've fantasized and what actually happened by a process called reality monitoring. When the distinction between imagination and the real world is blurred, such as in the first few minutes after waking from a vivid dream, reality monitoring is working to catch up. And one brain structure that seems to be involved in reality monitoring is a furrow or wrinkle in the prefrontal cortex called the paracingulate sulcus or PCS. And since delusions in several psychiatric conditions such as schizophrenia have been linked to PCS variability, it's not a structure to be trifled with."

"So, Kluge unleashes his nanobots on the PCS, tells you this intricate story, and it becomes your reality because the PCS is overwhelmed?" asked Rebecca.

"I'd guess it's something like that," Doc responded. "If you let the nanobots zap all different parts of the brain randomly, you get seizures and the bizarre dream world that I experienced. But if you get them to congregate at the PCS, reality monitoring is suppressed and elaborate focused delusions form. So, how Kluge got them to focus on that one structure is the real breakthrough. I don't suppose you have any idea how he did that?"

"Yeah, I think I heard the little devils talking before I swallowed the drink." After Doc's roll of his eyes, she said, "I have no idea. And I kind of think it's going to stay that way. When he gave me the stuff, I asked what it was. He just said it was his secret formula with the recipe right here. And he tapped his head."

"Well, if he found a way, it won't be long until others do the same. I hope Congress takes this threat seriously, and any technology that invades our minds gets a ton of close scrutiny."

It was a lot to think about, and Rebecca took a moment to do just that. Finally, she said, "It's hard to believe. All this killing because of a wrinkle in the mind?"

"Well, it's actually the lack of a wrinkle that can cause problems. In this case, wrinkles are good."

Rebecca smiled. "You're not going to convince many women of that. And I guess mine must be as smooth as a baby's bottom."

"Actually, I'd guess just the opposite. You came out of his spell rather quickly, unlike Jackson who apparently maintained her deluded thoughts for nearly a year. So, I'd guess there's a big beautiful wrinkle right in the middle of your prefrontal cortex."

Rebecca laughed but soon found her pleasure overtaken by resolve. Her questions had been answered, and Doc knew all she could remember about being Kluge's sacrificial assassin. The moment to confess her half-truth about their night together was at hand. But before she could speak, Doc did.

"You know, we promised ourselves when the case was over, we'd take up some unfinished business ... if you know what I mean. Well, other than the paperwork, the case is over. And it just so happens that I'm free tonight."

The mischievous smile she should be wearing to answer his innuendos didn't come because there was no more time for stalling. "There's something we need to talk about first."

She got no farther, however, before she heard her outer office door opening. She leaned over to look beyond Doc and found an unfamiliar woman walking slowly through reception. Her simple white shirt and cutoff jean shorts highlighted lightly tanned and well-toned arms and legs. She almost looked like a bodybuilder straight off the beaches of southern California.

"Can I help you?" Rebecca called.

"Yes, you can," the woman said.

At the sound of her voice, Doc spun around in his chair so quickly he nearly knocked it over. Even from the side, Rebecca could tell that all the color had drained from his face. "Nicole," he said softly. "What is it?"

"Nothing that has anything to do with you, Doc," Nicole replied. "I came to see Ms. Marte."

One of the things Rebecca recalled from Doc's stories was that Nicole had never called him by his nickname. Even before they were engaged or even dating, he had always been Sam. But then, a lot had changed since then.

Doc turned back around, hitting his knee against the desk, but he hardly seemed to notice. His eyes darted around the room as if looking for an escape. After a moment, he took a long breath and said, "I'll get out of the way, let you two talk business."

"Hold on just a second," said Rebecca. She turned to Nicole. "Can this wait until Monday? It's the weekend, and I was getting ready to go home." It wasn't her usual greeting to a potential client, but Rebecca could see this being many things other than a case she wanted.

"That's up to you," said Nicole. "I wanted your help because ... I killed a man."

The End

AUTHOR'S NOTE

A beta reader for this book asked me the following: "BTW, could any of this stuff actually happen or is this just your mind at work?"

I love getting that question. It suggests that I did at least part of my job, because I want to make much of what you read sound possible or even probable. A looming capability that promises us great things is exciting. One that is used malevolently, however, also creates tension and suspense. And it raises the question that was in this beta reader's mind. Where is the line between fact and fiction?

In a sentence, we're straddling the line described in this book already.

We could, using current technology, over-stimulate the paracingulate sulcus (PCS) and see if there was a breakdown in reality monitoring. We'd need to use surgically implanted electrodes rather than nanobots, but that approach has already been perfected for the treatment of Parkinson's, dystonia, epilepsy, and other diseases. And if the direction of commercial research remains unchanged—perhaps best epitomized at the time of this writing by Elon Musk's Neuralink project—we may see implanted chips allowing our brains to interface directly with the Internet or with the brain of another person. The possibilities are exciting, but at the same time, a bit disquieting.

So, where's the fiction?

First, in the use of nanobots rather than implanted electrodes for brain stimulation. Nanobots have been used for this purpose in the lab, although I know of no human trials ... yet. But if the technology is perfected and has the same risk/benefit ratio as electrodes, the choice between swallowing a pill filled with nanobots or having holes drilled through the skull seems clear to me.

Second, there's fiction in how widespread, random electrical stimulation of the brain would have affected Doc's behavior. There is, however, reason to believe the description in the book is close. Epileptic seizures are accompanied by sudden, intense electrical activity that may be localized and last a few seconds or may spread across the brain and last for minutes. Doc's behavior was dramatized; no seizure would produce the range of bizarre actions he showed. But on the other hand, Rebecca's first aid was based closely on the recommended treatment for seizures.

Perhaps the largest leap across the line into the world of fiction, however, was in postulating the effect of overstimulation of the PCS. Research has rather consistently found a correlation between the prominence of the PCS and the tendency to experience hallucinations. Correlation, however, does not prove causation. It does not eliminate the possibility that other brain structures or some unidentified neural process affect both PCS development and proclivity for delusions. Basically, exactly how PCS variability is related to reality monitoring awaits further research.

Finally, the book implied that the PCS could be present or missing; that it could be a prominent crease or an area "smooth as a baby's bottom." In fact, research on this structure classifies the PCS as "absent" when it's small, generally 20mm in length or less. The book adopted this terminology without getting into the fact that PCS presence is actually a matter of degree rather than all or none.

So, while the book suggests a testable hypothesis—that PCS overstimulation would cripple reality monitoring—given how little we know about the relationship between this brain structure and hallucinations, I would expect (and hope) for a cautious approach to this question.

ACKNOWLEDGMENTS

This book would not have been possible without the help of a number of talented individuals, and I've been fortunate to work with several who have continued their support of my work, story after story.

First, I'd like to thank Ms. Janet Harrison for reading and providing numerous helpful comments on an earlier draft of the manuscript. A special thanks go to Dr. Liz Gehr for helping me watch my technical Ps and Qs. Any inaccuracies in the technical content are mine; hopefully, they're all intentional to build the fiction.

The diligence of my editor is greatly appreciated. She even investigated the question of whether Rebecca should sit "in" or "on" an armchair. Who even knew there was a difference?

Finally, thanks go to my talented daughter, Ms. Courtney Perrin, for the design and creation of the cover art. Clearly, I tie her creative hands by the branding of the series—same font, same color scheme, same profile on the covers. Even so, she finds a way to make them interesting and unique.

ABOUT THE AUTHOR

Bruce Perrin has been writing for more than twenty-five years, although you will find most of that work only in professional technical journals or conference proceedings. After receiving a PhD in Industrial/Organizational Psychology and completing a career in psychological research and development at a major aerospace company, he's now applying his background to writing novels. Not surprisingly, most of his work falls in the techno-thriller, mystery, and hard science fiction genres, examining the intersection of technology and the human mind now and in the future. Besides writing, Bruce likes to tinker with home automation and is an avid hiker, logging nearly 2,500 miles a year in the first nine years of Fitbit ownership. When he is not on the trails, he lives with his wife in Aurora, CO.

Thank you for reading *A Winkle in the Mind*. If you'd like to help others find this story, please consider leaving a review on Amazon, Goodreads, or the website of your favorite bookseller.

For all the latest on my new releases, promotions, and book reviews, please subscribe to my blog: BruceMPerrin. com